*Sign*
*of*
*the*
*Crescent*

## About the Author

Debbie Federici has a love of contemporary fantasy with unexpected twists and turns in her novels for teens. Born and raised in rural southeastern Arizona, Debbie enjoyed growing up on a ranch, then later moving to the city and attending the University of Arizona, where she majored in Journalism. She has three sons and has been married to her college sweetheart for a really, really long time. Debbie currently lives in the metropolitan area of Phoenix, Arizona, where they have cacti in the front yard and a swimming pool in the back, along with a golden retriever, a cocker spaniel, and a cockapoo who love hugs and kisses. Visit Debbie at her website:

www.debbiefederici.com

## Other Books by Debbie Federici

*L.O.S.T.*
>	(with Susan Vaught)
>	LLEWELLYN, 2004

*ShadowQueen*
>	(with Susan Vaught)
>	LLEWELLYN, 2005

# Sign
## *of the*
# CRESCENT

**DEBBIE FEDERICI**

Llewellyn Publications
Woodbury, Minnesota

FIRST EDITION
First Printing, 2005

Book design and editing: Rebecca Zins
Cover art: background © Digitalvision,
landscape © Digital Stock
Cover design: Kevin R. Brown

Library of Congress Cataloging-in-Publication Data
Federici, Debbie Tanner, 1965-
 Sign of the crescent / Debbie Federici.
   p.  cm.
 Summary: Orphaned, seventeen-year-old Taryn, troubled by bizarre dreams, incapacitating vertigo from Ménière's disease, and strange sensations of power emanating from her crystal pendant, finds herself drawn to the mysterious Erick, a knight from a parallel world who could ultimately be her greatest enemy.
   ISBN-13: 978-0-7387-0808-9
   ISBN-10: 0-7387-0808-9
   [1. Fantasy.] I. Title.

PZ7.F3133Sig 2004
[Fic]—dc22

                                                            2005044142

Llewellyn Publications
A Division of Llewellyn Worldwide, Ltd.
2143 Wooddale Drive, Dept. 0-7387-0808-9
Woodbury, MN  55125-2989, U.S.A.
www.llewellyn.com

Printed in the United States of America

## Dedication

To my cousin Lora Decker, who has been one of my best friends and biggest supporters since age one.

To my best bud Jan Gentner, who has shared with me many major milestones, from college to boyfriends to family to hitting the big one.

I love you both!

## Acknowledgments

What would I do without my two wonderful critique partners, Susan Vaught and Sheri Gilbert, who have visited with Taryn and Erick so many times? I love you gals!

Love goes to my husband Frank and my three sons, Tony, Kyle, and Matthew, for paying attention when I put out the "Do Not Disturb" sign. Sometimes. Nothing like being the only girl in a houseful of guys! At least our dogs are girls—it evens the odds a bit. Hugs to Honey, September, and our little gal Sugar.

To my agent, Erin Murphy, who told me *Sign of the Crescent* isn't weird—or did she say that it's a *good* weird? Much appreciation goes to Kevin Brown for the fabulous artwork, to my editors Megan Atwood and Becky Zins, and to all the other terrific folks at Llewellyn for believing in *Sign of the Crescent*.

I can't forget to say thank you to dreams. Without that vivid dream I had one night, this book wouldn't be here. Without shooting for my dreams and making them happen, neither would I.

# PART ONE

. . .

*Seek the Crescent*

*Seek the crystal*

*Find them or perish*

*Find them and perish*

*Only fate can decide*

. . .

## October 13
## Tucson, Arizona

### *Taryn*

*"The epidemic of unexplained disappearances continues in Tucson, despite the increased number of police patrolling the city. Another six teenagers were reported missing last night.*

*"Similar statements are pouring in from authorities in four other cities in the southwestern U.S., all reporting record numbers of young adults vanishing over the past two months . . ."*

Silence hangs over the high school cafeteria as the news channel goes to station break, and it's as if cold fingers skim my spine. Murmured conversation picks up and I turn back to the rally poster I'm working on, coloring in block letters with a red marker.

My free hand goes to my throat. Lost in my thoughts, I pull out the chain from beneath my shirt and caress the half-moon pendant. Strange warmth flows from the black crystal through my fingers, and my arm tingles. A feeling of power rushes through me. Incredible, intoxicating power—

"Taryn?"

I jump at the sound of Jen's voice and my marker slashes red across the white poster board like a half-moon streak of blood across pale skin. Like my birthmark.

"Taryn Simons."

"What?" I blink and turn to see her brown eyes focused on me.

"I've called your name at least four times." She frowns. "I'm not sitting on your bad side, am I?"

"No." I shake my head. "I was just zoning."

She sighs and puts her hand on my shoulder. "Thinking about your grandmother?"

Avoiding her gaze, I trace block letters on the poster in front of me and don't answer.

"Hey, it's me you're talking to."

I take a deep breath and look up again. "I—I'm not ready to talk about Gran, okay?"

Jen cocks her head and I notice the elegant curve of her neck. I've always envied her high cheekbones and runway-model build. I'm considered full-figured, which is a nice way of saying I'm not thin by any stretch of the imagination. Jen has beautiful coffee-colored skin, as smooth as silk, where mine is pale and I have freckles scattered across my nose.

"You know I'm always here for you," she says. Gold bracelets clattering, she smiles and hugs me. Her beaded braids, pulled into one thick ponytail, swing forward and pop me in the eye.

"Ow!" I feign an injury by covering my eye with my hand. "You're lethal."

Grinning, Jen reaches across me for a blue marker. "Two more posters left."

"Hey, Jen. Taryn." The male voice draws my attention and I look up to see Phil, a good-looking guy from our biology class. "What time is the rally Saturday, and where's it at?"

As usual, I'm too tongue-tied around a gorgeous guy to say a word.

"Hiya, Phil." Jen hands him a neon pink flyer. "Three o'-clock, city hall."

He smiles at Jen and then me. "Great job organizing the rally, you two."

"Thanks." Jen waves. "See ya."

*"Lamflg,"* is about all I can get out. My cheeks heat and I bury my head on my arms. *I'm such a dweeb.*

As I raise my head, Jen lowers her voice and says, "That guy is a one-hundred-percent-fine-looking male."

"Better watch it or Josh might hear you."

"Yeah." A wistful look crosses her face. "I barely get to see him these days."

"That stinks." I reach into the backpack at my feet and pull out a tube of raspberry-scented lotion, then squeeze the lotion onto my dry hands and rub it in. The smell of raspberries mingles with the acrid scent of markers. "Your dad giving you grief?"

"What's new?" Jen raises her hands in exasperation, jingling the gold bracelets on her arms. "I'm almost eighteen, yet I can't even date? Cripes, I have to sneak around just to see the guy who's been my steady for the last two years. You'd think I'm still in middle school."

"Wonder what my dad would've been like?" I slide the lotion into my pack, picturing my father's handsome face from the photo at home. Well, at my foster home.

I wish I'd had the chance to know him. For a moment, I allow myself to indulge in the daydream of the perfect father who would have been around when I was growing up, if he hadn't died when I was a baby.

"Let me tell you," Jen's voice interrupts my daydream, "dads are *always* protective of their little girls." She drops a blue marker onto the table and grabs a black one. "I should

5

consider myself lucky to have a dad who cares. I know he's just concerned, and especially now, with all the kids vanishing."

"I hope we can get some action stirred up Saturday." While I sip my drink through a straw, I glance around the room at all the students busy helping with preparations for the rally. I set down my soda, pick up a marker, and start working on the poster again. "What I don't understand is why more people aren't upset about what's going on."

Jen nods. "I think our rally will kick butt. Get some attention."

"Too bad I don't have any magical powers." I grin and wave my hand as if I'm wielding a wand. "I'd fix the problem like that."

She giggles and rolls her eyes.

Buzzing fills my bad ear, like a bee has slipped inside my head. I drop the marker.

An overwhelming lightheadedness overcomes me. I clench my fists on the tabletop. The world shifts and I feel as if I'm on the low end of a seesaw. Up and down make no sense, and only my grip on the table keeps me from falling over.

*"Oh, no,"* I murmur, trying to focus on something to keep the vertigo at bay. The garbage can across the room—I stare at it, willing the dizziness away.

From the corner of my eye I see Jen's lips move, but the buzzing is so loud I can't hear what she's saying. An expression of concern crosses her face. She moves beside me and ducks under the table to grab my backpack.

Not this. Not now. It's been so long since I've had an episode.

I keep my eyes on the garbage can, afraid to blink, afraid to move. Paint chips scar its green sides and rust scatters like scabs across the can's surface—like wounds. Like the marks on my heart from Gran's death and the loss of my parents.

Sweat breaks out on my forehead and my stomach churns as Jen opens my fist and presses a tablet in my palm— meclizine from the bottle in my backpack. In my other hand she places my drink. I have to get the meds down before I start vomiting.

My hands tremble as I bring the tablet to my mouth and follow with a drink of soda through the straw, never taking my eyes off the garbage can. At first I think my throat is going to refuse the meds, but I manage to swallow it.

Just a few minutes and the episode will pass. It has to. I can't spend days flat on my back, unable to move. Unable to walk. Unable to eat. Unable to function. Damn Ménière's. It's rare for anyone under twenty to get the disease, but I've battled it since I was ten years old. I'm so sick of it, and it will never go away. In all probability, it will only get worse.

*Meditate. I need to meditate.*

The world slips away as I shut everything out and draw on my inner strength. I hear nothing but the buzzing in my head, see nothing but the garbage can in front of me, am aware of nothing but Jen's gentle hand stroking my back.

Inhale. Deep breath. Exhale.

I don't know how much time has passed when the buzzing fades and my stomach calms. Gradually the hearing returns in my good ear, though my more affected ear feels dead or stuffed with cotton. I can hear the talking and laughter of students around me. My body has been clenched so tight my muscles ache as I begin to relax and lean against my friend.

Jen. I had all but forgotten she was there.

"Thank you," I whisper.

"You gonna be all right?" She gives me a quick hug. "This is why I worry about you being alone. Your foster parents are practically never there. What's going to happen if you have an episode and nobody's around to help you?"

"I don't need Richard and Carolyn to be there. I can take care of myself."

She sighs. "All right. But I'm going to drive you home."

I start to shake my head, but stop myself. Sometimes the slightest head movement can bring on another episode. "I'll be fine."

"Don't start. I'll take you home so you can rest." Jen massages my shoulders, easing tension from my neck. "I'll get your homework from journalism class."

I want to argue, but I know she's right. I can't take the chance of having a full-blown episode while driving. Just a little rest and everything will be back to normal.

## Newold, Zanea

### Erick

Crimson-robed guards stand watch at the chamber entrance while Elders' Council members sit stiff-backed behind the crescent-shaped table. The room smells of must and age, along with burning pitch from torches mounted in sconces. It is unusually warm in the room due to all the Haro knights and Council members present for the session.

Adorned in their pristine white robes, the attention of every Elder is focused on Van, my twin, who stands before them. We are only eighteen years of age, yet have trained to be in the service of the Haro knights from the time we were toddlers.

Torchlight flickers across Van's calm face. She wears the garb of the Haro knight—black leather tunic, breeches and boots, her sword sheathed in its scabbard.

"The number of Oldworlders stolen by the Sorcerer Synomea has increased threefold." Van's gaze is direct as she speaks to the Council. "This in the last two cycles. It is more than the Haro can keep up with. Last night, in the Oldworlder city of Las Vegas, we lost ten of their youth—saved only eight."

"Lady Vanora, *esteemed* Haro knight." Council Voice Osred leans forward, dark eyes narrowing, his skin like ink in the low light. "Of this we are quite aware. Do not waste our time repeating knowledge common to the Council."

I clench my fists at my sides and open my mouth to speak, but Cole's grip on my shoulder stills me.

"No, Erick." My friend leans close to my ear, his voice so low only I can hear it. "Do not risk the wrath of the Elders. Let Van speak."

My friend is right, but it is difficult to bite back my anger at the complacency of the Council. At the stupidity of Osred. If I do not watch myself, I may be confined to the dungeons. I would not be able to join my friends in the fight to save our people, as well as those of Oldworld.

Van raises her chin, her mahogany braid falling over her shoulder. Her gray eyes appear calm, yet I know my sister and sense the frustration simmering beneath her skin. "It is only a matter of time," she says, "before Synomea's wickedness spreads across the Neguriän Sea to Newold."

Osred's brows furrow so deeply they become one. "You dare to imply the Council is lacking in its ministrations to Newold? To our sister cities?"

"Pardon, Voice Osred." Van straightens, tall and proud, her tone clear and even. "It is not my intention to make such an implication."

"Then speak." Osred waves his hand, as though brushing away an irritating fly. "We waste valuable time."

Van takes a deep breath and clasps her hands behind her back. "Several of our best Haro knights are willing to dispatch to Zumaria and infiltrate the Sorcerer Synomea's fortress."

"What say you?" Osred's look is one of incredulity. The other members of the Elders' Council stir and look from one to another.

"Synomea would not expect such a direct attack." Van speaks more quickly now, as if fearing Osred will not allow her to finish the proposal. "This elite team could dispatch within his fortress, find the sorcerer, and eliminate him."

What amounts to a small uproar follows Van's words. Council members whisper to one another. Haro knights murmur words of assent or dissent. Only the faces of the Council Guard remain impassive.

Quenn, the senior dispatch officer, brushes her short hair behind her ear. Her brown eyes flash at Finella, Van's closest friend. Finella returns Quenn's stare and shakes her head.

"Silence!" Osred slams a stone on the table, the sound cutting through the melee.

When all is again silent, he turns his dark gaze to Van. "And who would lead this team, Lady Vanora?"

"Lord Erick and myself." She nods in my direction and faces Osred again. "We would choose four among the most loyal of our knights."

Osred stands, as do the other Council members. "Council will consider your proposal and notify you when we have reached a decision." He inclines his head to Van, then leaves the chambers, all Council members following in his wake.

I grit my teeth and glare at Osred's backside as he retreats.

Van and Finella join Cole and me as we leave to head to Haro Command, the stone building beside Council chambers. From Command we will dispatch to Oldworld, as we have every night for the past two years.

It is early evening, the sun setting over the Vandre Peaks. Smells of wood smoke and pine from the surrounding forest linger in the cool air. The twin moons of our world glimmer faintly in the sky.

"That went exceedingly well," Finella murmurs, the frustration in her voice matching my own.

Cole shakes his head. "What now?"

The sound of boots against stone echoes into the night as we walk the short distance to Command.

"We wait," Van replies. "Maybe Council will vote in our favor."

"Not likely." I settle my hand on the hilt of Navran, my sword, and feel the familiar warmth of its magic flow through my palm. "The Elders believe it is enough to slow the pillaging of the young in Oldworld. They believe if Synomea's attention is on Oldworld's people, he will ignore ours."

"Osred is an idiot," Cole grumbles.

"Who are the other two knights you would suggest for this team?" Finella asks as we turn and walk up the steps to Haro

Command. "It goes without saying you would include Cole and me."

Cole grunts.

"Of course." With a smile, Van nods at our friends. "I believe we should choose Gareth and Basil. They are loyal to us and have been our friends since we were children."

Aye, we have been friends for a long time. We are all seventeen and eighteen years of age but are among Newold's finest swordsmen, and all willing to die for our people.

The squire opens the door to Command for us to walk through. Finella brushes by me into Command, her jasmine scent hanging in the air behind her.

Quenn, the senior dispatch officer, is already at her post at the na'ta command when we arrive. "What you proposed to the Council is foolish," she says, her face twisted in a scowl, brown eyes flashing.

Van smiles, but I can tell it is with effort. "Where's Albin?"

"Likely at the tavern. It is his night off," Quenn replies.

Van frowns as she and Finella mount the na'ta platform.

The mood of our group sobers as we dispatch in pairs to the Oldworlder cities we are assigned to—to what seems like a futile effort to save their people and our own.

# October 14

*Taryn*

*I dance in the shimmering light of the crescent moons. Beneath my bare feet, grass is soft and damp with dew. Joy sweeps through me, so sweet and intense it's almost painful. Around the glade I twirl, spinning at the edge of forest thick with silver-shaded pine. Night air tickles my nose with scents of spring rain and juniper.*

*Lion, always my companion, walks at my side. I stop to caress him, his golden mane coarse beneath my fingertips and his silvery eyes luminescent in the night. To my astonishment I can hear his deep-throated rumble strong and clear despite my bad ear, and the sound pierces my soul.*

*Even as I walk with the ever-trusting and loyal Lion at my side, I feel amazing power rising within me—a feeling I could control destinies, that I'm invincible, that I could—*

A cruel voice shatters my dream. *"Ta'reen, it is time. Come, Ta'reen!"*

I bolt upright in bed, pressing my hand to my racing heart. Goose bumps prickle my skin.

*"Come, Ta'reen . . ."*

The voice, so loud I swear someone is speaking in my head. I've never heard anyone so clearly. Like a surge of ice water, fear crashes into me. I can't breathe.

Silence.

My breath whooshes out, leaving me gasping, and I collapse onto my pillow. "Your imagination's running wild again," I tell myself. Why would I hear someone calling me Ta'reen? My dream. It must have been part of my dream.

Blessed silence is all I hear now.

Since when have I welcomed silence?

Raindrops patter against my window, and I turn my good ear to listen. The sound is strangely comforting. For Tucson, it's been raining far more than normal. Outside, a car's engine roars like Lion as it passes by, and I shiver. Shadows and light stalk one another across my ceiling.

Absently, I push up the sleeve of my T-shirt to rub the half-moon birthmark on my biceps. I blink sleep from my eyes and check the glowing digital clock. Almost midnight. I need to get some sleep since I have school in the morning, but I'm wide-awake. I had so much trouble falling asleep to begin with, because I keep having these strange feelings of danger. And now the dream—I'll never get back to sleep.

Why this dream? Over and over, these visions of a world with twin moons. I wake feeling as if I've been in that very meadow.

But what's more frightening is that feeling of power. It's almost . . . evil. And it's like I crave it, *want* it.

*No!* I could never be like that!

I've had these dreams every night since my seventeenth birthday, one month ago today, and exactly a week before Gran passed away.

My eyes ache and I grasp the only thing of real meaning to me since Gran died—the last piece of my parents: my heritage. My half-moon crystal pendant.

Just holding it in my palm soothes the ache, as it has soothed all my fears and heartaches since I was a child. As I touch the black crystal, that odd warmth flows through my limbs, and my hand tingles. Tension eases from my muscles and I relax.

I slip the pendant beneath my T-shirt so that it is close to my skin and try to go back to sleep.

*"Ta'reen! Outside, now!"*

Chills course my spine as the voice shouts in my head. In both ears.

Dizzy and bewildered, I sit up and swing my legs over the side of my bed. A force compels me to move. "I—I'm coming." My feet hit the floor.

Outside. I need to go outside.

Why? I don't know. I just know I must. Now.

The tile is cool to my bare feet as I rush through my foster family's dark house.

Hallway . . . foyer . . . alarm pad.

The code. Seven—two—one—four. *Beep!*

Damp night air against my skin. Wet concrete under my feet.

Hurry, I must get to the street. "I'm coming!"

---

## Erick

"What do you find so desirable in this place, Erick?" Cole asks as we talk in the shadows of the darkened street.

I shrug and swipe rain-soaked hair from my eyes. It is true this world is not as fair as our own. With the odd machinery, queer customs, strange-smelling air, and pale stars, Oldworld cannot compare to our beautiful Zanea. Yet it calls to me.

"Newold is more beautiful," I finally say, "but I rather enjoy this Tucson."

Cole's black eyes glitter in the faint light. "Give me Vandre Forests over this desert anytime."

With a laugh, I clap my friend's shoulder. "Some desert with all this rain of late." I glance at the na'tan at my wrist. "Portal. We had better go."

Cole nods, then vanishes.

I touch my na'tan and familiar tension vibrates my limbs. Air shimmers from silver to black as I appear at Cole's side on another Tucson street. In the distance, a young woman walks barefoot and unsuitably clothed beneath the glow of a street lamp.

"Damn! What is wrong with Quenn? Why did she dispatch us so far?" As I rip Navran from its sheath, I measure the distance between the girl and me with my eyes. "The portal will appear where she walks." I sprint toward her, racing on asphalt slick with rain. Around us thunder rumbles, masking the sound of my footfalls.

"We are too far, Erick. It is too risky!" Cole's voice fades as I run.

Even at such distance, I sense the portal's void before it opens. My gut tightens. By the gods! I cannot understand why Quenn dispatched us so far from the portal. At least a furlong! Racing, I clench my sword hilt, blood pounding in my veins.

The portal appears. A hum like a thousand berrymoths fills my ears.

The portal grows. Expanding. Blotting out all it touches.

A Zumarian warrior emerges through the blackness of the portal, its hulking form illuminated by the streetlight. From behind, Synomea's warrior looks like nothing more than a leather-clad man, but like all the sorcerer's minions, the beast's skull is burnt flesh and bone.

When she sees the warrior, the girl halts and for a moment seems frozen in place. She turns to run but her foot slips on the wet sidewalk. My hopes sink as the Zumarian clamps the girl's wrist with his claw and drags her toward the portal. I'm still charging forward, as if there might be some chance to save her.

"Let me *go!*" she screams and yanks her arm. With a howl, the warrior loses his grip and the girl tumbles to the concrete.

*She fought him off.*

Impossible!

The warrior lunges for her, his boots scraping the sidewalk.

Yet again the girl attempts to flee, but slides and falls to the ground. She twists and kicks at the warrior with her bare feet. "Get *away!*" she screams, her voice shrill and filled with fear and fury.

As I draw up behind the Zumarian, I barely have a chance to wonder at the girl's courage or the miracle of her escape from the warrior's grasp.

Runes glitter along my sword and my arm burns with familiar fire. The warrior's back is to me, and in one powerful stroke I behead it. Fluid spurts, drenching my tunic and the girl's. The head rolls into a puddle and stops, sightless eyes spattered with rain.

I spit on the ground in disgust for the sorcerer who sends these empty souls to steal Oldworlder lives. I shove the body and head of the warrior into the void. In moments the sorcerer's

17

portal vanishes, as if it had never existed. Black gore smears the street and metallic blood stench pollutes the air.

Heaving a sigh of relief, I wipe rain and Zumarian blood from my face. From where she sits on the sidewalk, the girl stares at me, mouth open, eyes wide. Her hair is red-gold in the streetlight's radiance, but darkening as it becomes wet from rain. She must not have been outside long.

The girl bleeds where the warrior's claws scratched her arms, and the beast's gore stains her tunic. Her breath comes hard and fast, and she shudders. I do not know what possesses me, but I reach out. Her eyes grow wild, and she flinches and draws back. Before she can escape, I crouch and clasp her hand, using the Old Magic to soothe her fears.

An odd sensation travels my arm the moment I touch her. It does not make sense, but I feel bonded with her—like she has always been part of me. I pull her to her feet and she trembles in my grasp. I catch her sweet scent. She smells of moonlight and raspberries.

Such intense eyes, almost fey. Even in the pale glow of the streetlight, I see they are green as grass, sprinkled with flecks of sunlight.

She tilts her chin to look into my eyes, then blinks the rain away. The top of her head just reaches my shoulders. "Th-thank you." How pleasant her voice is. It is low and breathless. "What happened? What was that? Who are you?"

The Old Magic. I should erase her memories and send her home. But the urge to know more of her nearly overwhelms me.

"I am Erick of Haro," I reply. "And you, milady?"

She looks taken aback and hesitates. "Taryn."

"A beautiful name." I grip her hand tighter. "It is not safe to be out at night."

"I—I'm not sure how I ended up out here." Taryn shakes her head. "I'm so confused. I was asleep and then a voice woke me. Next thing I know . . ." She presses her free hand to her temple and closes her eyes. "This is a dream and I'm going to wake up any minute now. I am not talking to a huge guy who just saved my life."

I smile. I have never felt such a need to protect another, as if I must. "Allow me to take you to your home, where you will be safe. Do not stray after dark again. It is dangerous."

"What?" She opens her eyes, a puzzled expression crossing her face, as if she cannot hear my words.

"Where do you live?" I pass my fingers over her forehead, using the Old Magic to coax the words from her lips.

Taryn glances to a house across the street. "There—" With a gasp she steps back, but I do not release her.

"It is all right, Taryn." I look over my shoulder at Cole, who stands tall behind me. His sword and his frown no doubt frightened the girl. "This is my friend, Cole."

"Are you out of your mind, Erick?" Cole shouts. "Calling an Oldworlder by her name?"

"I wish to take her to safety."

"No involvement. You know the rules."

The desire to clout my friend swells within and I clench my fist. One solid punch. "We will discuss this later."

Taryn attempts to pull her hand from mine. "Hey, I don't need you—ah, whoever you are—to take me home." Like wary prey, her gaze flits from Cole to me. "I'll be going," she says, her voice trembling.

The rules. I cannot allow her to remember. Before she can fly like a falcon-hunted sparrow, I place two fingers to her forehead and catch her to me as she collapses.

# October 15

## *Taryn*

*Burnt flesh and bone. Steel claws glittering in the streetlight. Flashing sword. A head rolling on the ground. Sightless eyes staring at me.*

"Are you okay, Taryn?" Jen touches my hand.

I shiver as she brings me out of that horrid daydream, back to reality and the high school library where we're studying. "You were saying something?"

She scoots her chair closer to mine and I catch the scent of her baby powder perfume. "Is something wrong?"

"Nothing. Not-a-thing." I force a smile and shake off the strange feeling I've forgotten something.

A sense of the surreal creeps over me as I check my watch and see scratches. Five on top of each forearm. There are more on my legs, but thankfully they don't show since I'm wearing jeans. The scratches were there when I woke up this morning, but, for the life of me, I can't figure out how I managed to cut myself.

My pillow and clothing were damp and my hair straight and matted, as if I'd soaked it in the shower before going to sleep. When I noticed the scratches, ice water chilled my veins. I tried to convince myself I must have scratched my arms in my sleep, but how could that be? And the T-shirt and boxers I slept in . . . where did all that black tarry stuff come from? It got all over my sheets, too.

Jen yanks her biology textbook from under a mountain of papers. "I'm worried about you."

"There's nothing to worry about." I try to make my voice sound lighter than I feel. I snap my notebook shut and stuff it and my algebra book into my backpack. "I've gotta run."

"I'll pick you up tomorrow for the rally." Jen taps her pencil on the tabletop. "You know it makes me nervous, you being alone at night when your foster parents are working. And those scrapes on your arms—I still can't believe you don't remember how you got them."

I shake my head. "I'm fine. I had a weird dream last night, and I'm sure I scratched myself in my sleep. Stop worrying so much about me."

"Somebody's got to, now that you're all alone."

"I told you, I'm *fine*. And I'm not alone."

"Well, you are, sort of. And there are way too many strange disappearances going on around here," she says. "Do me a favor and get a dog. A big one." Her grin sparkles mischief. "Or better yet, get a big guy."

I roll my eyes. "Like *that's* gonna happen."

"Why not? You're way too hard on yourself. A little on the pale side, but you're a fine-looking lady. Your problem is you're too quiet and you study too much."

"In case you haven't noticed, I'm not thin and gorgeous, and I'm going deaf in one ear."

With barely concealed irritation, Jen narrows her gaze. "Stop putting yourself down."

I shrug. "Whatever. The day some guy meets my strict criteria and falls for me, well . . . I'll buy you those beaded sandals you've been wanting."

"You're on." The spark comes back in her expression and she grins, her white teeth flashing against her dark skin. "I like the ones with the gold beads."

"Yeah, right." My chair scrapes tile as I stand and pull on my light jacket and swing my worn backpack over my shoulder. "See you tomorrow."

"Later." Jen waves, then cracks open her biology book.

I head out of the library, cross the campus, and breathe in the smell of fresh-cut grass and rain-soaked earth.

Jen's right—I study too much and keep to myself. I put all my focus and energy into being a straight-A student. I really want to be a top journalist and make a difference in the world.

But I can't help feeling that twinge of fear threatening to consume me. What if I start losing hearing in my good ear, too? Then the only way I'll be able to do interviews will be to read lips.

Oh, right. Like that'll work.

No. I can't dwell on the possibility of going completely deaf. If I let myself think too much about it, I might shatter into a thousand pieces. My grandmother had forced me to take sign language classes, and I was so angry with her for that. It was like admitting defeat.

While I walk across the parking lot, I free strands of hair caught in my chain. Out of habit, my fingers find the half-moon pendant and I feel that familiar surge of comfort, and the newer sensations of warmth and power. It's not simply a feeling of confidence, it's more a feeling of domination, of command, of mastery—over other people.

I drop my hand away and shiver. I don't like these feelings I've been having . . . yet I almost crave them.

No. This is ridiculous.

The horn beeps as I use the keyless to unlock my red VW Beetle. The new-car smell washes over me as I slide into the driver's seat and toss my backpack onto the floorboard of the passenger side. When I grip the steering wheel, my stomach clenches. The Bug was my grandmother's last gift to me on my birthday.

But now, just a month later, Gran is gone. I'm alone.

I choke down the knot in my throat, turn the key in the ignition, and the engine purrs. I drop the Bug into reverse and cut my eyes to the rearview mirror.

My foot slams on the brake pedal. A strange vision fills my mind, blocking out everything else.

I freeze.

*Skull-like, disfigured face. Claws of steel. Smell of rot.*

A terrifying sense of evil rushes me. A daydream—like the one in the library?

Another vision floods my mind, but this one is somehow soothing. *Silvery gray eyes. A gentle touch.*

I press my palms to my temples. "Flu. I must be coming down with the flu." I try to shrug off the eerie feelings as I back out the car and head home to another lonely Friday night.

---

## Erick

"Have you gone completely insane?" Cole snaps his reins as we ride our horses through the village of

23

Newold toward Haro Command, where we make our nightly journeys to Oldworld. "A Trendorian troll has more sense."

The sun hangs low to the west, and our shadows are long. I force myself to breathe and consider my words. "If you were not like a brother to me, I would not have told you of my feelings."

This gives Cole some pause, and his frown deepens. For a moment, the only sounds are our steeds' hooves against cobblestones and a mule braying in the town square. "But Erick. An Oldworlder?"

The twist in my belly could be no sharper, no hotter if it were made from a sword fresh from the forge. I turn and gaze into the depths of his coal-black eyes. "Do you think I do not know what I risk?"

With one hand, I gesture toward the west, and then the village. "Look there. The sun on Vandre Peaks. And around us, the glory of this city. Of Newold—and beyond, each of her sister villages. All these lives, so squarely on our shoulders.

"Gods!" I clench my jaw and rake my hand through my hair. "I would sooner rip out my own heart than lose a single soul, from our world or theirs. You know me. If I could deny this—this *recognition* of my heart's true mate, I would do it."

Cole averts his eyes. "Aye. You would." He sighs. "Of course you would. Your damnable honor. Sometimes I have feared it would steal you from us too soon. Erick, you know you and the others—you are the only family I have known. The only family I will ever know. If you are banished . . . the Council—"

I clench my steed's reins, the leather biting into my palms. "The people rely too much on the Council to protect them. It has been countless years since anything has posed a threat to our way of life—so many years our people forget the past, and may yet lose our future."

Cole's sigh scatters a bit of lingering smoke from a nearby smoldering cook stove. The air smells of pine and dying fire. It is evening, and shops have closed. I run my hand over my face and glance into the quiet marketplace where only a few villagers mill about, thinking of nothing beyond their own cares.

"Let us hurry," Cole grumbles. "It is almost time."

"Maybe I am crazy." As we ride, a feeling of weariness overcomes me. "But I cannot stop thinking of the girl. I do not understand what compels me, but I know I must see her. Just this once. Not tonight. Tomorrow."

The clatter of wagon wheels upon cobblestones interrupts our discussion. The driver cracks his whip and the horse whickers. Bits of straw tumble from the wagon as it rumbles onto the road leading to farmlands outside Newold.

When the noise fades, I turn back to Cole. "Well?"

He snorts. "You will see this girl whether I help you or not. My aid will only slow Voice Osred's tracking and get me banished along with you."

"We have been friends since we were children," I reply. "I trust no one else, save my blood sister. And she would never agree. You know I would never put you at risk, Cole. If Voice Osred raises the alarm, I will take full responsibility."

Cole brings up his mount in front of Command, beyond the hearing of Kean, the young squire who mans the doors this evening. My steed halts beside Cole's. Hands twisting his horse's reins, he studies the stone building where we dispatch to Oldworld. The building is older than I am. My father, one of the first Haro knights, served as Chief Commander and Council Voice.

Beside Haro Command is another building of stone, yet far more grand. Crimson-robed Council Guards stand watch at the entrance. Within the opulent building, where we so recently stood before the Council, dwell the Elders' Council members, growing lazy in their comfort.

Or perhaps treachery? Is that what keeps them blind to Synomea's threat?

Cole mutters, "Lady Vanora will surely have my head if she finds out I aided you."

"This has nothing to do with my twin." I manage a low chuckle. "And you had better not let her hear you refer to her as Vanora or Lady. She will be certain to have your head if you call her anything but Van."

A smile flickers across his face. "Aye. Van." With another heavy sigh, Cole shifts his weight in his saddle. "I am sure no good shall come of you seeing this Oldworlder." He shakes his head. "You are the only one I would do this for. Besides, if you are to be banished, I would just as soon keep you company."

I clap him on the back. "Thank you, my friend. Tomorrow night we will dispatch early."

When we dismount at the foot of Command, a groomsman takes our horses to the stables. Cole and I hasten up the steps, nod to the door squire, and head into the building. Only Council members and Haro knights are permitted through the doorway. Few know what lies within, and of our nightly missions. Often I wonder how our people can turn their backs on the dark shadow that lies far beyond our mountains and beyond the Neguriän Sea—the dark shadow sure to expand to Newold as Synomea's power grows.

So many Oldworlders—men and women, someone's child, brother, or sister—taken as slaves. It isn't right the people of Zanea are kept unaware of the extent of the Sorcerer's evil deeds. We are a compassionate people—or we used to be. Now, we are told not to think of it as a rescue of innocents, but rather as a protection of our own people. I am sure if this ignorance continues, it will prove fatal to our world.

When we enter Command, Council Voice Osred strides across the chamber and nods, his pristine white robes scrubbing tiles as he sweeps past. "Lord Erick, Sir Cole."

I return his nod. "Voice Osred."

Cole scowls. "Osred is an idiot," he mutters under his breath as the Council Voice leaves Command.

Albin, the pale dispatch officer, stands behind the granite na'ta command where he controls the na'ta magic. His hands are quick, his magic strong, and most nights he has no problem managing the dispatch of ten Haro teams, two teams per Oldworlder city that Synomea opens portals to each night.

Lady Quenn is the only knight with more skill at dispatching than Albin, but lately I have seen little of her. She is a difficult person to contend with, but I have great respect for her.

Cole's dark eyes narrow when he sees Albin. As usual, I have the feeling he does not like Van's beau.

I am not sure I like him either. "Good eve, Albin."

"You just missed Gareth and Basil," Albin says.

Grinning, I shake my head. "Why the Council partnered those two is beyond comprehension. They are as likely to kill each other as they are to slay the sorcerer's beasts."

My sister Van and raven-haired Finella enter Command as Cole and I step onto the na'ta platform. I smile at my twin and at my sapphire-eyed former flame. Finella and I ended our courtship months ago, but we remain friends. Finella, whose blood is said to be part Elvin, is a bewitching young woman.

Albin kisses Van, and when they part, she smiles at him. Beside me, Cole growls, and I attempt to hide a scowl. If Van finds Albin worthy, then he must be. I trust her judgment. However, I cannot help but feel no one is good enough for my sister.

"No portals are set to open in your quarter as yet." With fluid movements, Albin's fingers move over the na'ta command. "May the gods be with you tonight."

My gut churns as the dispatch begins. In the two years I have traveled from Newold to Oldworld, I have yet to become used to the difficult journey. Once we arrive in Tucson, it is easier to dispatch from one street to the next, and the return to Newold is fair.

I grind my teeth as every muscle in my body tightens, drawn so taut each fiber might snap with a movement. All around me radiates silver until I see nothing.

Air shimmers again from silver to purple to black, and I arrive on a deserted Tucson road devoid of light. I drop to one knee. My breath comes in short gasps.

Cole appears at my side. His breathing is heavy and he sways, but keeps to his feet.

"If we continue this madness for long, we shall become old before our time." I glance at my na'tan. "Gods—so soon? Portal."

We dispatch again and appear behind three girls who walk along a street that is empty save for darkened houses and Oldworlder machines that sit like black beasts of night. Windows glitter on the machines like a Trendorian dragon's scales.

"Damn!" I have yet to recover my full strength from the harsh dispatch from Newold. My knees threaten to buckle and I stumble toward one of the girls. At the same moment I grab her arm, the portal opens and a Zumarian warrior steps out.

The girls shriek.

I use the Old Magic as I press my fingertips to the forehead of the female I hold, and she slumps to the ground. Cole grabs another girl.

The warrior throws the third over its shoulder before Cole and I can attack. The moment the beast touches her, the girl is rendered unconscious. Her hair is gold and for a moment I fear it is Taryn, but in my gut I know it is not.

Cole and I leap toward the Zumarian, but he steps into the portal and vanishes with the girl.

"Damn that beast!" In disgust I kick the ground.

Cole bends over the girls to attend them. "Two is better than none."

"Every life has value." I help him administer the Old Magic and send the girls to their homes with no memory of this night. The Zumar never open a portal on the same street in a single night, so the girls are safe. They will wonder what happened to their friend, but I can do nothing about that.

She is lost to them forever.

The thought of Taryn being taken by such beasts tears at my heart. I must see her again, if only to warn her, to use the Old Magic to ensure that she will never leave the safety of her home at night.

# October 16

*Taryn*

After we have dinner out, Jen drops me off from the rally at city hall. I let myself into the house and key off the alarm. It was an intense day, but we made the evening news and we hope to get more people in the community involved in stopping the disappearances. What has happened to all the teenagers who have vanished these past couple of months?

I toss my keys and my backpack onto the kitchen table and make myself a cup of hot cocoa in the microwave. The sweet smell of chocolate fills the room.

I head outside to the back porch with my mug of chocolate and settle into the swing. Moonlight seeps through clouds, lacing their edges with silver and black. A ghostly haze shrouds the stars and I wish they were visible.

Other than gentle moonlight, the only illumination comes from the kitchen window. A soft breeze cools my cheeks, but my light jacket keeps me warm. The backyard is cozy and comforting, and a place where I can escape.

Sweet-smelling honeysuckle climbs the trellis and hibiscus bushes crouch along the wall. Their blooms are shadowed and I can barely see them in the dim light. I drink the rest of my hot chocolate, the warmth spreading through me as I unwind.

After I set my cup on the table beside the swing, I close my eyes and meditate. I take deep breaths and exhale. Relaxing. Melting into the worn cushions.

Meditating is something I've done instinctively since I was a child, when I began to lose my hearing to Ménière's disease. I would withdraw within myself and focus, as if that act alone could allow me to hear things more clearly. Meditation helps me make it through the fierce episodes of vertigo.

A strange sensation prickles my skin—I feel like I'm being watched. The sound of a footstep startles me out of my meditation. My lids fly open and I jerk my attention toward the yard.

My heart stops. I can't breathe.

A stranger. Towering over me. Night shrouding his face.

Panic almost paralyzes me. "What are you doing here?" My voice trembles, but I manage to stand to my full five feet seven inches and lift my chin, my hands clenched into fists.

The guy must be a full foot taller than me. What can I do? I can't get around him. I take a deep breath. Think, Taryn!

He steps into the light. A rugged face and tentative smile that roots me to the spot. And those eyes—almost luminescent. *Silvery gray.*

My dream!

My heart revives, hammer-strikes against my breastbone. I glance to a sheath at his side. A sword? Who carries a sword? And the way he's dressed—like he's going to a Halloween party a couple of weeks early.

He extends his hand.

I step away, set to dodge around him, but the backs of my knees hit the seat's edge. Losing my balance, I fall into the porch swing.

The stranger slides next to me and traps my hand beneath his. For an instant I'm frozen.

I feel a jolt throughout my body and see flashes of memory.

*Terror. Evil. Clutching me. Dragging me . . . to a black hole. Then this guy with the silvery gray eyes. Protecting me.*

Everything that happened that night comes back in a rush, like cold rain sweeping over my body. I remember the horrible man grabbing me, raking his nails down my arms. I remember this guy . . . cutting the man's head off, saving me. But it's all so surreal I can hardly wrap my mind around it.

And I feel something more, something strong and urgent. It's as if I've known this guy all my life. As if I've been waiting for him. His touch is soothing, drawing every bit of fear from me. From the depth of my being I know I can trust him. How? I don't know. But it's like . . . *magic.*

"You rescued me." It's all I can think of to say.

His strong hand grips mine even tighter and he smiles.

"Wh-who are you?"

"Erick." As he speaks, a thin scar whitens along his cheekbone.

"I—I'm Taryn." No—wait. Why am I telling him? I can't seem to help myself. It's like he's coaxing the words from my mouth and comforting me at the same time.

"I know." He grins and the sensation in my midsection intensifies. His deep voice portrays an old world kind of accent, like he comes straight from the Middle Ages. Intelligent eyes convey passion and perhaps a bit of recklessness.

That's right. I remember telling him my name the night I met him. I shake my head. "But who are you?"

"Erick of Haro."

I attempt to pull my hand away, but it's trapped beneath his fingers. I should be frightened, but I'm not. I don't understand it, but he makes me feel comfortable. Confident. "Okay, then. Why are you here?"

Erick moves closer and his leather-clad thigh brushes my leg. He clasps both my hands in his. "The Elders would ask me the same." His voice is low, but his words are clear and forceful. He's sitting on my left, so I don't have much trouble hearing him.

"It is difficult to put into words," he continues, "but I knew I must see you."

"Me?" Confused, I blink at him. "Why would you need to see me?"

"You have remained in my thoughts since that night." Erick brushes a loose strand of hair from my eyes, and I shiver. "You have bewitched me."

"Bewitched?" My voice nearly fails me.

He leans closer. His musky scent of sun, leather, and horse fills my senses.

Before I realize what's happening, he brushes his lips over mine. Soft, sweet. Everything inside of me melts.

Cold realization splashes over me. I put my hands on his muscled chest and shove. "Stop!" I jump up from the swing and stand on the porch, every part of my body shaking. "This is crazy. I can't kiss you. I don't even know you!"

"I beg your pardon, Taryn." He looks down at his scuffed boots, then glances at me with a guilty grin. "I am not sorry for kissing you. But you have my apology for not asking."

"Oh." I can't stop a brief smile. I love the way he says my name. Lyrical, like the sweetest music. "I don't kiss guys I've just met." Heck, I don't even kiss guys I've known for a while, but I don't tell him that.

"Sit with me. You have my word I will not take such liberties again. I must leave soon, but until then, may we talk?" His gaze flicks to a black wristband, then back to me. His features are earnest, eyes pleading.

My heart melts like ice in the desert heat. I want to throw myself at him and feel his lips against mine again.

What am I thinking?

"All right. We can talk. But you have to promise to behave." It takes all my control not to touch my tingling lips.

Erick moves to the far end of the swing. He's dressed in black, from sleeveless tunic to tall leather boots, and looks like a swordsman from some medieval tale.

"I want to know more of you." His eyes are sincere, his gaze never leaving my face.

I sit at the opposite end. On the edge of the seat—I can run if I have to. But I feel I won't need to. My attraction to him is overpowering. I feel a link between our souls, drawing me closer to him. And it's not because he's good-looking—there's just something about him.

*Soul mate.*

At the turn of my thoughts, I shake my head. Confusion and curiosity war within me, my thoughts in chaos. "Now, wait a minute. You're supposed to tell me about you, not the other way around. Prove to me you're not some kind of maniac." I fold my arms and eye Erick with what Gran called my "Ms. Stubborn" look.

He grins. "It is most attractive." A cleft dimples his strong chin.

Goodness, he's cute. Maintain, Taryn. Keep your cool. Some Ms. Stubborn. "What's attractive?" I manage to ask with a straight face.

"You are a fighter. To the last. It was no easy feat to escape the Zumar."

Unease spreads through me like a thousand worms crawling under my skin, and I wring my hands in my lap. "I was terrified."

"I saw no fear. If your eyes could have struck the warrior down, my blade would have remained clean."

"Hey, we're supposed to be talking about you, remember?"

With a shrug, he replies, "There is little to tell."

I raise one eyebrow. "Yeah, right."

Erick gazes at the dark sky, blond hair brushing his broad shoulders. "I am not from here. But I have been coming to this place a long time. The evil being that tried to take you— it is my job to stop its kind. I am a Haro knight. It is what I have trained for from childhood."

"A Haro knight? Evil beings? What I saw was a man, not some creature." I inch farther away from Erick, and almost fall off the swing.

*A skull-like face.*

*The stench of blood.*

*Erick, taking my hand and helping me to my feet.*

*The beast's claws scraping my arms.*

The scratches!

"Taryn, you must know that . . . creature . . . was no man."

"You—you cut its head off."

"It is the only way to kill the Zumar."

I'm not sure why, but faith in Erick grows within me. "I— I do believe you. I remember a man. Your friend. He was upset with you for calling me by my name."

"That was Cole. He is fit to slay a dragon over my desire to see you. But a good friend." Erick looks back to the sky as if it holds answers to all the world's problems. "I should not be here. It is forbidden for Haro to interact with Oldworlders beyond our duties."

I don't know what possesses me to lean close and place my hand on Erick's. Mine is so small against his. He turns back to me. His crooked smile alone draws me to him.

"Thank you for saving me," I say. "I'm confused about all this, but I'm glad you came."

Erick glances again at the wristband. "Alas, I must go."

"Oh." Disappointment ebbs through me, leaving only emptiness. "Will you come back?"

What am I saying? What's wrong with me?

"Perhaps tomorrow night." He squeezes my hand between both of his.

Erick's face is so close to mine, I catch my breath. With a casual gesture, he raises his fingertips to my forehead . . .

Sleepy and bewildered, I make my way into the house, lock the door, and set the alarm.

What was I doing outside? My thoughts feel fuzzy. Strange. I go to my room and change into a T-shirt and boxers, then tumble into bed.

*Erick*

I shake off the tension of the dispatch as I wait for Cole. The night has a breathless silence to it until a shimmer stirs next to me, and Cole appears.

36

"What kept you?" I say to Cole. I stride toward a boy who jogs toward us along the darkened street. Thank the gods not another person is in sight.

The boy stops. "What the—" he shouts when I grab his arm.

"Your whim satisfied, Erick?" Cole presses his fingertips to the boy's head and catches him when he collapses.

"I must see her again." A humming noise tells me the next portal is opening, and I ready my sword while Cole settles the boy upon the street. I raise my weapon as the black void appears.

A Zumarian steps through. My blood pounds. Charging forward, I swing my sword at the beast's neck. It deflects my blow with its claws and flings me to the ground with the strength of three men, knocking breath from me.

As I scramble to my feet, Cole attacks the warrior from behind and severs the Zumarian's head. A fountain of gore and blood drenches my tunic. Cole shoves the carcass into the sorcerer's portal and I kick the head into the void as it closes.

After Cole wipes his blade on a patch of grass, he drives the sword into its sheath. "This girl is not worth the risk."

My muscles tense. Resisting the urge to pummel my friend, I fight to keep my voice calm. "Choose your words with care."

"Your life." Cole scowls. "You wish to lose all for an Old-worlder? Hell, Erick. Do you not remember years ago?"

How could I forget? It was my own father. I stare into the darkness, measuring Cole's words. This place called Tucson, it is one of the better assignments. But to never return to Newold?

"Your family was a great power," he says. "Your father risked all. And lost all. Lady Van and you have done well to recover what he cast away. Do you dare gamble as your father did?"

Silence weighs heavy between us. "Your concern is noted," I finally say. "The future, what it holds for me, I do not know." I run my hand over my head and glance up at pale stars. "But I must see Taryn."

Cole clenches his hands. "No names! Do not think of Old-worlders as people. If taken by the Zumar, they are lost forever. No emotion, no involvement—it is the only way."

I cut my eyes from the dark sky to Cole's face and shout, "You speak like the Elders! Night after night, you see lives torn apart. How can you not care when the Zumar abduct innocent people?"

His gaze is steady; not a muscle flinches. "It is my job. We save these people only to protect our own world. I dare not think of their pain—their suffering." A pause, and my friend's face creases with pity before hardening with resolve. "It can be no other way, Erick, lest we become soft—unable to serve in even this way."

I sigh. "I will consider your words."

Cole reaches down to the boy and wakes him with a touch, then uses the Old Magic to send the youth home with no memory of this night.

I glance at my na'tan. "Gods, we are late." Without waiting for a response from Cole, I touch my na'tan and dispatch.

---

Frustrated, I stomp into my bedchamber and remove my tunic and breeches. This night we dispatched to seven portals. We saved five lives, but another six we lost to the Zumar. The memory of the Oldworlders taken by Synomea's minions seethes in my belly. If only they could resist the Zumar touch as Taryn did.

Dark thoughts of the night's failures threaten to consume me, and I force them away. I turn my mind toward more pleasant memories.

*Taryn.* From the moment my eyes met hers, I knew I needed to see her again. To be with her. Like a berrymoth to lotho trees, she draws me closer. Taryn's beauty rivals any in Newold, but it is her courage and strength of soul that calls to me.

By the light of Nar, what am I thinking? Am I willing to gamble everything—my blood sister, my home, my lands—to spend stolen moments with a girl of a different world? That I am willing to involve Cole?

My father. Did it not lead to his death at the whim of that evil sorcerer?

I must not see Taryn again. I was a fool to risk everything to see her tonight. But the briefest touch filled me with such warmth. Her hand on mine. My lips against hers.

I fling myself on my berth and slam my fist against the mattress. Feather quills poke my knuckles as my hand sinks into the tick. With a heavy sigh, I turn over and stare at the beams, and see nothing but Taryn until I fall asleep and dream.

# October 17

## *Taryn*

In the front yard I rip a dying ragweed from the wet earth, then sneeze before tossing it near a prickly pear cactus. The smell of dirt and marigolds surrounds me and a rogue horsefly zooms by my face. It's starting to get dark, but I'm just about finished with the yard work. Leaning back, I wipe sweat from my eyes.

When Gran passed away, I was forced to live in this foster home until I turn eighteen, a year from now. Richard and Carolyn, my foster parents, are all right, and I don't mind at all that they're not around much. I do what I can to help out with the yard and housework.

More than anything, I wish my grandmother were here. Missing her is an ache digging away at my soul, an anvil of pain permanently lodged in my chest.

Through my grief these past weeks, I've realized my grandmother was preparing for her death all along. Somehow Gran knew she was dying, though she never warned me. Not in so many words.

Damn! If she loved me, why didn't she tell me? I know I'm being selfish and unfair, but it hurts so much. She could have prepared me—could have let me know she wouldn't be with me much longer. If she'd let me know, I would have made sure every second counted!

Without realizing it, I had finished weeding the front yard. I dust off my clothes, head into the house, and lock the door behind me. After I enter the foyer, I pause at my bedroom and glance at the photo sitting on the bureau of my parents and me. Ian and Stacie. My family. My mother appears so youthful, so full of life. The look on her face as she gazes at my father is pure adoration. My handsome father stares down at me as an infant, an odd look on his face. Pride? Longing? A feeling of déjà vu washes over me.

In the kitchen, I throw a bag of popcorn in the microwave and click on the radio.

*"More teenagers were reported missing last night."* The DJ's voice holds more concern than I'm used to hearing from him. *"The police have beefed up patrols, but the disappearances have only increased . . ."*

With a grimace, I switch off the radio. Being alone most of the time with all the disappearances going on makes me scared enough, without listening to those reports.

I wash the dirt from my cheeks and hands at the kitchen sink. The smell of popcorn fills the room as I dry my hands and face on a dishtowel. I grab a pitcher of lemonade from the fridge and, while I pour a glass, I again notice the scratches on my arms. Where did they come from?

*Metal claws rake my arms, tearing into my flesh.*

*Terror dashing into me like a tidal wave.*

*I scream and try to fight off the skull-faced beast—*

I hear the splatter of fluid and glance down to see I'm still pouring, my glass overflowing and the lemonade spilling onto the counter and tile.

What's wrong with me? Why do I keep having these strange daydreams?

Once I sop up the mess with a dishcloth, I take the cloth to the laundry room and toss it in with my dirty clothes. On top of the pile are the pink T-shirt and boxers I usually sleep in—covered with that black tarry stuff . . . *that looks like dried blood.*

My hands shake as I pick up my T-shirt. The fabric is stiff where it's coated in that dark substance. It smells strange, like rotting garbage left in the sun too long. It's the shirt I slept in the night I got these scratches. But my wounds couldn't possibly have produced so much blood—if that's what the stuff is.

Even stranger, every time I try to think about what happened that night my mind grows fuzzy, like something is preventing me from remembering.

The microwave beeps, bringing me back from my thoughts, and I toss the shirt onto the pile. I'll deal with it later.

When I'm armed with popcorn, lemonade, and a fantasy novel, I head out through the back door and sit on the porch swing. It's late afternoon and a balmy breeze sweeps over me. The bougainvillaea bush tumbles in a purple riot to the side of the porch and the red hibiscus blooms bob their heads. The garden waterfall chuckles as water tumbles over the rocks.

While I munch popcorn the strange daydream nags at me, but I don't know what to do about it. Could it have something to do with these scratches? How could something have happened Thursday night that I don't remember?

When I'm finished eating, I set the empty bowl and glass on the little table beside me, along with the book. The swing rocks back and forth, my weary muscles melting into the cushions.

*A charming grin, a gentle touch.*

My eyes open and I press my fingertips to my mouth. What kind of daydream is this, that I can feel the pressure of lips against mine? A dull ache spreads throughout my limbs, and gentle warmth in my chest.

With my hands clasped behind my head, I stretch out so that my ankles rest on one arm of the swing, with my head below the other. Honeysuckle vines shade the porch, enveloping me in their thick perfume.

The hummingbird feeder swings in the afternoon breeze, back and forth, lazy and hypnotic. A comfortable feeling of weariness overcomes me as the trickle of the garden waterfall lulls me to sleep.

---

## Erick

Van and I guide our horses through the forest from Newold Village to the wizards' cottage. It is a short journey to the meadow where I often played as a boy. Ancient beyond comprehension, the wizards are revered, even feared, by most of Newold. The powers the wizards control are rare indeed.

"I am surprised the wizards summoned us," Van says.

"What could they want with you and me?" I reply. "It has been a long time since anyone has seen L'iwanda and L'onten."

"It is a sign. Like a song on the wind." Van tightens her grip on her horse's reins, her white knuckles the only indication of what must simmer beneath her calm exterior.

My horse snorts and tosses his head.

Wind cools my neck and sun dapples the ground through pines. I swipe at a berrymoth that nears my face and it buzzes away. Only hooves hitting stone, creaking saddle leather, and a lark's trill interrupt the quiet afternoon. As always these past few days, thoughts of Taryn weigh heavy on my mind. I try to dismiss this longing to see her again, but it consumes me, a constant fire burning within.

No. I will not give in to my desire. I will not go to her today.

"I do not believe this meeting with the wizards would cause you to appear so concerned." Van's voice cuts into my thoughts. "What is wrong?"

"Nothing." I let up a bit on my charger's reins. I want to tell my blood sister of Taryn, but I cannot find the words. And I know it would worry Van.

My twin looks at me beneath her dark lashes, her gray eyes studying mine. I never could fool her. Even as a child, she knew when I was up to mischief or troubled.

To my relief, the wizards' cottage comes into view and I am saved Van's scrutiny. Silver-leafed oaks surround the rambling home. Roses, tulips, and foxgloves flourish in the front. It is early spring, yet the wizards' flowers bloom year-round. To the back lies the herb garden. As I dismount, I catch a whiff of rosemary and sage, mint and thyme.

Before I lift my hand to knock, the aged door creaks open. It is too dark to see within.

"Come," a voice says, resonant with authority.

"We have been expecting you," says another.

My gut tightens. By force of habit, I rest my hand on my sword hilt. I glance at Van, then duck through the doorframe. It is so dim I squint until my eyes become accustomed to what light is offered by fat candles on bookshelves and tables. The cluttered recess smells of cloves and burning tallow.

"Pray, sit." L'iwanda, a pale woman of my height, sweeps rolls of parchments from a wooden bench to the floor.

"Little time we have." L'onten, a man taller than I, settles onto the frayed cushion of a divan. L'iwanda joins him. Their faces are ageless. I wonder if the tales are true and they are indeed as old as rumored.

Van and I sit next to one another on the bench, across from the wizards. Unease stirs within me as I see L'iwanda and L'onten's troubled expressions, and I pull at the neck of my tunic. It is stifling in this room.

"You are present for the knowing," L'onten says. He is clean-shaven, and his bald head shines as brightly as one of our moons.

Her hands clasped, Van leans forward. Mahogany tresses spill over her shoulders, not confined by her customary braid. "We came as soon as we received your summons."

L'iwanda tilts her head, her silver hair shimmering with the movement. "You fear for Newold, that the Council has become incompetent."

Surprise crosses Van's face and my own gut betrays my alarm. How do they know? The Elders would consider it treason to hear such words spoken aloud.

"Aye," Van admits, her voice soft, even in the stillness of the room. "We fear the indifference of our people spells doom for the world of Zanea. Your guidance would be of great benefit."

I snort. "Our kinsmen think only of bread on their tables and fat rabbits in the stewpot."

L'iwanda's enigmatic smile is filled with a sinister mystery. "This is the dark time foreseen."

Candlelight reflects on L'onten's bald head as he nods. "When the actions of the few answer the unspoken prayers of the multitude."

L'iwanda holds out her hand to me. "Your sword."

"Let us see Erickson's blade," L'onten adds.

I only hesitate a moment. I unsheathe Navran and pass it to L'iwanda, hilt first. Wizard's runes glitter along the blade at her touch.

"Oh, aye." L'iwanda's black eyes sparkle, a foil to her silver hair. "It has been many years since this sword was needed for such a cause." She gives it to L'onten.

"Five centuries." L'onten smiles, and green sparks drip from Navran's edge. "As the prophecy foretells, 'twill be soon it shall fulfill its destiny. The L'iwanda and L'onten magic shall be Lion's to wield."

The hilt burns in my hand when L'onten returns it to me, and I sheathe the weapon, saying, "Are you certain? The prophecy is as old as the sword. Navran was handed to me from my father, and from his father before him, and before. The prophecy has never come to pass, yet we have always prepared."

"Aye," L'iwanda replies with a nod.

"So, it is true," Van murmurs as her gaze meets mine. "The descendant of Erickson the Great, our grandfather many times removed, will wield Navran against tremendous evil. You are the keeper of the sword, and its fire is yours alone."

I shake my head. "I have felt a measure of its power. But to be the one . . ."

L'onten takes L'iwanda's hand and they both close their eyes.

Cold blankets the room, vanquishing all warmth. I shift in my seat and glance again at Van. Her face is wan as she watches the wizards. Unay, our housekeeper, says Van is so like our father was. Calm, with an inner strength I can only envy and fierce loyalty few people would dare challenge.

"By the fire of Navran," L'onten says. A vase rattles on the bookshelf.

"And the power of the crystals," L'iwanda adds. Candle flame sputters.

"On Allhallows Eve . . ."

"Under the light of the moons . . ."

"Loyalties will be tested."

"Blood shall spill."

"And be it love or power . . ."

"Good or evil . . ."

"The choice of the Crescent . . ."

"And the will of the Lion . . ."

"Seal the destiny of Zanea."

L'onten's voice trails away and ice fills my veins. I have never thought much about prophecy, yet I cannot help but feel disturbed by the wizards' haunting tones.

"What must we do?" Van asks as she rubs her arms. Her skin is roughened like goose flesh and I know she must feel the same chill I do.

The wizards open their eyes.

L'iwanda links her fingers in her lap. "You know what must be done, my children."

I nod. "We need to travel to Zumaria and confront the sorcerer himself."

Her eyes wide, Van looks from the wizards to me. "The Elders' Council will never approve. They do not believe the sorcerer's evil ways will reach across the sea. They believe it is enough to slow Synomea's hand in Oldworld."

"They become more complacent with every day that passes." I clench my fist and hit my thigh. "It is as though Synomea's will already extends to Newold."

My sister's mouth tightens. "If we do this, it will mean our exile. Or imprisonment. Assuming we survive."

L'onten stands, his face a pale moon against the midnight blue of his robes. "Time runs quickly, like a river after a spring thaw."

L'iwanda's arms float upward, as if drawn to the sky. "Seek the Crescent."

"Seek the crystal."

"Find them or perish."

"Find them and perish," L'onten says, and then . . . he is gone, as smoke swirling in the wind.

L'iwanda drifts from her seat, arms still reaching for the stars. "Only fate can decide." She flickers and vanishes, like a snuffed flame.

Freezing, crushing coldness slams into me.

Candles extinguish. Darkness.

Before I can get to my feet, everything vanishes around me.

Brightness. I blink light from my eyes. The smells of sun-warmed loam, pine, and herbs surround me. Outside the cottage, I sprawl on the ground next to our horses. Van sits at my side.

"The audience," Van says, with no emotion, "is over."

# October 18

*Taryn*

I head out to the cafeteria's courtyard to meet Jen at our usual lunch spot. We prefer to eat outside because the weather is usually great—and inside, students chatter so loud it is hard to carry on a conversation, especially with my bad ear.

"Hey there," I say when I see Jen's exasperated look. "Having a Monday from hell?"

"Is there any other kind?" She slams down her lunch tray and the sandwich bounces off like a plastic-wrapped football. "Monday was created by Satan, right? I bet if I poke hard enough in my father's Bible, I'll find that part."

I laugh as I slide onto the bench, clattering my own tray on the table and dropping my backpack next to my feet. "Your dad again?" I ask as I unwrap my sandwich.

"What else?" She grabs her plastic spork and picks at her pasta salad. "Until something's done about these disappearances, I have zero social life."

Something tugs at my subconscious. What is it? What's with all those disappearances? I brush the vague feeling away and take a bite of my turkey sandwich.

Jen scoots closer to me and drops her voice. "You remember Sid Stewart from history class? The one with the spiked pink hair?"

I nod while sipping a drink of soda through a straw.

"I heard from Josh that Sid's been missing for two weeks."

Goose bumps prick my skin and I hurry to swallow. "That's the third person I've heard of from our class."

Jen frowns. "Jon Blake's been gone for a year, at least. Who's the other?"

"Micki Reese."

"Duh." Jen slaps her forehead. "I knew that. Poor kid. She was a snot, but no one deserves that."

My sandwich doesn't look so good now, and I toss it on the tray. "On the radio this morning, I heard they're doubling the number of cops patrolling the streets at night. I think our Saturday rally did some good."

"Let's hope so. It's getting way weird out there." Jen takes a sip of her lemonade. "That's why you need to get a big dog."

I give her a faint smile, and then my gaze trails across the courtyard as I speak. "All of this has given me some strange dreams." I turn back and toy with my soda's straw. "I dreamed some bizarre creatures are taking everyone. These things are tall, with skull-like faces and charred flesh." My skin crawls. "And they drag people through a black hole to another world."

Jen giggles and snorts, definitely not ladylike. "Girl, you should be writing fantasy novels instead of planning to report the news."

With an embarrassed grin, I say, "Maybe I can turn all these weird dreams into a book. I've always loved to write, but I've never had such a vivid imagination as I do now. It's as if someone or something has a hold on me."

I don't tell her about the feeling of power that has been consuming me lately—like I could rule the world and have everyone on their knees before me.

"Don't know about you." Jen shakes her head and smiles.

I caress my pendant, and for a moment I'm lost in my thoughts, enjoying the feelings that now rush through me when I touch it. I shouldn't like them, shouldn't want them, but somehow I do.

Jen taps my hand with her finger and I look up to see her warm brown eyes watching me. "Hey. Is there something wrong?"

"I'm fine." I do my best to smile.

"Remember who your best friend is if you need to talk." Jen waves to someone, then scoots off her seat and dumps the contents of her tray in the garbage can. "Wrap it up. We've gotta get to algebra."

"I'm coming, I'm coming." I clean my own tray, grab my backpack, and we head off to class.

I slip my pendant under my shirt as we walk, and feel its tingling warmth against my skin. I enjoy that sense of power overcoming me . . . intoxicating . . . incredible . . .

I shake my head, trying to rattle the thoughts out of my mind.

---

After I finish my homework, I talk with Jen on the phone for a while, then head to my bedroom, put on a V-neck T-shirt, and lie down. It's dark, the only light coming from my bedroom window.

As I drift off to sleep, I feel like I'm waiting for something—or someone.

A presence wakes me, and I open my eyes.

The Nordic god from my daydreams stands above my bed, a silhouette against a background of black night. He leans closer, into the light from the window, and smiles.

What a dream.

I bolt upright, my feet thumping onto the floor. My heart thuds. This isn't a dream. A guy is in my bedroom.

"Get—get out of my room!"

His lips move, but he speaks too softly and I can't hear the words he's saying.

"I said leave!"

With a quick movement, he grabs my hand. His touch electrifies me—and unlocks my memories.

A sigh of relief escapes me. "Erick."

"I could not stay away." He moves to my left side and folds his long frame onto the bed beside me, and the mattress squeaks from his weight. His silvery eyes caress me with a glance. "I apologize for waking you."

"Ah . . . that's okay." I ruffle my sleep-tousled hair. I feel like I've known him all my life. "I hope I wasn't snoring."

Erick laughs, and his cleft deepens. "No. You are truly beautiful."

"Now I know you're feeding me a line—I'm a mess."

"Perhaps a stray hair or two, but it becomes you." Erick brushes hair from my cheek with his knuckles, and I breathe in the smell of him—of earth and sunshine. He trails his fingertips across the bridge of my nose. "So many faerie kisses."

"Faerie kisses?" I ask, and then smile. "Oh, you mean my freckles. My grandmother called them angel kisses."

A strange look crosses his features and, for a moment, I think his face pales beneath his tan. His hand travels to the throat of my T-shirt to rest on my half-moon pendant. "This stone. How did you come by it?"

I glance down to see my crystal resting in the palm of his large hand. "My parents gave it to me when I was born. On my fifth birthday my grandmother let me wear it, and I've never taken it off since." My smile grows wistful as I remember the day Gran gave me the necklace. "It means a lot to me. This charm's the only thing I have left from my parents, since everything else was destroyed in a fire."

Erick runs his thumb over the pendant. Iridescent glimmers, like sparks of green fire, glint in the black crystal as he turns it. "It reminds me of another. It is quite pretty."

"Thank you."

His gaze moves to mine. "But not as fair as you."

A warm blush sweeps over me. "I didn't remember you until you took my hand. The same thing happened the other night you were here. I had no memory of you saving me until you touched me."

"I apologize. For now it must be this way. When I am with you, you will remember everything. But when I leave, you must forget."

"Why?" I frown. "I don't understand."

"It is a commandment to all Haro knights. We must not allow Oldworlders to remember us, and we use the Old Magic to suspend memory. I am breaking many rules by being here with you."

"What do you mean by Oldworlders? And magic?" I shake my head. "None of what has happened since the night we met makes sense. Please tell me what's going on."

Erick sighs. "Very well. But when I leave, you will remember nothing until I see you again."

"Until you touch me."

"Aye."

All I can think about is his kiss. His lips against mine. What's wrong with me? I've never been one to swoon for a handsome face, to fall recklessly into a relationship with any guy. But Erick . . . it's as if he's a part of me. That touch of his must be seriously affecting my judgment. And my heart.

I fidget on the mattress and fold my arms, pretending an indifference I don't feel. "Okay. Go for it. Tell me what this is all about."

Erick rakes his fingers through his thick, blond hair. "This may be difficult for you to understand."

"Try me."

He glances again at the wristband. "I am not from here."

"It's obvious by the way you dress and your accent you're from another country."

"Not another country. Another world, which we call Zanea."

My jaw drops and my eyes must be as wide as my mouth. "Another world? Did you say another *world?*" I shake my head. "Yeah, right. Let me guess. You expect me to believe that?"

Yet as soon as I say the words, somehow I know he's not lying to me.

"It is the truth." His gaze never wavers from mine. "Zanea exists on what is called a parallel."

"Okay." I take a very deep breath and try to remain calm. "If that's true, how is it you speak our language?"

"Long ago, this was our world."

I shake my head again, the impossibility of what he's saying rattling around in my head. "How can this be? You're telling me you're from another planet, but your people once lived here, on Earth."

"Aye. Most magical folk left this world over five hundred Earth years ago from a place called Europe and traveled to Zanea through a portal created by the great wizards. It is home to my people, as well as a force so evil it is beyond comprehension of those in your world."

"How do you get here? In a spaceship?"

Erick gives me a quizzical look. "Haro travel by dispatch, a window from our world to yours. Much like Zumar portals, but using the Old Magic of our wizards, not sorcery."

Questions overwhelm me. Perhaps it's my journalistic instinct. But it's more likely my desire to know more of this guy. "Tell me about this Old Magic."

"Ours is a spiritual magic. Many among us are born with the ability to perform magics, and we are trained to use them from birth." He sighs and drags his hand over his face. "But the strongest of our magic is governed by the great wizards L'onten and L'iwanda. It is their powers that allow the Haro to travel from Newold to Oldworld."

*Magic.* It's all so unbelievable. "What exactly are Haro?"

"Haro are an elite force—knights, or soldiers if you will. I am a Haro knight, trained to protect your people."

I frown, trying to absorb all he is telling me. I feel like I'm in the middle of a fantasy or sci-fi movie. "What are you protecting us from?"

Erick leans closer and takes both my hands within his. His touch, so warm; his hands, strong and calloused. A fluttering sensation tickles my stomach. Maybe I shouldn't be in my room, sitting on my bed with a practical stranger.

55

"The evil force is the Zumar," he says. "One of their warriors attempted to take you."

I glance at my arms. "My scratches. I keep thinking I'm losing my mind because I can't remember where they came from. I still don't understand how I ended up in the street."

He runs his fingers over the scabs. "You were fortunate the beast did not take you through the portal. When we arrived, I thought I would be too late."

"How do you know where to go—where a portal will be?"

"As soon as the Zumar set to open one, we are notified by the na'tan, which is linked to the wizards' magic." Erick holds up his wrist. A leather band anchors a round disc of about an inch wide and a quarter-inch thick, a lot like a wristwatch. Its black surface seems to absorb all light that surrounds it. "With the na'tan, we dispatch directly to the void, usually before it opens. There is always only one Zumar warrior per portal, whereas Haro travel in pairs."

He moves closer to me, his gaze so intent, so serious. "I do not understand what happened the night I met you. Cole and I dispatched so far you would have been lost if you had not fought off the beast. It was no small miracle you were able to escape his grasp."

I've never felt so confused, and his nearness disorients me even more. "What do they want with us? Why do these beasts come here? Why do your people care?"

"So many questions, Taryn." He smiles and rubs my wrists with his thumbs. "Synomea, the most powerful sorcerer in our world, sends the Zumar to abduct young Oldworlders to serve as slaves in his fortress."

I catch my breath. "The disappearances!" A cold wave sweeps over me. That would explain everything, if what he's telling me is for real. And would explain why I've felt like I know something about all the kids vanishing.

"Some of our people are sure the sorcerer has been biding his time until he has enough slaves and a large enough army of Zumar warriors. When he does, we believe he will attempt to extend his realm by attacking Newold and our sister villages." Erick's voice grows tight with anger. "Yet our Elders' Council believes that by stopping the beasts from stealing your people, that is enough to keep Synomea from taking over our world."

"How long has this sorcerer been kidnapping people from Earth?" I ask, still barely able to comprehend what he's telling me.

"The sorcerer has taken people from Oldworld since before my birth. But not until recently has he stolen enough to be of notice in your world. With my world's magic, we can save some of your people. But unfortunately many more are lost forever."

His large hands squeeze mine. "Once taken by the Zumar, Oldworlders are never recovered."

Icy fingers trail my spine and hair prickles at my nape. "Never?"

Erick shakes his head. "We are commanded to rescue only those here, on your Earth. It is all the Elders allow." He puts his fingertips to my forehead and odd warmth spreads through me. "Do not leave at night. Stay in your home and be safe. Promise me, Taryn."

"How can I promise if I can't remember you?" I murmur, enjoying the melting sensation of him being so close and touching me.

Smiling, he moves his hand, slipping it into my hair. "Old Magic." He cups the back of my head, his mouth inches from mine. "May I?"

The rational part of me knows I should say no. I barely know him. Barely. But a larger part of me feels I've known him all my life.

"Yes," I whisper, and close my eyes.

In a whirl of color and emotion, he kisses me. I wrap my arms around his neck and hold him tight, his warm lips moving over mine. The kiss lasts for an eternity, yet ends too soon.

With a soft groan, Erick pulls away and glances at his wristband. "I have to go now, little one. A portal is about to open. But tomorrow night I will be back, if you allow it."

*Little one?* No one has ever called me *little* anything. I want to ask him if his magic has anything to do with the way he makes me feel, but all I can say is, "Please come back, Erick. I'll miss you."

He smiles and kisses me. "No, you will not. But I will miss you."

Fingertips brush my forehead.

---

*Erick*

My muscles ache as I tread up the stone steps of our manor, then enter the foyer. While I unfasten my sword belt, the heavy door swings shut behind me. It is good to be home. It was another long night, yet I do not feel like sleeping.

"Down, Xen. Off with you, beast." The mastiff sniffs the Zumarian blood on my tunic and growls. He slobbers his greeting over my boots, threatening to spread it onto the seat of my breeches. I scratch his mangy head, then nudge him away with my knee.

"M'lord, your breakfast awaits." Unay snatches my sword, still in its scabbard, before I can abandon it onto a chair. She has been cleaning up after me since I was a small boy. She is so petite, I fear she will tip over from the weapon's weight.

"When will you learn to put your belongings in their rightful places?" Unay bobs her head. Her gray hair reminds me of the dust balls dwelling beneath my berth. "You should be more like your sister—now she be a good lass. Hurry along, Scamp! Eat a proper breakfast."

I grin and hold out my hands, palms up. "Unay, my love. What would I do without you?"

"Starve, in truth." Unay sniffs, her nose to the air. "And this fine manor. I shudder to think what 'twould look like."

"Is Van home?"

"In her library." The echoes of Unay's footsteps fade as she trundles off to my study.

I head to the kitchen and find my breakfast waiting, still warm. The kitchen smells of Unay's baked bread and pork sausage. I manage to eat only four eggs, six sausages, and two slabs of bread with honey and white butter. I do not have my normal appetite.

When I am finished eating, I head to the only place I find calm. The study smells of books and leather. Often as a child I imagined the scent of my father's pipe tobacco in this room, though he died when Van and I were babes.

Perhaps it was Unay's tales that kept him alive in my mind. Or the oil painting of Father and Mother hanging above the desk. When I was a boy, I thought their eyes followed me about the room, and I never did perform mischief here. But, away from their watching eyes, I surely drove Unay and Rufus near heart failure.

"I wish you had not died so soon after our birth," I complain to my mother's image in my regular but useless litany. "And Father. Murdered a year later by that bastard."

And all for an Oldworlder woman.

My thoughts flash to Taryn and I clench and unclench one fist. I used to think my father foolish, but now . . .

From a hidden compartment within my desk, I withdraw the yellowed letter my father wrote to me before his exile. Over the years the parchment has grown fragile and the writing faded. I unroll it and read again the words my heart has memorized:

> *My son,*
> *By the gods, how it pains me so to leave you behind.*
> *But it is my own choices that have brought me to this fate.*
> *With all my heart, I long to take you and your fair*
> *sister with me. But no, you must remain in Unay and*
> *Rufus's care. One day, this you will understand. It is my*
> *hope we shall be together as a family once again. That the*
> *Elders' Council will see the folly of their ways.*
> *Erick, let not the strident voice of the few outweigh the*
> *needs of the many. Let not complacency bind your soul to*
> *the will of the one who would choose to enslave our people.*
> *As sure as the twin moons watch over Zanea, evil will*
> *find a way into our world. Evil that will not rest until it*
> *conquers all that is good . . . unless you are true to your*
> *destiny.*

*I bequeath Navran, the sword of light and fire, to you. It is your birthright. Generations of our family have trained for the day Navran will be needed to defeat the worst evil ever known to our lands. I know now I am not the one. I believe—and aye, I fear—it is your fate. And while I fear for you, there is a quiet confidence in my soul that tells me I have nothing to fear except your choice.*

*Should you choose to ignore your calling, the doom of Zanea shall be sealed. Should you choose to wield Navran against our greatest foe, then I know our world may survive.*

*Blessed be, my son.*

*Your loving father,*

*Roland*

With a sigh, I roll the letter and slip it into its hiding place. Damn Voice Osred and the Council! Perhaps they will listen to what we have proposed and allow us to go to Synomea's lair. In truth, I am afraid they will vote against us.

I retrieve my sword from its resting space on my desk where Unay put it. The leather grip is smooth and comfortable in my hand. With my feet apart and shoulders squared, I stand in the center of the spacious room.

Hand to hand I toss Navran, feeling its familiar weight, feeling the stirring of the magic along its blade. The crystal within the lion's mouth upon the hilt catches the light and sparkles with the wizards' magic.

Over and over I perform the drills Rufus taught me when I was a child and could only practice with a wooden sword. Navran's power pulses through my arm, growing with each repetition. If what my father believed is truth, it may not be long until Navran is needed.

Yet even as I think of the prophecy, my heart denies the truth in it, and Navran becomes cold in my hands.

With disgust, I sheathe the sword and toss it onto my desktop. I shove papers and inkwell aside, kick off my boots, and sit behind my desk, resting my feet atop its surface.

Taryn fills my thoughts—I can think of little else. No other girl exists for me any longer. She is pure and good, a loving and caring person. I can see everything in Taryn's fey green eyes . . . they are windows to her very being.

I sigh. I knew I should stay away, yet I could not. As the hour drew near, I found myself again at her home, Cole scowling his disapproval as I left him.

This night, Taryn wore a blue tunic and short breeches. Her red-gold hair was loose about her face and like fine silk to my touch. And her lips . . . soft as rose petals. Her scent . . . always of raspberries. If only I could allow her to remember me, so she might think of me as often as I think of her. Would she? My heart tells me yes.

I grab my sword from the desktop and unsheathe it once again. The lion on the hilt scowls at me, its mouth open in its ageless roar. The crystal between its jaws is the exact size of what was removed to create the crescent crystal many years ago. If it had not vanished, the crescent would have belonged to Van.

Unbidden, the wizards' words come to mind. *Seek the Crescent . . . Seek the crystal . . . Find them or perish . . . Find them and perish . . . Only fate can decide.*

What crescent am I meant to seek? Did they mean the crystal—the crescent crystal that has been missing since I was but a babe? The crystal that is sister to the one imbedded in Navran's hilt?

Damn! Riddles and portents. Yet the wizards spoke the prophecy yesterday, and tonight I went to Taryn and saw her pendant. Can it be the crescent crystal? In my heart I know it is, but I cannot imagine how she came to own it. Should I tell her what value it holds? Perhaps danger?

It is an object of terrible power, one that should not be used for any purpose lest it override that purpose with its own drive for power.

Taryn is surely safe with the crystal. She could not possibly have the ability to use it, since she is not of my world. And no one from my world would think to look for it on Earth.

# October 19

*Taryn*

With a sigh, I throw my keys on the counter once I get home from my after-school shopping marathon with Jen. Can that girl ever shop, literally 'til we drop. One new pair of jeans, two sweaters, tennis shoes, and six pairs of socks later, I'm ready for bed.

I'm so tired my head aches and my eyes water from yawning so much. I'll head off to bed as soon as I finish straightening up the kitchen. Unfortunately, my foster parents aren't the neatest people on the planet.

I take a drink of ice water, then set my glass on the countertop and put the last dirty dish into the dishwasher.

As I close it, a hand grips my shoulder.

Fear erodes every practical explanation I can try and come up with. I press my hand to my pounding heart. And in that moment I know who touched me. I turn to Erick, who brushes hair from my face. His smile is so tender.

"You scared me!"

"My apologies, little one."

"How did you get in, like you did the other night?" I glance at the door and back to him. "The alarm is set."

With a shrug, Erick says, "Old Magic. Do you mind?"

I hate being snuck up on and I'm tired and irritable. I want to say, "Yes, I mind," but I realize there's no other way. If he dared to knock on the door instead of coming right in and touching me, I wouldn't know who he was and I would probably call the police. And I'm so happy to see him that I feel some of my tiredness slip away.

"No." I smile up at him. "I don't mind. I'm glad to see you."

He brings my hand to his lips and kisses my knuckles. Such a gallant gesture, like a knight in a medieval romance. I start to laugh as the kiss tickles my skin, but a familiar popping sensation fills my bad ear, and fear fills my heart.

*Damn it! Not now!*

I snatch my hand away and turn to grab my clear vitamin box from the countertop. Vaguely I hear Erick asking me what's wrong, but his words are faint to my good ear. I flip open the one day in the box I keep filled with the meds to fight off vertigo. I bring a tablet to my mouth and grab my glass of ice water. My hand is trembling so badly as I drink, the cold water splashes down the front of my shirt. I set the glass down and grip the countertop and focus on a pair of salt shakers.

"Taryn." Erick's hands are on my shoulders, my back to him. "Tell me what is wrong."

"Just a moment," I whisper. "I'll be fine."

"A portal will open soon," he says. "I must go. You will be all right?"

I'm filled with disappointment that our meeting is spoiled by my attack—that I don't even know when I'll see him again. Tears ache behind my eyes. "Yes. Go."

Fingertips brush my forehead.

I blink as I notice my vitamin box, the tab filled with meclizine open. A glass of ice water is half empty next to the box. Did I take one? I don't remember.

What happened? I was tired and loading the dishwasher, and then I closed it and . . . *a hand on my shoulder?*

I clench my fists and turn around, slowly.

Nothing's there. My legs weaken with relief, and I sag against the counter.

I seriously need a vacation.

---

## Erick

In my study I polish Navran. L'onten's magic sparks along the keen edge, and L'iwanda's runes glitter upon the blade.

It was difficult to tear myself from Taryn tonight. I was with her for only a few moments before she appeared to become ill, and then the na'tan demanded my leave.

A hint of laughter was in her eyes when I kissed her hand, and then fear. What was that odd pebble she put into her mouth? It must be some kind of healing herb for whatever ails her. Gods, how it tore at my heart to leave her in such a state!

Cole and I dispatched to portal after portal. I have never seen so many, and often we arrived too late. Disgust twists like daggers in my gut and anger burns a fine fury in my head. The sorcerer has not dared to open this number of portals in one night—why now?

I put away the bit of soft leather I use to clean Navran and sheathe my weapon. If the prophecy of the sword is true, I might defeat Synomea myself. Do I dare to believe it?

Synomea. That beast murdered my father. Yet he lives, stealing the souls of Oldworlders to do his wicked deeds. If the Elders do nothing, I am sure his power shall grow and all of Zanea will fall to his sorcery.

The front entrance slams and boots slap stone. Xen raises his head and scrubs his tail against the floor. When Van flings the study door open, Xen nearly knocks her down in his excitement to see her.

"Xen, I am not in a pleasant mood. Begone!" She pushes him away and settles into the wingchair. The mastiff ignores her command, driveling over Van's hand before returning to my side.

I raise an eyebrow. Rarely does anything ruffle my sister. "What troubles you?"

She removes a linen handkerchief from the pocket of her breeches, wipes slobber from her hand, and glares at me as if I should know her thoughts. "For one, this night. In the Oldworlder city of Las Vegas, Finella and I hardly arrived at one portal before another opened. There are too few Haro to keep up with so many portals."

My disgust matches hers and I nod. "The same in Tucson."

Van pulls her braid over her shoulder and picks it apart until her mahogany tresses fall to her waist. "Tonight I received notice the Elders' Council sent word regarding our petition for action against the sorcerer."

I raise an eyebrow. "And . . ."

Her gray eyes flash and her mouth tightens. "Albin said the Elders will not grant our request."

67

My anger mounts, knotting my shoulders and neck. "He is sure they have refused?"

"Aye."

"Damn!" I jump to my feet and Xen yelps as I tread on his paw.

Sprawling on the chair, Van stares at the ceiling. "Shall we gather our friends, then?"

"The Elders leave us no choice." I unsheathe Navran and begin working out my frustrations through my ritual exercises in the center of the den. "We must stop Synomea before his power rises and our world is lost."

"Agreed. We and our friends can accomplish this mission. I will speak with Finella, Gareth, and Basil. You inform Cole." With a sigh, she kicks off her boots next to mine. "This is what the wizards talked about."

"Wizards." I shake my head. "I have no use for riddles. We go because it must be done."

"And the prophecy. You know in your heart it is the truth." Van's gaze wanders to the portrait of our parents. "Think Father would have done what we plan to?"

"Aye." I feint with my sword and then pause. "If the Elders had not banished him . . . if they had not left him vulnerable to Synomea's attack."

"He was foolish to risk all for an Oldworlder."

A shadow of discomfort sweeps over me and I turn to my desk so she cannot read my eyes. "You had better eat your breakfast, then sleep. Tomorrow night we will meet with our friends."

# October 20

## *Taryn*

*By the glow of the moons I run through the meadow, pine needles wet beneath my bare feet. Like water gurgling in a stream, happiness bubbles up within me. Moonlight sparkles on snow-capped peaks that stand stark and vigilant beyond the forest.*

*I stop near Lion, my precious dream beast, his silvery eyes glinting. He's a lion, yes, but I've never been afraid of him. He is my friend. My true heart.*

*He trusts me implicitly . . . should he?*

*Lion is alone, his friends absent tonight. He rubs his head against my thigh, and I stroke his mane. He smells earthy—of dark loam, sunshine, and leather. Such odd scents for a lion. Clearly I hear a low rumble, a sound like a sudden summer storm, rising in his throat.*

*Like a warning.*

*A cool breeze kisses my cheeks, and I turn my face to the sky. Crescent Moon sails at a distance, but Full Moon is close enough to touch. I admire Full Moon and long to embrace it—to make it mine.*

*Power . . . all that power could be mine . . .*

*I reach out . . . my fingertips caress its luminescent façade . . . and ice creeps along my arm. Numbing cold. Freezing me to my very core. Its frost fills me, taking over my mind, my soul, my spirit. I snatch my hand away, my heart pounding, my stomach clenching.*

*Full Moon changes . . . thinning . . . to a Sickle.*

*The meadow vanishes, and I stand in the middle of a horrid wasteland. A volcano belches clouds of ash, illuminated by fiery lava. Jagged cliffs and treacherous slopes of black surround me, the wicked rock beneath my feet cutting into my soles.*

*Sulfur fills my lungs . . . I can't . . . breathe.*

*Where's Crescent? And my dream beasts . . . my Lion?*

*Only Sickle. Dominating the sky . . . glowing crimson . . . drenching everything in blood.*

I sit upright in bed, chest heaving, hair soaked with sweat. My hand trembles as I reach for my pendant. The crystal warms upon my touch, calming me, and my breathing slows.

My dream was so vivid! I felt pine needles beneath my feet, a breeze on my face, Lion's mane under my palm . . .

And the iciness of Sickle.

In all the time I've dreamed of the beasts and moons, I've never seen Sickle. The instant I touched Full Moon and it began to turn, I felt violated and deceived. I rub my arms, trying to scrub away the abhorrent feeling sliding under my skin.

My birthmark. It's been there my entire life, so much a part of me that I forget it. I pull up my sleeve and study the mark. Yes, that's what Sickle reminded me of. The birthmark on my left biceps. It's vermilion, shaped like a crescent moon.

These dreams grow more powerful every night, and they've become so real. Not only Lion but Bull, Tiger, Serpent, Scorpion, and Bear. Usually the beasts roam together, in one strange place or another.

70

Except the volcano and the midst of a wasteland. I've never visited that lava field in my dreams before. What a dismal, hideous place. I'd never want to be stuck in a place like that.

I climb out of bed and glance at the clock on my bureau. Only five A.M. With a groan, I shuffle into the kitchen. I could never get back to sleep, so I might as well start the day. A power breakfast. That's what I need.

I'm quiet as I fix breakfast, trying not to wake my foster parents. They come home in the early hours of the morning and sleep until noon. They work the late shift at the airport. Richard is a mechanic and Carolyn works at a car rental booth.

Soon the smell of scrambled eggs, bacon, and toast fills the kitchen. It's been so long since I've had much more than cold cereal and skim milk for breakfast. Three weeks—no, another week has past, so it's been four weeks now.

A month since Gran died.

I shove all depressing thoughts out of my mind as I grab my vitamin holder off the counter. It's one of those long and narrow seven-day boxes, with a separate lid for each compartment. I normally refill the box on Sunday, because I save that compartment for my meclizine so it's always handy and I don't have to unscrew the darn childproof cap on the prescription bottle when I have an episode.

*W* for Wednesday—I pop that tab open and drop the vitamins into my palm.

Ugh. I hate taking them. Something about swallowing horse tablets with water first thing in the morning doesn't agree with me. But Gran was insistent about supplements, and it's a routine I haven't had the heart to break. I set the box on the counter, grab my glass that matches the fruity wallpaper, take a gulp of water and swallow the tablets.

I close my eyes, leaning against the counter, and last night's dream of Lion comes to mind. His fair mane coarse beneath my fingers. His scent of earth and leather. So familiar, those scents . . .

*Silvery gray eyes.*

And that feeling of awesome power that filled me, made me want more.

My skin chills and my eyes open. Something's there. At the edge of my mind. I can't quite grasp it and it's driving me crazy. I grit my teeth and clench my fists in frustration.

The vitamin holder moves. It rises at least four inches above the countertop.

My eyes widen and I stumble away from the counter. My knees wobble and I grab the handle of the refrigerator to hold myself up.

The box clatters to the floor and most of the lids pop open. Meds and vitamins scatter across the tile.

Lightheaded, I cling to the fridge and glance around the kitchen, as if I might find something that could have caused that tablet box to lift off the countertop and throw itself to the floor.

Nothing. No one. Only me.

I take a deep breath and hold my hand to my pounding heart. It was my imagination, and that did *not* just happen.

No way.

Maybe I'm going crazy. Surely, I'm losing my mind and I should pick up the phone and make an appointment with a psychiatrist.

I grab the cordless, but the number I dial is Jen's. Before the first ring, I hang up. I realize it's barely after five-freaking

A.M. Besides, what could I tell her? That my vitamin box happened to throw itself off the countertop?

A logical explanation has to exist. And if I can't figure it out, I'll make that appointment with a shrink.

---

## Erick

"What troubles our fair Erick?" Finella purrs. She settles down in the grass, her legs curled under her.

Cole snorts.

"By the looks of him, I would say he is in love." With a grin, Van jabs me in the ribs with her elbow. "Although we never see him with any of the village girls."

I swig water from my flask, then return my gaze to the crackling fire. Smells of damp earth and burning pine fill the glade. We gather outside the village of Newold, not far from the wizards' cottage, where my friends and I are able to meet without risk of being noticed.

An odd yearning builds within me to get to Taryn and make sure she is safe. But why would she be in any danger?

"Well?" Finella interrupts my thoughts like a cat prepared to pounce on a mouse.

"We're here to discuss our options, not my life." I withdraw my dagger from my boot and a sharpening stone out of my pocket. "Where are Basil and Gareth?"

"They'll arrive soon." Van finishes plaiting her brown hair, ties it off with a leather strap, and tosses the braid over her shoulder. "We have time. Who is she?"

I shrug as I hone the dagger's edge, the sound of blade against stone echoing in the glade. "You do not know her."

Finella raises an eyebrow and her eyes widen. "Our Erick has truly fallen for a girl?"

Again Cole snorts.

"Ah. Cole does not approve." Van stretches her leather-clad legs before her and looks from him to me.

I glare at Cole.

"Hmmm, a challenge." Finella grins and smoothes a lock of raven tresses behind her pointed ear. "Do we need to get it out of him by force or trickery?"

Van laughs. "Likely both."

I slip my sharpened dagger into my boot. To my relief, Basil and Gareth approach.

They argue as usual.

"No. We slew six Zumar last night. My four to your two."

"Clod, your memory is as poor as your aim. *Seven.* My four to your three."

"Ha! You son of a whore," Gareth growls.

Perhaps it is unwise for a man to point out another's questionable parentage. But then Gareth has never been accused of being wise.

"Ah, here we are." After Basil claps Cole's back, he ruffs my hair, pulls Van's braid, and blows a kiss to Finella.

"Stop being such an ass," Gareth grumbles, shaking his straggled mane. "You've delayed us again."

Basil winks at me, pale green eyes glittering under a cap of red curls. "Erick and Cole have dispatched first the past few nights. They seem to want extra time among the backward and wayward souls. I think there's something of interest to them in Oldworld."

Cole and I exchange glances. If Basil noticed, the Elders might.

"You cannot be interested in one of *them?*" Finella's slanted eyes widen. At one time, I had been infatuated with her black hair, sapphire eyes, and Elvin features. "You have fallen for an *Oldworlder?*" She says the word as if it is the worst of fates.

At this moment I would like to throttle Finella. "This is not up for discussion."

"It is too important." Van lays her hand on my arm. "Erick, what have you done? What you say here goes no further than the six of us."

Cole snorts. I shall break his nose if he does it again.

Do I dare tell my friends? If I do, and word leaks to the Elders, I will be banished. Yet it would be better to put myself at risk than allow my friends to be kept unaware.

I sigh. "Her name is Taryn." Cole rolls his eyes to the forest canopy. I ignore him. "I met her a week ago. She was almost taken by the Zumar."

"Along with thousands of others." Finella's voice hangs heavy with sarcasm, and I struggle to control my anger. "What makes this girl so special?"

"I do not know how to explain it, but my soul seems to know her." I thrust my fingers through my hair. "And what Taryn did that night . . . you will not believe it." In the flames of the fire, I visualize all that happened. "The portal opened where she stood, but we had dispatched too far. It should have been hopeless, but I went after her." I look at each of my friends. "The Zumar warrior grabbed her arm, yet she escaped his grasp. She flung his hand away from her as if he were no more than an overgrown child."

Finella gasps.

Van's jaw drops.

Basil, for once, has nothing to say. He begins his usual restless circling of the clearing, hands behind his back.

"That isn't possible," Gareth mutters, his dark skin glowing in the firelight.

"Tell them, Cole."

Cole looks glum. "The girl fought off the Zumar."

"I was still too far away to save her," I continue. "Taryn fell into the street and fought the Zumar, kicking at his claws. She held the beast off and gave me enough time to reach her and slay the warrior."

"Unbelievable," Van whispers.

I glance at the group of stunned faces. "To my knowledge that has never happened before."

Basil shakes his head as he paces faster yet. "No Old-worlder could escape the Zumar grasp. Only someone from Zanea could withstand the warrior's touch."

"That was what interested you in this girl?" Finella says.

I would think she was jealous if I did not know better. "It captured my attention. And then, when I saw her eyes, I was lost."

In my mind I see those eyes, so fey, so exquisite, and feel myself drowning in their depths. "Beyond killing Synomea, my only desire is to see Taryn. To understand her better and find the source of her great will and strength."

"Is she beautiful?" Finella prods.

"No." Cole says, and my skin crawls with the desire to pound him. I am not certain he will live through the night.

Finella lowers her lashes and looks pleased.

"Taryn has her own beauty, one radiating from within, as bright as the moons of Zanea." If my gaze could slay Cole, he would surely die on the spot. "She is beautiful to me. Far more lovely than any lass on this world or theirs."

Cole drops his eyes.

Finella's pleased expression vanishes.

"How often have you seen her?" Gareth growls.

I hesitate, then reply, "Four times since that night."

A collective gasp.

"Erick, you could be banished." Van reaches out and captures my hand. "Remember our own father."

Gareth moves to stand before me, hands on hips. "Have you no more sense than to chase this wench like a rutting hog?"

I bolt to my feet. Chest to chest with Gareth, my fist is drawn back, ready. "One more word and I shall beat you to a bloody mess." Like a drawn bow, tension binds me. "One more word."

Cole and Van move between us, blocking Gareth from my sight.

Van pushes my fist down. "We do not need fighting amongst ourselves."

"Pah!" Gareth kicks a chunk of wood into the fire.

"Although I question his choice of words," Basil says, "Gareth is right to be concerned with your actions, Erick."

"What we are here to discuss has nothing to do with Taryn. I will not tolerate a single word against her." I resume my seat. "However, I need to tell you something."

I pause, questioning my decision to inform my friends, but again, I cannot leave them unaware of the whole truth if they are to battle beside me. I would have told them soon enough. "The third time I saw her, I noticed it. It has nothing to do with my desire to see Taryn, but perhaps it is best you know."

Van leans closer. "What?"

"Taryn wears the crescent crystal."

Dead silence hangs over the glade, followed by uproar.

"Not *the* crescent crystal?" Disbelief fills Van's voice.

Gareth scowls. "It cannot be."

"That explains the attraction," Finella says.

Basil stops pacing. "You must be mistaken."

Cole stares at me.

"I am sure of it." I turn my gaze to Finella. "As I said, the crystal has nothing to do with what I may feel for Taryn. If you value our friendship, you will watch what you say."

Finella's blue eyes widen, but she does not speak.

"*The* crescent crystal?" Van repeats. "The one that belongs to our family?"

"She wears it around her neck, on a gold chain. L'iwanda's and L'onten's fire sparks within."

Basil resumes pacing. "You are sure of this? It is the crystal? L'iwanda's and L'onten's? The crystal disappeared when you were a babe."

"I have seen drawings, and the shape is the same. The crystal matches the one in my sword. But it was more than that." I search for the right words. "As soon as my fingers passed over it, I knew. I could sense its power."

"Van spoke of the prophecy only days ago." Gareth leans forward, a greedy look in his eyes. "The crystal could be the answer to our war with Synomea."

"By birthright, Van should have the crescent," Cole mutters.

"She is an Oldworlder. We cannot allow her involvement," Van replies.

With a scowl, Gareth jumps to his feet. "Erick can take the stone. He can use the necessary magic. The girl would never remember owning it."

"No!" I shout.

Silence. Startled looks.

"I will not take it. It was a gift from her parents, now long dead. It is a thing she treasures." I rake my hand through my hair. "It is not certain this crystal would end any war, and it is not certain any one of us could wield its power."

"The crescent crystal belongs to our world, not hers," Gareth growls. "The wizards could teach us."

"The stone belonged to my family and it is my decision to leave it with her." I look to Van. "Do you agree?"

Van's eyes meet mine and I see understanding in the gray depths. "Aye."

Gareth kicks another rock into the fire. "Idiocy!"

Her eyes narrowing, Finella edges closer, her thigh close to mine. "If this girl gave the crystal of her own will?"

I shake my head. "We must find another way to defeat Synomea. We will not involve Taryn."

# October 21

*Taryn*

"Algebra. Ugh." I open the textbook on my kitchen table, but don't notice what page it's on. The vision of that handsome face wanders through my mind. "Get real, Taryn," I grumble, and scoot my chair closer to the table.

Then I remember tomorrow morning is garbage day and I'd better get that recycle bin out to the curb. Since algebra is my least favorite class, I don't mind the interruption.

It's cool, so I slip on my jacket. After I flick on the porch light, I grab the trash and head out the back door.

And stop dead.

A muddy print mars the porch, right in front of my door.

My heart revs like a racecar. I hold one hand to my chest and struggle to calm myself. Settle down. It's probably mine.

I set the trash can on the porch and step next to the print. It's much too big to be mine or Richard's or Carolyn's.

No—I know it in my heart. This boot print shouldn't be here.

Slowly, I ease back through the porch door. The cool evening breeze sweeps past me. My algebra instruction sheet flutters on the table, threatening to flee. I turn and slap it down onto the table.

A large hand closes over mine.

An instant of fear rushes me, followed by unlocked memories. And relief.

"Erick." I withdraw my hand and stand to face him. Or to face his chest. He's so big, I actually feel small next to him. All my life I've felt like an Amazon—tall and heavy. And this guy makes me feel petite.

"Hallo, Taryn." Erick's hair falls forward as he leans over me. "May I?"

I stand on my tiptoes, my face close to his. "You don't have to ask anymore." I kiss him.

"Let's sit on the swing," I say after the sweet, delicious kiss. Erick stares at me as if I'm a goddess. Taking his hand, I lead him out the door, dodging the garbage can.

Once we settle on the swing, I glance down at Erick's boots. Could it have been his? But the print seemed different than his boots. For a second I wonder if it could be a Zumar warrior's. I open my mouth to tell Erick, but something holds me back. I don't want to ruin what time we have together by making him concerned. Worries can wait. I'll tell him later.

Erick pulls me close to him, resting my head against his chest, and he murmurs something I don't understand.

I withdraw and look up at him. "I can't hear you with my—my good ear against you."

His gaze is steady, his silvery gray eyes boring into mine. "You have no hearing in your other ear?"

With a sigh, I shake my head. "Very little."

"An injury?"

"It's called Ménière's disease, and I've had it since I was ten." I shrug, like it's no big deal. "Most of the time I'm fine, but sometimes I have episodes of vertigo that make it hard for me to function—to even walk straight."

"Ver-ti-go?" Erick says slowly, his face puzzled.

"It's like the world is spinning around me," I explain. "And then I can't understand up and down anymore. I can become very ill. When you were here last, I felt an episode coming on, so I had to take a pill to help prevent it. Sometimes it takes me awhile to get myself together."

"Ah." No emotion crosses his face, and I wonder if he thinks less of me for not being . . . whole. But then he says, "I was very worried about you. I could hardly keep my mind on my duties when I left you."

"You were?"

"Aye." He smiles and eases his arm around my shoulders. "I would like to know more of you."

"First tell me about you. We've known each other for a whole week now, and I still don't know enough. The last time you were here, you had to leave almost as soon as you arrived. And you didn't come to see me last night."

"I wanted to, but it wasn't possible."

I smile at his seriousness. "So, tell me, how old are you? Do you have any family? What do you do during the day?"

Erick laughs, his lips close to my hair. "I am eighteen. I have only my twin sister Van for family, as my parents died when I was but a babe. And nearly every minute I think of you."

"You're such a flatterer." A warm flush spreads through me. His embrace is so comfortable, so safe.

Erick kisses my hair. "Now tell me about you."

"As a coincidence, I'm an orphan, too—except I have no family left at all. My grandmother, who raised me, passed away not long ago." My voice catches before I continue. "I'm seventeen and a student, so I go to high school during the day. And if you'd let me, I'd think about you all the time."

"If I could, I would. But it is not possible, the way things are."

"You sound worried."

"Aye."

I smile at the quaint expression. "What's bothering you?"

"Other than my desire to be near you, even when I cannot be?"

With my finger, I poke him in the ribs.

He squeezes me tighter. "In recent months Synomea, a terrible sorcerer, has grown in strength. We are powerless to stop his warriors from taking larger numbers of your people. We Haro are too few, and I believe the problem will only become worse."

I bite the inside of my lip as my thoughts turn to the vanishing teens. "Our police department has doubled the amount of officers who are out at night, but the disappearances have increased. They tell everyone to make sure they never go out at night alone."

Erick shakes his head and frowns. "That will only make it easier for the Zumar to take more of your people at a time."

"Can't something be done? Have your people tried to stop him in your own world?"

"Some among the Haro favor an attack against the sorcerer at his Zumarian stronghold, but the Elders refuse to allow it." Erick tenses, and bitterness edges his words.

"Do you agree? That your Haro should attack the sorcerer?"

"An invasion, of sorts. A small force sent into the fortress to attack Synomea from within. We do not have enough knights to wage a war and would not wish the loss of so many lives."

"And you would like to join or lead the group that wants to infiltrate his fortress," I say, my voice flat.

A heavy weight settles in my chest at the thought of Erick venturing into the Zumarian stronghold—possibly to his death.

Feelings I've had since Gran died creep over me. Being totally alone, with everyone gone. Me, wandering through the world, deaf and isolated, with no one to talk to. How could I even begin to think anything permanent could develop between Erick and me? For goodness' sake, we're from two different *worlds*.

Enjoy it while it lasts, Taryn. And don't lose your heart while you're at it.

"Would you fear for me, little one?" He caresses my arm along the healing wounds, sending shivers down my spine.

I swallow past the lump growing in my throat. "Yes."

Erick moves his hand to my chain, pulling my pendant out from where it's hidden beneath my shirt. "But you would not remember me." He turns the half-moon over. Glints of green fire spark in the black crystal, somehow looking more brilliant as he touches it.

"A part of me would. When you're not here, I don't have a conscious memory of our times together, but at some other level, I'm aware." I untangle myself from his arms, look into his fathomless gray eyes, and see a puzzled expression cross his handsome face. "I have flashes of memory, or visions. And I feel more alive—with a new sense of purpose."

"I do not understand. You should remember nothing." He releases the crystal and takes my hands within his. "I should not be here. It is unfair to you."

"I'm so happy when I'm with you, Erick. Please don't risk your life going to that place." I reach up and trace the scar along his cheekbone with my finger, then move my mouth close to his. "May I?"

He smiles. "You never have to ask me, Taryn."

I brush my lips against his. He presses his mouth to mine and kisses me with such tenderness that a strange desperation wells within me and I don't want to let him go. Like a stone tossed in a glistening pool of water, silvery ripple after silvery ripple travels through me.

Erick rains kisses upon my face, my eyelids, my nose, my hair. "I must leave. Tomorrow night I will be back." He stands and pulls me up beside him. "Good night."

A brush of his lips, a touch of his fingertips.

---

## Erick

"We must come to a decision now," I say, eyeing each member of the Haro team. We have just returned from our daily journey to Oldworld, and huddle 'round the fire in the glade outside Newold. "We must take action since the Elders have voted against us."

"Damn Voice Osred," Gareth mutters. "He is not fit to lead a council of fools."

Van leans forward. "It is time to take matters in hand. While the Elders do nothing, Synomea and his Zumar grow in strength. Many Council members have become soft, with no thought to how this will affect Newold."

Finella pushes her raven hair behind her pointed ear. "My mother said Council will convene in two days. It will last at least a week, and their attention will be turned away from all but their own deliberations. Mother is one of the few Council members who would favor our actions. Yet I do not dare tell her."

"We must keep this among the six of us." I rub my neck, attempting to ease the tenseness of my muscles. "If we are successful, we will return from Synomea's fortress before any of the Elders notice. We have no better time."

"Truth," Cole grunts.

Gareth spits into a patch of red foxgloves. "Voice Osred will be consumed with his own importance and will not notice our absence."

Pacing, Basil tosses a stone and catches it. "Let us not be rash. It is a dangerous mission Erick and Van propose."

My innards knot in anger at Basil's words, but before I can speak, Gareth says, "Always one to think of yourself. If you are so concerned about your pretty face, you can stay. We have all known this plan is the path we need to take."

Finella yawns, covering her mouth with her fingers. "I tire of your arguing, the two of you. This task must be done, and the wizards' wisdom guides us. Basil, this leaves you alone. What is your decision?"

Basil rocks on his heels, still tossing the stone. Up and down. Up and down. He stops and, for an instant, I can picture him flinging the rock at Gareth's temple.

Lips curling into a grin, Basil chuckles. "Someone must speak for reason. Many commandments we would break. We have nothing but the Old Magic and brute strength of six."

Gareth looks to me. "The crescent crystal."

"The crystal is not an option." I withdraw Navran, then a bit of soft leather to clean the blade.

Finella curls her legs under her. "Why are you not willing to take the crystal from the girl? She is an Oldworlder and it does not belong to her."

I look up from my sword, into her sapphire eyes. "We do not need it to rid ourselves of the sorcerer."

With a scowl, Gareth says, "Why are you willing to forsake the one thing that would help our cause?"

Gritting my teeth, I glare at him. "I do not believe any one of us is the so-called chosen one who can wield the crystal's power. It would be worthless in our hands and it is safer in Oldworld, far from the sorcerer's reach."

Finella cocks her head to one side. "Erick, you may be the chosen one, or Van. Your family controlled the stone for generations, and the crystal belongs to you both. You must recover it and use it."

*"No."* I return to the task of polishing my weapon.

"Why do you think we can defeat Synomea?" Basil unsheathes his sword, puts the point into the dirt, and twirls it as he speaks. "How will we enter the Zumar fortress to reach him?"

"By the grace of the wizards, our plan shall work," I reply. "The sorcerer will not expect such an attack, so surprise will be on our side. Cunning shall gain us entry to the fortress."

I run the cloth along the blade that glints in the firelight, the flames' reflection dancing along its keen edge. "Our might shall give us victory."

## October 22

*Taryn*

"Goodbye, Carolyn," I say, and wave at my brunette foster mom as her heels tap down the sidewalk.

"Keep the alarm set," she calls back. "I'm worried about you and the disappearances."

"I will." I smile. "See you tomorrow."

She waves and I close the door behind her. For a moment I rest my head against the door, a sense of loneliness passing over me.

A noise shatters my thoughts. A footstep on tile. Behind me.

My heart hammers as I whirl around.

Oh. My. God.

A man. A huge man.

Before I can say a word, before I can do anything, he grabs my arm.

"Erick!" Warm pleasure and relief sweeps over me at his touch, and I melt against him. He embraces me, replacing my fear and confusion with sheer happiness.

"Taryn." He kisses my hair and my forehead.

I think I'm going to lose my mind not being able to re-member Erick.

He feels so good, smells so good. He's so right for me. I turn my face up to his, and his expression freezes my core.

I push him away. "You're not coming back."

Erick brushes hair from my eyes, a caress along my cheekbone. "Is my face so easy to read, little one?"

Why didn't I see it? He's abandoning me—leaving me. Like everyone else. I should have known. I should have seen it coming. I never really expected a guy like Erick to stay interested in me, did I? Please. I'm not that stupid.

I tear away from his touch and turn my back to him. My head throbs and my eyes ache.

He grips my shoulders and I feel the warmth of his hands through my light jacket. His familiar, musky scent surrounds me. I want to fling myself into his arms and never let go.

"Pray, understand." The grasp on my arms tightens. "I have been so selfish. I never should have come here."

I swallow, struggling to keep my voice steady. "Leave."

"Taryn, I—"

"Just go!"

Erick reaches around, takes my hand, and presses something cold and flat into my palm.

I feel his lips kiss my hair.

Fingertips brush my forehead.

---

## Erick

As I lie upon my berth, my gut aches. How could I have allowed myself to develop a relationship with Taryn? An Oldworlder, for Nar's sake.

Gods. The look on Taryn's face when I told her I was leaving tears at me. It was as if I had ripped her heart from her chest. I try to feel better, knowing she will not remember me because of the Old Magic. Yet she claimed to have flashes of memory when I am not there.

How could that be? Could it have been the crystal? No, she is an Oldworlder and she has no magic. The crystal is nothing more than a bauble for her.

The crystal. Should I have—

No. I will not allow myself to challenge my own decision. I must go forward from here and complete our mission as planned.

My eyes fix on a spider's web at the corner of my ceiling. My fingers are laced behind my head as I rest upon my mattress. Perhaps our mission will be successful and we will rid Zanea of Synomea, and then I can go to Taryn with a free heart—if she will have me.

Yet, even if we destroy the sorcerer and return to our world, my friends and I face prison or banishment. We can only hope the Elders have the wisdom to see we are doing what is best to save our world.

Even as I believe I shall never sleep, my mind grows hazy, and I dream.

*Murmuring her name, I hold her tight, my lips against her hair.*

*She vanishes. My arms, empty . . . aching.*

*A shadow, ahead. Taryn!*

*I run until I am close to her—I try to clutch her hand.*

*Gone.*

*She flits by, and I sprint after her. Farther and farther, she is always out of reach.*

*My hope wanes.*

*There! Within my grasp.*

*I capture her hand and pull her to me—*
*Horror slices me like a dagger's blade.*
*It is the twisted face of a Zumar warrior.*
*In the distance, Taryn screams my name . . .*

## October 23

*Taryn*

My head feels stuffed with pillows, as if I just got over an episode of vertigo. I push myself up from my bed and my feet hit the floor. My dreams last night were so disturbing, so strange, and so achingly painful.

And I had that dream of power again. Like I was a queen, a ruler, someone masses would bow down to.

The turn of my thoughts jars me and I reach for my pendant—and freeze.

It's gone.

My hands tremble while I grope around my neck, as if I'll find my necklace there from sheer will. Calm down, Taryn. It has to be here somewhere. I fling off bedclothes, shake the sheets, empty pillowcases, pull out the bed, shift my mattress, search under, around, and over the nightstand.

Nowhere.

"No, no, no, no, *no!*" My pendant must be here. I fell asleep with my hand on it. I know I did! I tear apart my bedroom and the bathroom. I search everywhere, including the porch swing and the refrigerator. As a last-ditch effort, I even search my car.

When there is nowhere else to search, I lay on my bed and put my arm over my eyes. Like everyone and everything else I ever cared about, my pendant is gone.

---

I can't believe it's late afternoon when I awake, the light in my bedroom dim. My eyes feel weighted with bricks. I feel so much pain inside, and it won't go away.

I force myself to get out of bed and take a shower. It feels warm and comforting, washing some of the hurt down the drain. I want to swirl down that drain and vanish, like Alice slipping into the rabbit hole, leaving all my hurt behind.

Perhaps I'd find another world—there's certainly nothing here but pain. The pain of losing my grandmother, never knowing my parents, being lonely, losing my hearing, and the pain of losing . . . *Erick*.

Erick? Where did that come from? I don't even know an Erick. Perhaps mentally I've already gone down that rabbit hole.

At last, I step out onto my bathmat and wrap myself in a towel. It takes long minutes to comb out and blow-dry my hair, and still it falls limp in my face.

I hate my hair in my face. I cram it in a scrunchie and pretend I don't notice how pale my face looks in the mirror.

Habit tempts me to throw on makeup, but I decide there's no need. Who will I see, anyway? I smooth raspberry lotion over my body, the scent relieving some of the stress. A little. I slip on faded jeans, a pink long-sleeved shirt, running shoes, and my jacket.

After I snatch my house key from the hook in the kitchen, I automatically grab my tablet holder so I'll have my meclizine with me in case I have an episode while I'm walking. I shove it in my pocket, head out the front door, lock it, and walk. The memory of the tablet box rising above my countertop flashes through my mind.

It floated, then clattered to the floor.

*No.* It had to be my imagination. Somehow I set it at the edge of the counter and just imagined I saw it rise almost half a foot before it fell.

Maybe if I tell myself that enough times, I'll believe it.

I walk and walk. Through the neighborhoods of ranch-style homes, palo verde and mesquite trees, and cacti. Pale earth, yellow grass, and telephone poles.

My shoes make soft squishing noises as I walk. Quail calls and the distant sound of traffic meet my ears. The smell of fall in the desert permeates the air. Soon it will be the holidays.

I hadn't even thought of that. Thanksgiving and Christmas alone? Well, with people who aren't really family.

I sigh.

The sun is setting behind the mountains and it's almost dark by the time I realize how far I've gone. Another spectacular sunset spans the sky, blazing streaks of pinks and oranges.

Words ring in my mind and I halt, mid-step. A guy telling me to stay home when it's dark. The voice, masculine and unknown . . . yet familiar. I feel a vague sense of unease and rub my temples.

I'm in the middle of nowhere, on a stretch of road where there are no homes, just lots of desert and an occasional car passing by. When I check my watch, I'm surprised to find I've been walking for an hour.

With growing apprehension, I dig into my jacket pockets and pull out what's in there. Great. No wallet. No change. Only my house key, the vitamin box, a silver button, and a shoelace. Lovely. I didn't even bother to bring my pepper spray.

I stuff everything back into my pockets, then pause.

Silver button?

I pull out the button again and squint to see it in the dimming light. It isn't a button, but a disc, engraved with a strange picture. The figure reminds me of the hunchback, flute-playing Kokopelli, the ancient Anasazi symbol for life and love.

Where did the disc come from? No, the picture isn't of a Kokopelli. What is it? I run my thumb over the design. It feels almost comforting, like my pendant. How on Earth did I end up with it?

I'll have to study the disc when I get home. I slip it into my pocket and look up, feeling the approaching darkness closing in on me. Panic wells within, like scratches in my mind. Since when do I fear dark? Automatically, I reach for my pendant.

Gone.

The half-moon stone has given me so much strength and comfort, for as long as I can remember. Now it's gone. But how? And where?

I turn and start to walk back home.

*Faster. Walk faster.*

Wonderful. Just peachy. It'll be well past dark by the time I reach home. Who knows what kind of loonies may be out?

The memory of that boot print on my porch comes to me. I've been keeping the doors locked and the alarm set, but what good does that do me here? What am I doing out alone?

Dusk.

Streetlights flicker to life. At least another mile to get home. How did I manage to walk so far? Why didn't I pay attention?

It's getting cold. Too cold.

A strange tingle starts from my scalp, traveling all the way to my toes. I stop. Air shimmers and shifts, like a mirage before my eyes. Something blots all the light in front of me, like a giant casting a shadow. An enormous black hole spreads from sidewalk to street, blocking my path.

Terror sears me as two men step from the hole. Not men—monsters! Grotesque faces. Metal claws.

Blood pounds in my veins. "No!" I scream and turn to run.

Claws clamp on each of my arms.

And I *know*.

*Zumarians!* Oh, my God! The Zumarian monsters have come back to get me!

I fight the beasts, struggling to wrench myself from their grasps. The stench of rot and decay makes breathing nearly impossible.

The Zumarians lift me, and I dangle. White-hot fire sears my shoulders. I kick, trying to make contact, but my feet flail, hitting nothing. Desperation and fear churn my gut.

The black void grows closer and closer. "Let me go! Let me GO!"

*Once taken . . . never recovered . . .*

"Erick!"

## Erick

Again my friends and I meet in the glade outside Newold, and I struggle to focus on the decisions at hand. My mind, my heart, and my soul continue to return to Taryn.

I force my thoughts away and look at my friends' faces. "Tomorrow night we meet here. Agreed?"

Cole nods, but looks troubled.

Basil paces, rubbing his palms together. "Everyone is sure?"

With a rush of anger, I narrow my gaze. "If you are not with us, say so."

Gareth stands and blocks Basil's path. "Stop your whining, or leave. We cannot afford your disruptions if we are to be successful."

Laughing, Basil settles next to Finella. "My dear, whatever are we to do with them?"

Finella shrugs a slim shoulder and grinds a leaf beneath her slender boot. "Enough of your mindless chatter. Erick and Gareth are right. You are with us or against us, and there is no middle ground."

Basil says nothing. He only leers at Finella and tries to pinch her, but she elbows him.

"Damn, Basil!" I shout. "We have a lot to work out. If you do not wish to join us, then leave!"

"You are my friends, my family." Basil straightens up, his arms wide, and grins. "I will go where you lead."

Van rests a hand on my shoulder. "Is something wrong, Erick?"

I shrug off her touch. "I am fine."

Finella moves close to me and strokes my other arm, tracing a finger down my biceps. "The Oldworlder from Tucson?" Finella smells of jasmine, thick and heavy, unlike Taryn's soft scent of raspberries and moonlight.

At her touch, my muscles tighten and I shrug her off as well. "Nothing is bothering me. As I said, I am fine."

Cole glares at me. "You had better be speaking the truth. We need no distractions."

"Gods!" I leap to my feet and clench my fists. "If it is so important to you, I will not be seeing Taryn again. Not unless our mission is successful and we destroy Synomea. And then only if she takes me back. Does that please you all?"

"So you have some wisdom left," Gareth says as he walks toward me. "Did you have sense enough to take the crystal from the wench?"

The frustration that has been building inside me explodes into rage and my vision turns red. I slam my fist into Gareth's jaw.

He drops. I dive after him. I reach back to strike again, but Cole and Basil grab my arms and pull me away. I struggle, trying to jerk myself from their grasps. All I can see is Gareth's leering face, and I want to smash it.

"No, Erick." Van steps in front of me and puts her hands to my chest. "This must end. Stop fighting, or this is over. We cannot risk our lives only to destroy ourselves."

I take a deep breath, then lower my fists and nod. Basil and Cole release me.

Van spins on Gareth. "And enough of your asinine talk. Is that understood?"

Gareth glares at me, then Van, and spits blood into the dust at our feet.

"It is almost time to dispatch." Van picks up a flagon and douses the fire. "Tomorrow night, then."

―――――――――――――

I massage my sore knuckles as Cole and I head toward Command. My only satisfaction is knowing Gareth's jaw surely hurts worse.

Cole and I walk up the stairs of Haro Command and Kean, the door squire, nods to me, then Cole. "M'lord. Sir."

I stride past, not wanting to waste my time on meaningless chatter. As I enter the doors, I run into Quenn and almost knock her to the floor. I grab her arm to keep her from falling.

The senior dispatch officer yanks her arm from my grasp and stumbles back. She glares at me, her brown eyes gleaming with dark fire. "Watch your step, you overgrown Trendorian warthog."

Cole raises an eyebrow and I give Quenn a mock bow as she sweeps past.

"That one is trouble," Cole mutters when the doors close behind Quenn. "We had better make sure she never learns any of our secrets."

"Ah. Lord Erick, Sir Cole." Albin glances up from his station as we take our positions. "Rather large portal opening in your quarter. The beasts are starting early tonight. Wonder what it is they're up to."

With a curt nod, I acknowledge him and dispatch. Tension winds my body even tighter until we arrive.

"Damn!" I yell as Cole joins me on the Tucson street. I stumble, then run. My body is still weak from the dispatch from Newold. "We are too far to save that girl!" I withdraw my sword as I race, hoping some miracle will occur. As it had with Taryn. I am too far and I only see the lady's gold hair captured by the glow of a streetlight. She walks with purpose.

Faster! My lungs burn and the metallic taste of blood fills my mouth. I can sense the portal. I will never make it in time.

Hurry! I must try!

The portal opens and the girl stops dead. Two warriors step through the void.

*Two?*

The girl screams and turns to run, but the Zumar grab her arms. She cries out, fighting against their hold.

My gods, it is Taryn! Fear scorches my mind as I race even faster. I must reach her!

She fights, but the beasts drag her into the portal.

"Erick!" Her scream shatters me to the core of my being.

"No! Taryn!"

They vanish.

I reach the spot where Taryn had been.

Raspberries. Her scent mingles with the death stench of the Zumar.

"Gods, what have I done?" I drop to my knees and hold my head in my hands.

# PART
# TWO

. . .

*All that power—*

*that intoxicating power*

. . .

## October 23

*Erick*

A hand on my shoulder. I stiffen. Rage flares so fast, so furious, my body shakes and I can see nothing. I bolt to my feet, wrenching from Cole's grip.

Cole! Why him? Were it Gareth, Basil—I would tear them apart and soothe this wretched fury.

"Gods damn!" I ram my sword into the earth. The ground is still damp from the rains and the blade sinks easily.

Cole maintains his silence, surely saving his life.

"I must rescue Taryn!"

He studies the ground, toeing the dirt with his boot. "I am sorry she was taken."

"Ha! You never did approve of my relationship with her."

"For this very reason. I knew what would happen to your heart if she met with harm. I have no wish to see you so upset."

I yank my sword from the dirt and feel Navran's power coursing through my arm. Aye! Synomea shall regret taking Taryn. I shall find the bastard and kill him myself. I clench the grip in my palm and the wizards' runes more than glitter along the blade—they flash and burn, as though ready to do my will.

"I must go to Zumaria for her," I say as I sheathe Navran. *"Now."*

Shaking his head, Cole folds his arms. "You cannot do it alone. Tomorrow night we go after Synomea with our friends. Then we shall have strength in numbers."

"Do you think I am going to leave Taryn with the devil himself? No! Not for an entire night. Not even for an hour!" Heat rises within me in a fierce wave and I desire nothing more than to slay something at that very moment.

"Think, Erick." Cole's black eyes plead that I listen. "If you try something foolish, there will be questions. Even returning too early to Command might raise eyebrows. Questions would surely halt our plans, and how would you rescue the girl then?"

I shove my hands in my hair, desiring to rip it out. "How can I get through this night, knowing Taryn has been taken?"

"To truly save her, you know you must finish the night's task. Tend to the portals and slay the beasts as if nothing is amiss. It is the only way. You know it is the only way."

Silence surrounds us as I consider Cole's words. As much as I desire to attack Synomea's lair at once, as much as I need to rescue my heart's mate, it would be foolish to attempt to do so without my friends. Without ensuring the Elders' Council remains unaware of our plans.

Clenching my fists, I let out a furious sigh. "Then I must leave early in the morning."

"No. We shall all need our rest to regain strength. And preparations are needed to leave tomorrow night."

I lean my head back to stare up at the sky. The stars in this world are so pale. Do the gods rule over Oldworld as they do Zanea? Can they hear my prayer to keep Taryn safe and alive until I reach her?

Cole slaps my back, drawing my gaze back to him. "Portal," he says. "We must go."

His black eyes boring into mine, Cole grips my arm. "We shall make every effort to save the girl. You have my word."

A dagger twists in my heart, the pain lancing my soul. I dispatch without another word.

---

## Taryn

Darkness and shrieking winds surround me as soon as the Zumarians drag me into the black hole. The air is damp and smells like burning rubber. Tension and agony clench my body, tighter than the grip of the warriors. I'm sure the black hole will rip me apart. Any second I'll explode.

A whir and hum fill my good ear as the fierce winds settle. Numbness claims my body as the tension eases, and I can no longer feel my limbs. The sound of rushing water joins the whirring noise.

An instant of brilliance assaults my eyes, forcing me to squeeze them shut. I open them again and try to blink away the light, but I can't focus. The Zumar warriors step forward and release me.

My deadened legs refuse to support me and I crumple to the floor, my chin striking stone. My teeth crunch together; I bite my tongue and cry out. The metallic taste of blood fills my mouth. My arms quiver, and my muscles hang limp as wet strings.

When my eyes finally become accustomed to the light, I notice I'm in a chamber with a black platform in the middle of the room and something like a metal cage against one wall.

Waves of dizziness overcome me and I close my eyes. The smell of dirt and sewage surrounds me. I hear grunts and growls from the warriors, then heavy shoes clomping on stone, stopping by my side.

My mind spins out of control as vertigo overtakes me and my chest heaves. I vomit where I lie. I don't have the strength to move or wipe my face. Buzzing fills my head. If I didn't know I was lying on a cold stone floor, I wouldn't know which way was up or down.

I'm barely aware of something hard prodding my ribs and then claws clamping my waist. Everything spins even more wildly as I feel myself being slung over a shoulder like a sack of grain, dangling upside down. I puke again as I bounce on the beast's back. Metal grommets from its armor poke my face and chest. Vomit, moldy leather, and decay fill my nostrils.

I hear nothing but the buzzing, screaming noise in my head as I fight to keep the world from spinning. An agonizing creak pierces the noise in my mind, like nails scratching a chalkboard.

The warrior grabs my hips and flings me down. My head strikes the wall and sparks explode behind my eyes—and then, blessed darkness.

---

*Candles flicker, casting shadows that haunt the room like dark spirits in an ancient graveyard—wraiths searching for wayward souls to feast upon.*

*A redheaded teenager trembles as his eyes open, sweat beading on his upper lip. With a combination of fear and loathing, he glares at the gaunt man standing before him.*

*Clenching his fists, the boy states, "You killed Mother and Father."*

*"They were no longer of any use." The man reaches out a gnarled hand and digs his fingers into the boy's arm. "You have reached the age of metamorphosis. It is time to fulfill your destiny."*

*The boy straightens, his face pale and his eyes glassy. "Why did you deem their deaths necessary, Grandfather?"*

*"I have visioned your future." The man lets his hand slide down the boy's arm, almost a caress. "You will be a powerful sorcerer, revered by your followers and your many children, feared by all others. I have much to teach you and little time before my own imminent demise."*

*Flinching at the man's touch, the boy raises his chin. "But why kill them?"*

*The old man smiles, exposing rotten teeth. "To make you strong enough to meet your destiny, to take this world as your own."*

---

My eyelids flutter and I groan. Images from the dream flicker in my mind and my heart aches for the boy, who seems almost . . . familiar.

I struggle to open my eyes, to remember where I am, but spiral again into shadows.

## October 24

*Erick*

No Zumarian escapes my blade. I slay every beast with vengeance, as if each one has the power to bring Taryn back to me.

Cole's sword remains clean. I destroy ten warriors, save fifteen lives. I think of nothing more than to erase the encounter from the minds of these Oldworlders and send them to their homes. Cole and I do not speak.

Before dawn breaks in Oldworld, we return to Newold and Albin gives congratulations. "A single girl lost. A good night."

Fury knifes my body and I lunge for Albin's throat. Cole dodges between us and grabs my shoulders, and we almost tumble to the floor.

Albin backs away, his face as white as the crescent moon. "What ails Lord Erick?"

"Rough night," Cole responds as he maneuvers me out the doors. We jog down the steps and, when we are out of range of hearing of the door squire, Cole claps me on my shoulder. "This evening, Erick. Get some rest and we shall rescue the girl and slay the damnable sorcerer."

I turn on my heel and head to my home.

Time cannot pass any slower. I prepare my haversack and am ready for this evening, but I refuse to lie down.

Why Taryn? Twice within a week, and both times Cole and I dispatched far from the portal. It makes no sense. And two Zumar warriors—I have never heard of such. Does Synomea know Taryn has the crescent crystal, and that was why there were two attempts to take her?

The crystal!

Gods! That must be why she was taken. How could I have been so foolish to not even consider the sorcerer could find the crystal with Taryn? I thought she would be safe in Old-world.

If Synomea gets his hands on the crystal, he will exploit its powers. Our battle may be lost before it begins.

The door creaks and I look to see Cole standing in my bedchamber door.

"What?" I grumble. Cole's appearance at my home could only mean bad news or more words between us about Taryn.

"You must sleep. I have come to see you get your rest before we leave."

"Rest!" I rake my hand through my hair. "As if that is possible."

Hands clenched, Cole approaches me. "This is for your own good."

Too late I see his fist flying toward me. Pain explodes in my jaw and I tumble into darkness.

---

*Seek the Crescent . . . Seek the crystal . . . Find them or perish . . . Find them and perish . . . Only fate can decide . . .*

The wizards' words are echoing in my skull when I awaken. "Damn!" I mutter and my jaw aches. "I have no time for wizard babble. I must rescue Taryn."

When I check the light outside my bedchamber window, I see it is late afternoon. I dress in a clean tunic and breeches, grab my haversack, and head to the glade to meet with my friends.

The forest is quiet other than pine needles crunching beneath my boots. But then a strange whisper curdles my blood.

*Lion . . . Lion . . .*

I rip Navran from its sheath and crouch. Wind rushes pines, the sound like endless ocean waves. The scent of cloves swirls around me and the air before my eyes glistens.

I ready my sword.

Two forms appear, shadowy figures in the mist. My heart races as faint images become stronger and I realize it is the wizards. Relief floods my being, mingled with apprehension.

L'iwanda and L'onten come closer, until they are mere steps away from me.

"The time has come." L'iwanda inclines her head, her silver hair floating like wisps of silk in the wind.

"You must retrieve the Crescent." In the afternoon sunlight, L'onten's bald head gleams.

I clench my sword as I study the wizards, but I ignore what they have said. "Tell me what I must do to rescue Taryn from Synomea's clutches."

"Ah." L'iwanda smiles. "In the dungeon she shall be."

L'onten nods. "From outside the fortress, seek the lion stone."

"Along the west wall it lies."

"Behind the lion is an entrance long forgotten."

"Through it you shall find the one you seek."

"Your love and your blood shall live to breathe beyond castle walls."

My love, Taryn. But my blood? Ah, they must mean Van.

I shake my head. "No. I will not put my sister in danger. I travel alone."

L'iwanda extends her hand to L'onten. "Keep Tiger close."

"Beware of Scorpion." L'onten clasps L'iwanda's hand.

L'iwanda's face fills with concern. "Beware the Crescent's duality."

Riddles! Anger stirs in my belly. I have no time for this. "Tell me now. Will we defeat the sorcerer?"

"By the fire of Navran . . ."

"The choice of the Crescent . . ."

"And the will of the Lion."

Their forms waver and swirl, like tendrils of smoke vanishing with the wind.

I pause, willing the wizards' words to make sense, trying to puzzle the meaning. I shake my head and continue on through the forest to meet with my friends.

When I reach the glade, my friends are waiting. Each bears a haversack containing enough supplies to make it through a few days.

"I know how to find Taryn," I say. "The wizards have told me where I must go."

"Good news," Van replies as she approaches me.

Cole takes my haversack. "We have arranged our dispatch with Albin."

"With that oaf?" I scowl as I rub my sore jaw. Cole has a strong left.

Van gives a gentle smile, but it doesn't reach her eyes, as if she is uncertain. "If the stars themselves did not cloud your vision, you would know he is loyal."

"I do not have time for chatter." I fold my arms across my chest. "I must leave now."

"Cole explained everything." Van squeezes my shoulder. "All of us have discussed the situation and have reached an agreement. Although we do not approve of your relationship with an Oldworlder, we love you and will not allow you to go alone. Together we shall fetch the girl when we go after Synomea."

I shake my head. "I will not endanger your life or the others." Even though the wizards spoke of my blood sister accompanying me, I do not want Van to go. "You all must wait for my return. Then we can go after the sorcerer."

"No." Her fists at her hips, Van raises her chin. "It is too dangerous for you alone, and we would lose our element of surprise. Together we stand a better chance of winning her freedom and defeating the sorcerer."

My sister will never back down once her mind is made, and she is right. I am a fool for endangering the greater part of our mission in my haste to retrieve Taryn. We shall do both at once. I run a hand over my head and glance at my silent friends. They each stare at me, their faces staunch and determined. Even Gareth, whose lip is swollen from my fist.

Van swings her haversack onto her shoulder. "If all goes well, we should make our return before the Elders' Council session ends."

I take a deep breath, then eye each of my friends. "As you know, we may face exile or imprisonment for what we are about to do . . . if we make it back alive. There is still time to back out, if you wish."

Cole grips the hilt of his sword. "We follow you and Van."

"Aye," Finella says.

Gareth nods.

Basil twirls his sword, its point in the dirt, and grins. "Where you lead."

"Then let us rid Zanea of its filth." I grab my haversack from Cole, then head for Newold.

It is early evening when we reach Command. Van slips into the building, then returns. "Lady Quenn and Voice Osred just left. Albin is ready."

We go in pairs, as always. Albin mans the na'ta command, his lips tight, his jaw set.

"Are you prepared?" I ask. "You know where we need to dispatch?"

"Aye." Albin nods. "Outside the west wall."

With Albin's assistance, Cole and Finella dispatch first. The air around them turns silver, like liquid. Their forms undulate and waver, like a reflection in a pond, and they are gone.

Basil and Gareth follow, faces grim, and for once they do not argue.

When the na'ta platform is again empty, Van and I mount the steps. "This should not be as difficult as the journey to Oldworld," she says, just before the dispatch begins.

Van is wrong.

The dispatch to Zumaria is far worse than any I have experienced in the past.

Pain slices my chest like a dagger and the agony in my head is as if each of my teeth is yanked out, one by one. A screech assaults my ears and I am afraid they will burst. When the dispatch ends, I stumble and fling my hand against a cone of lava rock to avoid pitching into it with my face. The rock cuts into my hand and my palm burns. My ears ring like the bells of Nar.

"By the gods," Van gasps beside me. I can hardly hear her trembling voice. She collapses to her knees. I would reach for her if my own muscles did not quiver.

It is difficult to breathe. The air reeks of sulfur. Mount Zumar glows in the distance, belching clouds of poisonous ash.

"Damn!" Temptation to kick something swells within me. Alas, nothing but lava rock exists in this place, and I would surely break my foot. "Unless Synomea has moved his lodgings, we are not outside the fortress."

"I do not understand." Van struggles to her feet, throws her braid over her shoulder, and scans the horizon. "We should have dispatched along the west wall." She rubs her bare arms, as if warding off a chill. "Albin assured us."

"Perhaps Albin is not to be trusted and sent us to this hell on purpose."

Van frowns. "Something is amiss . . . but Albin?" She visibly swallows and points east to Mount Zumar. "The sorcerer's fortress is far below. By the looks of it, we have at least four nights' travel, perhaps five."

"Damn. It shall be a long trek, and Taryn in that bastard's hands. What of our friends? Are they at the fortress while we stand here?"

"I will speak to Cole to inform him of our misfortune, and to see where they have dispatched." She sighs, but not a flicker of discouragement crosses her features. She is solid. Strong. Independent.

Van retrieves her l'apitak, holds it in both hands, and closes her eyes. Her disk is gold, graced with Mipawa, the goddess of stealth. Cole retains the sister to Van's l'apitak, somewhere across this forsaken wasteland.

It is a warm night. A welcome wind dries the sweat on my neck. I pull out my own l'apitak. Silver, engraved with Nipenia, goddess of life and love. The discs are bound with the spiritual magic of the wizards, enabling the bearer to communicate via thought with the person who holds its twin.

I clench my l'apitak in my fist and pray Taryn has the one I left with her.

Within a few moments I feel Taryn clasp her l'apitak. *Erick!* she cries in my mind, and I sense her distress.

*I will find you, Taryn,* I reply with my heart and soul.

But she is gone, and I feel only emptiness. *Taryn!*

Van's voice cuts through my attempt to regain contact with Taryn, and I open my eyes.

"They dispatched far from target." Van slips her l'apitak into the pocket of her breeches. "Cole and Finella are at least two days from Gareth and Basil. All are five, perhaps six days' journey from the sorcerer's stronghold. Unfortunately, they are all to the east. We have arranged to meet at the Zumar Caves south of the fortress walls as soon as we are able."

"Damn!" I snatch a lava rock and fling it, but never hear it drop. "I believe it was more than a miscalculation in dispatch."

Van slings her haversack over one shoulder, but does not answer.

"Food and water are scarce in this wasteland. We each carry supplies enough for four days, no more." My gaze flicks to the horizon, where Synomea's fortress lies. "Our friends need to forget our plans and return to Newold."

"I told Cole so. But he refused. He says they all wish to continue."

"By the gods, Cole is a mule!"

Van laughs, the sound too pleasant for this desolate place. "No more than you, Erick."

"If only we had dispatched into the fortress as planned." Ghostly shadows writhe around us as I scowl at the bleak landscape. "If only we could do so while we are here." Once in Zumar, without the dispatch officer's guidance, we cannot arrive within the fortress without a na'tan to dispatch to. And we cannot risk contact with Albin until our task is finished.

Van squeezes my arm. "All will be fine."

With a glare to my sister, I say, "Do you always need to find light where there is dark?"

"Your temper is enough for both of us." Van grins. "Come. We have a girl to rescue and a tyrant to destroy."

When our strength returns, we walk. We must find a cave before dawn breaks and sleep until darkness shields us once again.

The barest good fortune travels with us. The twin moons are at three quarters, giving us light enough to pick our way along the treacherous volcanic fields. My boots are sturdy and I do not feel the rocks' sharpness through the thick soles. Loose stone crunches beneath our feet, the smell of sulfur and ash thick and heavy.

My thoughts are with Taryn, and I am thankful she has the l'apitak I left with her. It will make it easier to find her amongst the Zumar. Easier to locate her, yet what shall I find? Tension stabs my neck and shoulders like steel claws as I imagine her slaving in one of Synomea's mines. Or worse.

I sensed fear and confusion when I brushed Taryn's mind with the l'apitak. Such a brief, sweet second, and she seemed thrilled at our contact. And then she pushed me away. No, shoved me from her thoughts, as if I might be the last person she would choose to greet.

Is she safe? What of the crystal—has the sorcerer taken it from her? If Synomea so much as touches her, I shall rip him apart and serve him to the crimson crows of Trendoria!

Even the night air is foul and too humid to dry the sweat from my face and arms. Hours pass as we hike across the hostile wasteland, and we see nothing more than treacherous cliffs and the volcano's baneful glow. Van and I do not speak.

We can only pray Synomea's eye cannot find us and that he does not have sentinels to stand in our way.

My thoughts continue to stray to Taryn. It is my fault, her capture, as certain as if I handed her to the Zumar myself. Synomea must have seized Taryn to retrieve the crystal. Why else were there two attempts to take her? Why else would he have sent two warriors the second time?

And both occasions Cole and I dispatched far from the portal. It is obvious someone from within Haro consorts with the sorcerer—perhaps Albin or another dispatch officer. It could be Quenn, who manned the command the first night I met Taryn. Even Voice Osred is suspect, or perhaps another member of the Elders' Council.

How did Taryn remain conscious when the Zumar touched her—both times? No Oldworlder has withstood the grasp of a single warrior, let alone two. Only those of Newold are unaffected by the Zumar touch.

How could Synomea have known Taryn possesses the crescent crystal?

In my heart, I cannot believe one of my friends would be a traitor. We have been together too long.

But my head begs I ask the question. If one of my friends is a traitor, who would it be? Perhaps Gareth, who finds every excuse to quarrel, or Basil, who balked at this quest. Could it be Finella, whose advances I refused once our courtship ended? I could never believe my loyal friend Cole would betray me. And certainly not my blood sister.

By the light of Nar! If Synomea has indeed taken the crystal from Taryn, it may be too late for us all.

It is after midnight by the time we reach the shelf above the thousand caves. It will be a steep and dangerous descent. It is fortunate we have knowledge of the terrain from our studies and trainings as Haro.

Van calls to me as I trek downward. "Erick—pray, take care."

I test each foot and handhold as I progress. The rock wall is jagged but solid and bears my weight. My confidence grows. I yearn to reach shelter and contact Taryn with the l'apitak.

Still several feet above the caves.

*Taryn.* I sense her. Feel her. As though she is here.

I glance down and see a shadowy form. Taryn?

The lava rock beneath my boot vibrates.

And gives way.

Fleeing rock slices my hands, tears flesh from my arms. Fire rips my limbs as I fight to find purchase.

The cliffside vanishes from beneath me, and I plunge.

---

*Taryn*

"Gran, I had a horrible dream." I can barely speak, my tongue feels so thick. So dry. The sound of my voice pounds like a hammer inside my head and my chin aches from moving my jaw.

As I roll over, my temple strikes something solid. Fiery bolts shoot through my head and everything spins.

*Not my ears. Not again.*

But this dizziness feels different—not like what I usually feel from the Ménière's. At this moment, I'm not sure which dizziness is worse.

Several minutes pass before the world settles and I can pry my eyes open. A wall of stone is at my nose. Ancient stone, crumbling and green with moss.

It isn't a dream.

The smell of vomit and filth surrounds me, and I dry heave. My stomach cramps and I withdraw inside myself, meditating, trying to calm the fears raging within me and trying to keep another episode of vertigo at bay.

*Taryn!* The voice echoes in my mind, weaving through my deepest thoughts to the center of my soul. Erick. His husky, frantic words filled with fear. Did I hear Erick yell my name as the warriors took me into the black hole? Why didn't he stop them?

And if Erick saw the Zumar take me, will he try to find me?

*Once taken by the Zumar, Oldworlders are never recovered.*

Cold waves of fear and despair wash over me. Will Erick consider me just another lost "Oldworlder"?

I picture his face, so dear to me. The strong lines of his features, the scar along his cheekbone, his silvery eyes and blond hair. But his smile is what fills my heart. That smile, holding so much tenderness, so much caring.

When I shift to lie on my back, I'm sure the pain will fracture my skull, and nausea churns inside me. I touch my scalp and blood covers my fingers.

As I wipe my hand on my jeans, I notice the steady sound of dripping water and the smells of dank earth, mold, and urine.

I try to sit up, but whirl into darkness.

---

Wiry bristles brush my cheek. I open my eyes to find I'm nose to whiskers with an enormous rat. A poodle-sized rat.

I scream and scramble to my knees. Poodle rat's whiskers twitch and I swear the beast glares at me with beady red eyes before turning up its nose and scurrying into a dark corner.

My breath comes in short gasps, as if I've been running. I hold my palm to my throbbing temples and try to calm down.

Poodle rat? The absurd image of a rat in a jewel-studded collar with its hair sheared like pompoms pops into my mind, and I almost burst into laughter. I'm definitely losing my mind.

Taking care not to bump my aching head, I lean back against the wall. The only light comes through the small window in the door. I hear the hiss and spit of flames, smell burning pitch. Light flickers, the dance of shadows reminding me of the dream of the boy and his horrible grandfather.

It's dim, but I can make out my surroundings. I'm in a cell—no, a dungeon, like in one of those King Arthur legends. A room of stone and a heavy wooden door, its window complete with iron bars.

Manacles and chains hang from the walls, and I don't have to wonder what's worse—serving as a slave to these monsters, being alone during the holidays, or being abandoned altogether. If I make it out of here and back to Tucson, I promise never to whine about being alone again. Never.

I reach for my pendant. Gone, of course. I thrust my hand in my pocket, and my fingers find the silver button. An odd tingle travels through my hand, straight to my heart.

*Erick.*

I feel him. I clench the disc, the metal cool in my palm. As clear as if it just happened, I feel Erick placing it in my hand. I even recall slipping it in my pocket after he gave it to me. Somehow, all those memories were unlocked the instant the Zumarian warriors grabbed me. Even memories of Erick. Relief floods me at the fact that I can remember him now.

My stomach grumbles. I glance to the foot of the door and see a wooden tray and a cup. I have no desire for food, but I don't want to die of thirst and it won't do me any good to become weaker from hunger. Somehow, some way, I have to escape. No way will I give up.

When I try to investigate the tray, my body won't cooperate. My limbs feel heavy, like I could sink into the stone floor, and my head throbs. Poodle rat probably ate it all anyway.

Everything seems so eerily silent. Where are all the other people they steal from Earth? What do they do to them after bringing them to this awful place?

A long, shuddering sigh escapes me. I should have stayed home, but facing the loneliness seemed unbearable. Erick had come to say goodbye. How strange I could not remember him, yet the pain of his leaving was still with me. It can only mean one thing—we are soul mates. We belong together. Or perhaps this is just my desire to be wanted, needed? Am I that weak?

Did he feel the same way about me? Or did he decide I'm not worth the risk? It's true he broke his world's rules to see me. He seemed to care for me, really care. I believe he came to see me for the same reason I was drawn to him. A deep connection—that we belong together. Like we were together in another life.

The distant sound of heavy boots rattles me, sending shocks through my body. A shadow looms outside the bars. The lever scrapes and the door swings open.

A Zumarian.

I shrink back, trembling, wishing I could become one with the wall.

This warrior is huge. Taller than Erick. And what a hideous face! Charred, hanging flesh, like the beast was born from fire.

The Zumarian kicks aside the food tray, the clatter echoing in the hall. It grunts and motions. My legs freeze.

In a single stride, the warrior grabs my waist and throws me over its shoulder, causing everything to whirl. I clench its leather armor with my hands, grinding my teeth, and pray another bout with vertigo isn't starting.

The warrior stinks like the garbage can at my foster home. My body aches everywhere imaginable and my head throbs in time with the Zumarian's footsteps. The thought of my foster parents jars me. They must be worried sick. Jen, too.

After walking along dark corridors, up endless creaking stairs, and through two sets of doors, the warrior halts and drops me. I land on my rear. Pain shoots up my backside and I'm sure my tailbone is now bruised.

In mid-groan, I catch my breath. This is no dungeon. This is a castle.

Elegant tapestries with rich, vibrant colors drape the walls. Ornate couches, chairs, and divans cushioned in green velvet line the walls, and a fireplace commands one corner. As I ease myself to my feet, I notice crystal chandeliers and a table set for two. Gold plates and flatware, unlit candles next to a wine bottle.

It all feels surreal, like I truly did swirl down my shower drain to end up in Wonderland.

If so, this must be the Mad Hatter's tea party.

The room smells of musty books and a sickly odor of burnt sugar that makes me want to gag. A fire pops and crackles in the fireplace, but I feel as cold as I did in the dungeon.

The doors to my left are massive and guarded by two warriors. To my right, green velvet draperies hang from floor to ceiling and I wonder what's behind them.

Two enormous windows, also draped in green velvet, are in the stone wall in front of me. It's dark outside, but there's a red glow in the distance. I check my watch. Assuming the date and year function still works, it's only been a day since the Zumarians grabbed me. It feels like forever.

When I turn around, my blood races at the sight of another person. My arm aches as I move my hand to my chest. I feel my heart pounding against my palm. *Calm down.* It's my own reflection in a large mirror.

I look absolutely terrible. A smudge crosses my face and a cut and bruise mar my chin. I rub at the trail left on my cheek from when I vomited. The stench clings to my clothes and hair.

Blood also cakes my hair and my scrunchie is about ready to fall out. I pull it off and stuff it into my pocket, next to the silver disc, vitamin box, and shoelace. My jacket and jeans are almost black with filth.

What I wouldn't give to be back in that warm shower at home . . . the warm shower that seems a lifetime ago.

"Ah, my lovely Ta'reen." A voice cuts into my thoughts.

I whirl around.

My entire body goes numb.

*It can't be. It can't be!*

My eyes widen and my aches are almost forgotten as I raise my hand to my neck. "But—you—you're dead!"

"To be sure, I am quite alive, my daughter." The man steps toward me, his arms outstretched like he intends to hug me.

*Father?*

My knees threaten to buckle. I stumble back and almost fall.

*No, no! This can't be happening.*

But it's him. He's aged so little from the picture, but he's wearing flowing emerald robes instead of a suit and tie.

"Gran said you died," I whisper as my thoughts reel. "In a fire. With my mother." I don't know why, but I walk slowly backward, while he continues to advance.

My father smiles, but it doesn't quite reach his eyes. "Obviously not." He drops his hands to his sides, but he's still coming toward me.

"I—I don't understand." The mirror is cold at my back now. There's nowhere to run. But this is my father. Why do I feel like I need to run?

He comes so close I can see his pores, and that burnt-sugar smell is even stronger. I was mistaken about his hair in the black and white photo. It's not reddish gold like mine, but completely red, only graying a bit at the temples. He's almost as tall as Erick, and I have to look up to see his eyes. They're green, flecked with gold, like my own.

"'Twas quite necessary that you had no knowledge of me these many years. Your grandmother served her purpose well—in keeping you safe from my enemies."

I can't think—can't comprehend anything he's telling me.

"'Tis too complicated to explain in mere moments, my child." He strokes my face and I flinch. He grimaces. "You smell of filth."

"I haven't exactly received the royal treatment."

My father takes my hand, his own soft and fleshy against my palm. Rods of ice shoot through my arm—that same horrible feeling I'd had in that dream where I had touched Full Moon and it turned into Sickle. I try to snatch my hand back, but his grip is firm.

"Have dinner with me and I shall explain all." He sounds like a caring father, but I resist.

Boiling fury melts the frost of his touch. I yank my hand away and see surprise in his eyes. "I don't even *know* you. You walked out seventeen years ago. You allowed me to grow up thinking my father was dead."

I clench my fists. "And what did you just put me through? Monsters kidnap me, sling me around, and lock me in a dungeon with a giant rat. Then you bring me here and suddenly I have a father who's alive? What the hell is going on?"

An expression flickers across his face. At first I think it's anger, but then I realize it must be pain, and I've hurt his feelings.

He takes a deep breath and sighs. "You are right to feel such confusion. Come, and your questions will be answered."

His words calm me, or maybe I'm too tired to argue. He takes my arm, propels me toward the dinner table, and guides me into a chair. It's soft and comfortable after sleeping on stone. My aching muscles melt into the velvet.

Servants appear from nowhere, as if by an unspoken command. Dressed in brown robes, the two women servants keep their eyes downcast and they don't say a word. What's wrong with them?

"Drink, my dear." He pours water into a crystal goblet and hands it to me.

This man hasn't been around for my whole life. Where does he get off acting like he cares about me?

I pick up the heavy goblet and stare at it, wondering if it's poison. But if he wanted to kill me, he could have done that already. Besides, he is my father. Why would he want to harm me?

While he watches, I taste the contents, then drink the entire glass. The liquid has a heavy mineral taste, but it's water. I use a cloth napkin to wipe the moisture from my mouth. "I'm not your dear," I say.

He chuckles and raises an eyebrow. "I have no doubt you shall come to realize this is where you belong, now that you have reached the age of metamorphosis."

I blink. *The age of metamorphosis.* Where have I heard that before?

My temper snaps. "Metamorphosis—is that what you call it? I call it kidnapping. Where's my mother? Is she alive, too?"

Again he looks hurt, and I wonder if I'm being fair.

My father draws a deep breath and lets out a sigh. "Your mother perished almost seventeen years ago."

He turns to the women and says, "Leave us."

I lower my gaze to my plate as the servants exit the room. When I learned my father was alive, hope built inside that my mother still lived, too.

"Eat," he says, his voice surprisingly gentle.

I pick up my fork and push my food around. The plate brims with stringy meat that appears to be overcooked pot roast. Joining it are reddish blobs that look like mushrooms and some grainy stuff that could be pasta. I'm afraid to ask what everything is. The meat could be poodle rat, for all I know. It tastes like chicken. The pasta substitute has a buckwheat flavor and the mushrooms have a lemony tang.

My jaw aches as I chew and my eyes water. But the strange thing is, with all the injuries I have, I'd think I'd feel a whole lot worse than I do.

We don't speak while we eat, but I catch him watching me with an expression that vacillates between amusement and something I can't quite pinpoint. Pride? Irritation, maybe?

When we finish the meal, my father leaves, his emerald robes scraping the floor. I can see his lips move when he speaks to a guard at the door, but with my bad ear I cannot hear anything that is said.

I slip my hand into my pocket, grasp the silver disc, and close my eyes. That same electric current I felt in the dungeon travels through my arm, sending warmth within my chest. I can feel Erick again, as if he's not far away.

*Erick!* I shout in my mind.

*I will find you, Taryn.* Erick's voice. In my head!

My eyes fly open and I see the man who fathered me, standing inches away, watching me.

He holds out his hand. "Give it to me."

I freeze, unable to move.

"Now." Perspiration soaks his temple, and he's so close I feel his breath on my face.

"W-what?" The disc slips from my fingers to the bottom of my pocket. I feel so alone, the link to Erick severed.

"The crescent crystal."

I shake my head. "I don't know what you're talking about."

"The crescent." He speaks slowly, like he's controlling his temper. "The one you have worn around your neck since you were five."

Relief rushes me. He's not asking for Erick's disc. But how does he know I wore the pendant since I was five? Why does he want it?

"My necklace vanished yesterday." I raise my hand to my neck, as if searching for my pendant. "That's why I was taking a walk when the warriors grabbed me. I was upset the necklace had disappeared."

"Show . . . me . . . now." Gone is the fatherly expression. Barely controlled fury tightens his face, his eyes a brilliant green against his livid features.

I scoot back in my chair, afraid of what he might do. "But I—" Oh. Prove I don't have it. I open my jacket and pull at the neck of my shirt so he can see it's gone.

He collapses into his chair and stares at the ceiling. The room is dead silent. I can hear blood pounding in my ears, and I'm conscious of every breath I take.

"Is it in your home?" His clipped words scatter like ice cubes on tile.

"No. I searched everywhere. I tore the house apart."

"Do you have any idea who may have taken it?"

"I—I don't know why anyone would. I had it when I went to bed and then noticed the necklace was missing when I woke up."

128

An image flashes in my mind. Erick touching my pendant, his face pale, asking where it came from. He recognized it and must have known it was something of value. Could he have taken . . . ? *No.* Erick wouldn't steal from me. Would he?

"What are you thinking, daughter?" He leans forward.

"Nothing." I rub my sweating palm on my jeans. "I don't even know why you're interested. It was just a trinket I treasured because my parents gave—"

*Oh.* This man is my father. *He* gave it to me.

He leans even closer, his intense gaze drilling into me. "The Haro knight. He must have taken it."

A hot flush burns my skin, and I flounder to maintain eye contact with him. How does he know about Erick? "I—I don't know what you're talking about."

"Do not play games. I have knowledge of this knight, that he was aware you had the crystal. My minion believed Lord Erick would not take it from you, but it is apparent he did. This knight I shall find."

Heat within me shifts to ice, like an overpowering blizzard in hell. "I—no. It must have been someone else."

"Do not be such a fool, child. It is apparent he sought you for this reason—to win your trust and take the stone. Why else would he seek you out?"

His insinuation is like a slap in the face, as if no one would find me worthy of love. But what if he's right, and Erick started visiting me to get to my pendant? Yet I remember how surprised he was to see it.

With a weary hand, I brush strings of hair from my face. "Why do you want my pendant? What do you want with me?"

"Do you not know my name, daughter?"

"Of course. It's Ian Simons."

129

He smiles, and it's not nice at all. "In my own world, I am called Synomea."

"You're *Synomea?*" Blood drains from my head, trickling to my toes. My body goes limp, and I slump in the chair. Why didn't I realize it before?

A wicked glint sparks his eyes. "So, you have knowledge of me." He sounds pleased.

Overload—this is more than I can handle. This man is responsible for all the disappearances, all the people taken from Earth by the Zumar. This is the same man Erick and the other Haro knights are bent on destroying.

*My father.*

"You're a—a sorcerer."

"As are you."

I blink and would shake my head if it didn't hurt so. Maybe I didn't hear right. *"What?"*

"You carry the mark; thus, you have inherited my abilities and you are a sorceress."

*Sorceress?* What is he talking about?

"A crescent marks your left arm. As mine." My father pushes up the sleeve of his robe to expose the birthmark, a cruel red slash against his pale flesh. His is more like a thin crimson sickle, where my birthmark is almost a half moon.

*My dreams of Sickle and Crescent.*

My throat constricts and my tongue is glued to the roof of my mouth.

"The sign of a true sorcerer of our line," he says as he drops his sleeve. "If you had been born without it, you would have been useless. Like the others."

*Useless? Like what others?*

He stands. "Come, Ta'reen. I have something that may be of interest to you."

Another swell of ice water sweeps over my body. *Ta'reen.* The voice in my head the night Erick saved me. "It was you." I stare up at him, gripping the arms of the chair. "Somehow you made me leave my house to go out into the street the first time a Zumarian tried to take me."

My father's face twists into a scowl. "That spell required a vast amount of energy from my powers. I had prepared long and hard for that night and 'twas for naught."

The battle raging within him emanates in waves. "Had you not been out of your home long enough for my minions to track you last night . . ." His voice trails off, making it difficult for me to hear. But I catch a flicker of something passing over his features, as if he's said more than he intended to or wants to admit, and he slams his mouth shut.

He gathers himself and holds out his hand. "Now come." The tone of his voice tells me I don't have a choice. Do what he says, or else. Or else what?

I get to my feet and step away from him, avoiding his hand. A strange feeling shoots through me, as if a sense of what he's thinking flickers in my mind—he's genuinely pleased to have me, his daughter, here with him.

No. That's ridiculous. How could I possibly know what he's thinking?

His fatherly smile returns as he drops his hand to his side and walks past me. I follow him to the fireplace, confusion swirling like a storm. Sorcerer or not, this is my father. Can he really be that bad?

"I know 'tis late and you require rest, not to mention a bath." He pauses before a table filled with an assortment of containers made of jade, ivory, wood, gold, and glass. "But first, a lesson."

Synomea opens a cloisonné box and pinches indigo powder between his thumb and forefinger. " 'Tis truth you are indeed a young sorceress, as this mind-flight shall prove."

He takes my hand. "When I administer this powder, we will fly across the volcanic fields of Zumar in search of invaders. I will guide you. Pay close attention and you will be able to lead the next mind-flight."

The sorcerer swipes the blue substance from the base of my palm down my middle finger. Then he wipes powder from the center of my forehead to the tip of my nose.

At first, I'm too surprised to react. I open my mouth to speak, but no words will come. A bizarre sensation creeps over me like warm honey being poured over my body. Then it's like my brain oozes out my ears.

The room dissolves.

Something, some part of me—my consciousness, my energy, perhaps my mind-spirit—flies across a wasteland as I'm dragged along by Synomea. Flying in the night sky is an incredibly exhilarating feeling that takes my breath away. We come to an abrupt halt and I'm standing below a steep cliff.

My senses reel and spin. Everything seems too bright, too vivid. Sounds are louder than loud, smells are strong and pungent. And somewhere, deep inside me, something is stirring. A sense it's right for me to do this. A sense I've waited my whole life to be this aware, this free.

This powerful.

Jagged rock surrounds me in ebony waves, a sheer wall rising to one side. Where the sky is clear, far from the volcano, brilliant stars glitter across the sky like diamonds scattered upon a velvet jeweler's cloth.

I look up—the twin moons from my dreams illuminate a familiar figure scaling the sheer wall in front of me.

*It can't be.*

Slow and sure, one step, one handhold at a time, he moves down the wall, his muscles bulging from the strain of the climb. He glances down and I see his face.

Erick! I want to cry out, but I don't dare for fear of startling him.

Synomea steps to my side and raises a finger. A slight movement, like he's drawing a circle in the air, and the rock below Erick's foot crumbles.

*Noooo!* I scream, yet no sound comes from my lips.

He fights to regain his foothold, but falls and lands in a heap at my feet.

"Erick!" I'm screaming, even as I'm ripped from the sight and flown to the fortress.

I find myself back in the room with Synomea.

"How could you?" My entire body shakes as rage wells up in me at the sight of my father's face.

"You have feelings for this Haro knight, Lord Erick." The sorcerer raises an eyebrow. "How ironic, as you will learn. It is a pity for you he is probably dead from his fall. But I was able to determine he does not have the crescent crystal."

"You—you don't care that he might have died?" I can't believe it. I just can't. I stare at him, hoping for some sign of sorrow, of emotion. Any emotion. Please, God, don't let my own father be a monster.

Something flickers in the sorcerer's unnaturally green eyes.

Was it anger? Pity?

"Losing those we love makes us stronger, daughter." His voice is eerily quiet, yet I hear every word like the strike of a hammer against my heart. "Pain is necessary preparation for what lies ahead of you. The death of the knight is but one of many things you will suffer on your path to greatness."

I don't know what possesses me. I lunge for my father, intent on venting my rage.

A quick movement of his finger and my forehead strikes something solid between us. I stumble backwards and fall. Once again, I land on my bottom, and it's all I can do not to cry out from the pain shooting up my backside.

For a moment I can't see Synomea. It's as if he has disappeared.

The air flickers and he reappears, frowning. "You have much to learn, my child. Take this barrier, for instance. It is a simple spell. A matter of concentration and will—nothing more. And yet even this you cannot do. You will, though. Soon, you will be a master of the elements, as I am. It is in your blood."

I'm so confused. All my life I've idolized the image of the father I never knew. I've always pictured him as loving and caring. But this? Someone who kills because he can?

"How could you be my father?" I ease myself to my feet. "How can you expect me to—to *like* you when you're so cruel?"

He waves his hand, brushing away my words. "Your like or dislike of me is meaningless. You will learn your place and the proper use of your powers, and you will learn respect. In time, you will see what I can offer you, and then you will understand."

Synomea gives a cold, calculating smile. "Now I shall release the beasts that will ensure any invaders upon my lands are eliminated."

# October 25

*Erick*

Pain splits my skull as I awake and struggle to remember where I am and what has happened. My hands and arms burn and my body aches.

Fingers prod at my skin and when I open my eyes I see Van is tending my biceps. We are in the belly of a cave. Damp black walls form a dome around us and the sunlight at the entrance is more than I can bear. I close my eyes and turn my head away.

"Relax." Smells of comfrey and tea tree oil pervade the air as my sister applies a cool poultice to my arm.

"What happened?" My voice sounds hoarse to my ears.

"You idiot, you fell when climbing down the cliff to the caves. Too fast for your own good, as always. You are so damn reckless."

I open my eyes and glance at her. For Van to show such emotion could only mean she had feared greatly for me.

Van grits her teeth and grabs a strip of cloth. "It is fortunate you fell only a few feet and landed on that thick skull of yours."

I know better than to argue at this point, if I value my arm.

She wraps the bandage around my biceps and I flinch as shards of pain stab me. "We are blessed you managed to fall in front of this cave. It was not easy dragging you in here."

135

The memory of scaling the side of the cliff comes back to me . . . and the fall.

I try to sit up but Van pushes me back with a firm hand. "Do not move. I need to change your dressings or you may face wound rot."

"How long have we been here?"

"Half a day yet before noon. At least you slept."

I study my sister's tired face. "And you? Have you rested?"

Van tears another strip of cloth and wraps it around another gash on my arm. "Aye. Let us eat, then nap until dark." She finishes binding my wound, then moves away.

By the gods! We have lost precious time. I stare at the cave's ceiling and work through my steps down the cliffside. How did I fall? I am certain my foothold was solid. It was as if a force loosened the rock beneath my boot.

Taryn—I sensed her. Near me. Behind me.

When I glanced down, I saw a ghostly figure. For a fraction of a moment, I was sure it was Taryn. And as I fell, I thought I heard her scream.

I close my eyes and remember when I last went to Taryn at her home. With the danger of this mission, I did not know if I would live to return. How I wanted to be with her one last time so that I might again see her face, feel her lips upon mine and her soft body in my arms.

How could I have been so selfish?

In my mind I can see the hurt on her lovely features, as if I had betrayed her. I should never have gone to her after the first night we met. But how could I not? She is a part of me, a part long missing. A part I must retrieve from that evil bastard.

"Damn!" I jump to my feet and hit my head on the cave's ceiling. White-hot agony sears my head.

Van lifts an eyebrow as she unpacks bread and hard cheese from her haversack. She withdraws a leather pouch and hands it to me. "Chew some white willow bark. It will lessen the pain in your head and your limbs, though not your heart."

My sister speaks wisdom. If anything should happen to Taryn, my heart shall never heal.

My hands and arms throb from last night's fall as I crouch beside Van and shake bits of the willow bark into my palm. "I fear Synomea may know we are here." The willow tastes bitter and unpleasant as I chew, and I grimace. "The surprise of our rescue and attack may be lost. Bloody incompetence! I shall throttle Albin myself when we return."

"Mmmm." Van braids her hair and gazes into the sunlight. Is there something akin to regret in her eyes?

"What is it?"

She continues to look outside the cave, her eyes focused beyond me, seeking something. Or someone.

"Van?"

My twin turns to me, but it is as if she sees through me. My gut twists with unease. I lean closer and squeeze her shoulders with my hands. "Van!"

Her eyes widen and she trembles beneath my palms. She drops her hands from her unfinished braid and shakes her head. "I—I—" Van stares at me as if she has seen an apparition.

"What? Tell me!"

Van pushes my hands away, then presses her fingertips to her temples. "A—a vision. But I am no visionary. Why would I see such a thing?"

"What did you see?"

Her face is pale, her gray eyes round. "The twin moons. One a white crescent, the other a crimson sickle. Blood dripped from the sickle onto a sword." She pauses and shivers. "That sword was Navran."

I take my sister's hands. "It is nothing but a daydream. Do not worry."

"No." She shakes her head. "It was a vision. As if it happened before my very eyes. I fear it means something shall happen to you, Erick. We must not go to Synomea's fortress without our friends. We must wait for them and go together, as planned."

"You stay where it is safe." I squeeze her fingers within mine. "I will go alone and bring Taryn to safety."

Van pulls away and gets to her feet to stand with her hands at her hips. "You must not go alone!"

I barely avoid hitting my head again as I stand before her. "The others are yet five days away. We are four. I cannot leave Taryn with that beast any longer."

The look in Van's eyes might well slay a smaller man. She sighs and shakes her head. Her voice is like steel when she speaks. "Very well. Then we go after Taryn together."

---

## Taryn

*Erick!*

*He tumbles in slow motion. I reach out to him, as if I can stop his descent, but he slams to the ground in a crumpled heap.*

I wake, a cold sweat breaking out over my body. Is Erick okay? Did my father kill him? Gentle warmth fills my heart, telling me Erick is alive and out there somewhere. He's my soul mate, and I would know it if . . . if he died.

Rubbing grit out of my eyes, I sit up in the unfamiliar bed and study my surroundings. Muted sunlight finds its way through the single window, barely lightening the room. Ruby velvet covers dark wood furnishings, from bedcover to curtains to armoire to four-poster bed. Plush rugs are scattered across the flagstone floor like pools of blood.

A velvet prison.

What catches my eye is a sunken tub with tempting wisps of steam rising from it. Oh, for a bath! I untangle my feet from the covers and head straight for it.

Red towels and a robe drape a nearby divan. On a small table, next to the couch, is a cake of raspberry-perfumed soap and a fat pot of something that smells like rosemary and I think is shampoo. I strip off my filthy clothes, jacket, and shoes I had not bothered to take off last night, and step down into the bath.

Mmmm. The bathwater smells of raspberries. The comforting scent swirls around me as I relax in the tepid water. A sense of unease nags me. Does Synomea know raspberry is my favorite scent? Has he been watching me that closely all these years?

My stomach twists. My father, watching me for years. Half of me wants to vomit at the idea. The other half of me wants to believe he actually cares for me.

After all, he's all the family I have left.

It might have been better if I had been born to a pack of wolves.

But how do I know he's as bad as Erick made him out to be?

*"You have reached the age of metamorphosis."* The words ring in my head and I remember where I heard them before—my dream of the boy and his horrid grandfather. That boy had looked so familiar to me, because he was my *father!*

My father's grandfather killed my father's parents.

The world seems to slip sideways.

What he must have gone through. I can't imagine having to live with something so terrible. Surely Synomea can't be as bad as his grandfather was, can he?

That is, if my dream was even something that actually happened.

A vice clamps my heart as my father's words come to me. *"Losing those we love makes us stronger, daughter . . . Pain is necessary preparation for what lies ahead of you. The death of the knight is but one of many things you will suffer on your path to greatness."*

Words that echo the dream.

It was real. It's all real.

A combination of terror and confusion surges through me. Numb, I sit and stare, seeing nothing.

The water has grown cold when I realize I'm still sitting in the tub. I scrub myself from head to toe, taking care as I wash the scrapes on my face and wound on my head. The blood in my hair is the hardest to clean, and I wince as the shampoo stings my scalp.

My body is still weak and my head aches, but I'm surprised at how much better I feel already. I can't help but wonder if this sorceress business has anything to do with it. Imagine how powerful a sorceress could be. Someone filled with magic, filled with awesome power—

No, good old Dad is out of his mind if he thinks I'm a sorceress.

If I were, that might make things easier. Like escaping and finding some way to help Erick, wherever he is in this wasteland.

My thoughts turn to my pendant—what happened to it? I had it the last time I saw Erick, and then it was gone in the morning. Erick had no problem getting into my house when the alarm was on. So could he have come in to take my necklace?

My heart tells me Erick would never steal from me. If not him, then who? It couldn't have been one of Synomea's warriors, or the sorcerer would have known. Not that I think the warriors have enough intelligence to even try.

Could it have been Cole, Erick's friend? He knows where I live and he could use that Old Magic Erick uses, too. I wonder if that strange boot print I found on my back porch has anything to do with my pendant disappearing.

I draw a deep, slow breath and my mind automatically begins to calm itself. For a moment, I sink into the quiet place I've been so many times through meditation. I turn my thoughts to Erick and I know he really is out there somewhere, and maybe, just maybe, he still cares what happens to me.

Until he finds out who my father is.

*Synomea.* I can't believe I'm the daughter of the very sorcerer Erick is bent on destroying.

The bath no longer feels relaxing. In fact, the last thing I want to do is stay in the water and keep thinking. Quickly, I finish rinsing off, and as I climb up the steps of the tub, my good ear detects someone removing the bar from the door.

I scramble to wrap the towel around me. Great. I'm naked, clad only in a bit of cloth, and I have no idea who, or what, is coming into my room.

141

Two girls, about my age, enter with heads bowed, and I breathe a sigh of relief. Before the door shuts behind them, I glimpse the metal claw of a Zumarian outside. The girls cross the floor and kneel at my feet.

"Don't do that!" I back up, horrified.

"Have we displeased you, Lady Ta'reen?" One of them looks up, a terrified expression on her face.

"No. Oh, no. Just don't bow to me. And my name is Taryn." I smile, but the girl doesn't. "What are your names?"

The dark-haired one glances to the blonde, whose head is still bowed. "I—I'm Maria, and this is Meg."

Meg scuttles for my dirty clothes, gathering them into her arms.

"No!" I say, my voice too sharp.

She drops them, but looks like she'll burst into tears.

I rub my forehead, holding back a scream of frustration. "I'm sorry. It's just that you don't need to take care of my things. I'll do it."

Maria shakes her head while grabbing the robe and bringing it to me. "You don't understand. If we don't do as we're told, his lordship will punish us."

His lordship? "You mean Synomea?"

"Yes," Maria replies as she reaches my side.

"I won't tell." I smile again, but it's hard. They are obviously terrified of his lordship. Is my father really that horrid?

"He knows everything. We don't dare disobey." Maria grabs one of my arms, stuffing it into a sleeve, and I wrangle with my precarious grip on the towel.

"Please!" she insists. "Assisting you is far better than serving *him*."

I stop struggling. When she puts it that way, it's hard to refuse her attention. "Okay. Leave my clothes, though. I'll wear them, even if they are dirty."

Maria shakes her head. "Oh, no, milady."

"It's Taryn. And why not?"

"His lordship ordered you to be clothed in clean robes and brought to him as soon as you're ready," Meg explains.

Maria pushes my other arm through the second sleeve, pulls the robe to my shoulders, produces a sash and proceeds to tie it around my waist. The towel drops around my ankles. Right now I'm tempted to tell *Father* exactly where he can stuff his robe and help him put it there. But after last night's little wall-in-my-face incident, I'm pretty sure I'd lose.

"Tell you what. I'll wear these robes, but leave my stuff. I'm going to make sure his *lordship* doesn't cause them to vanish." I gather up my clothes and dump everything but my jacket and tennies into the tub. "First, though, I'm going to clean them."

It's a battle royale to keep the girls from washing my clothes for me.

I lose. They win.

Maria forces me into a chair and starts to comb my hair, but I yelp in pain and beg her to let me do it. Gingerly I work out the knots, flinching with every stroke, tears in my eyes.

When I'm done, Maria spreads a lemon-scented cream over the laceration on my scalp and the cut on my chin. Next, she works my wet hair into a French braid. No rubber bands, and my scrunchie is too big, so we use the shoelace from my jacket pocket to tie the end. She hands me a silver mirror when she's done.

I study my reflection. The braid looks nice, and at least my hair will be out of my face. The cut on my chin is nasty, a purple bruise covers my jaw, and I have a nice egg-sized lump at my temple. But I'll heal.

"Where are you from and how long have you been here?" I ask.

Maria hesitates. "Las Vegas. As far as I can figure, I've been here maybe three years."

Meg scours my shirt, jeans, and undies with a vengeance, but glances up. An enormous bruise surrounds one of her azure eyes. In a soft drawl, almost too low for me to hear with my good ear, she says, "Las Cruces. It's been so long I can barely remember my mama's face." She ducks her head and starts wringing the water from the clothes. A tear falls onto my jeans.

How could he? Taking these poor girls from their homes and forcing them to slave for him . . . for me.

While they're cleaning my clothing, I shove my watch into my jacket pocket, then take my jacket and tennies and stow them under the bed, hoping no one will find them. I pray the disc is safe there—it's my only link to Erick.

Just as I finish hiding my belongings, the door swings open and Maria grabs my hand. "It's time to go see his lordship."

My throat is thick with fear as I go to the warriors, and then they escort me down a long hall. My crimson robes swish along the floor, the stones cool under my bare feet. Maria and Meg follow with their heads bowed, their subservience making my heart ache for them.

We enter the green room and Synomea is waiting, a broad smile plastering his face.

"Leave us." He waves off the warriors and the girls as if they're mere pests. They bow and leave. I'm alone with him. Again.

"Come, Ta'reen. We shall have our morning meal and then begin your next lesson."

"My name is Taryn, like Karen. Not Ta'reen."

He raises an eyebrow. "I named you Ta'reen. That is your given name and what I will call you."

"Then I won't respond."

He ignores my comment, guides me to the table, and pushes me into a chair. I swear there are rocks on my plate. Gray stones, the size of duck eggs. I glance from the plate to Synomea. He taps one of his rocks with a spoon, then breaks it with his fingers. Each half brims with a purple fluid, but not a drop falls on his plate.

"A true sorcerer's meal." He grins and drinks the contents of one half, then the other. "Eat."

Do I dare eat any more food in this place? I'm sure he doesn't plan to kill me . . . and what else can I do? I have to eat something while I'm here.

I pick up a rock. It's rough to my fingertips, like sandpaper, but feels only a little heavier than an egg. As I tap it with a spoon, a hairline crack forms at the center. I stop, grasp each end, and snap it apart like a fortune cookie. The whole mess crumbles in my hands, and I'm left with sticky goo and bits of gray rock clinging to my fingers and scattered across my plate. It smells like blueberries.

Synomea chuckles. "Another."

This time I take more care in opening the rock thing, but still manage to spill half the contents.

"Drink," he demands.

I grimace and bring a half to my lips. So much for not listening to him.

Here goes.

The moment the fluid touches my tongue, a strange sensation buzzes my body. Electricity crackles in my veins. The taste of the egg is sweet and thick, like melted chocolate. And suddenly I'm craving it. I drop the empty shell and drink what remains in the second half.

Warmth. No, I'm on fire. I'm the most powerful person on Earth, or on whatever this planet is called. My eyes meet Synomea's and I see his leering grin. But I don't care. I want more. The contents of the remaining two rocks I devour in record time, then clean my hands with a napkin.

"Only one of sorcerer's blood can feel the power of the Ta'sha eggs. Come, my dear, I will show you more."

Synomea takes my arm and leads me to the window. I feel so tall, so alive, so confident, every nerve vibrating.

I exist on another plane. Vivid colors fill the room, writhing in the air, surrounding me. And I *know*. Strange understandings, once buried deep inside, blossom and fill me—like there's a part of my brain that has stored so much knowledge from my birth, and it has all been set free.

The sorcerer draws open a velvet curtain and reveals the window extending from floor to ceiling.

The wasteland from my nightmare: as far as I can see, black rock void of greenery. In the distance a cone rises, spitting smoke and ash, vomiting black lava in slow rivers.

Somehow I feel no surprise at the sight, as if I knew one day I would come to this place. Still in the grip of the Ta'sha, I feel bound to the volcano, my body surging with the contents spewing from its mouth.

Closer is a pit mine filled with male and female workers. Some trudge into tunnels while others stagger out, struggling with baskets brimming with rocks of various hues. A water tower stands beside the mine and an odd-looking garden lies on the other side of the tower.

"What are those people doing?" I ask, though some part of me could care less.

"They are digging out the gifts of Zanea, things meant only for those of the truest sorcerer's blood."

I look at him, filled with desire to know more. "Will you show me all of this place?"

He observes me like he's gauging my intent. "Perhaps on the morrow we shall tour your new home."

I turn back to the window, the power of the Ta'sha making me feel almost invincible. Synomea stands behind me, so close now I can feel his robes brush mine, and he lays his hand on my shoulder. Way in the back of my mind, a part of me re- members who I am, and his touch sickens me. The magic's control weakens, or perhaps my own control strengthens.

"Here is where you belong, my fair Ta'reen. Do you not feel it? You are in the Ta'sha's grasp. Surely you realize you can never turn back."

My skin crawls. I move away and turn to face him, catch- ing the hard glint in his eye, and I force myself to smile. Something within tells me I can't allow Synomea to know I command any part of myself. Let him think the Ta'sha are controlling me.

If I play along and act dumb, leading him to say as much as possible, maybe he will teach me something I can use to get out of this place. Yesterday he showed me mind-flight. Today I will learn something more.

"Show me the next lesson." My words are clipped and devoid of emotion. I move to the fireplace and stand before the table of chests, my back to him.

His robes rustle behind me and my knees quiver.

"You are anxious." He's so close his breath stirs the hair at my nape. I struggle to keep from screaming.

"It is good, but no more than I expected of the Ta'sha," he murmurs. "Your powers have been released. You are indeed a sorceress, and with you at my side, we will rule this entire planet of Zanea. 'Twill not be long now."

*Rule? At his side?*

A part of me soars at the idea of ruling, of controlling people and destinies.

And I'm sickened as fast as that. How can I be thinking that way?

Synomea moves before the table and opens a jade vessel, revealing a pink powder. "This gives me complete mind control over our servants and anyone else I choose."

He replaces the lid and opens an ivory bowl filled with ochre dust, then glances at me. The smells are of minerals and earth, with a hint of cinnamon. "Used to torture those who fail to do as I command." My legs quiver at the insinuation.

Next, a purple jar with white contents. "So powerful, this." He chuckles and glances at me. "Allows the sorcerer to take any human form."

His hand stops over a wooden puzzle box. "Ah." I look up and glimpse his smug expression. He pulls out a peg, then removes the cover to expose scarlet powder inside. "This brings death to anyone I choose."

Goose bumps sprout over my entire body as I try to hide my burst of fear. Could the man who gave me life truly be that horrible?

He gives me a patient smile. "Surely you must realize we have enemies, my dear. Great power draws the jealous, the pretenders. They would kill us without a second thought, because they don't understand. Always, we must stand ready to defend what is ours; sometimes that includes our very lives."

I doubt him, but for a moment, he looks tense, almost hunted. I see him as an animal, and images of spear-wielding hunters make me shiver. Then I see him as the boy, in the clutches of that horrid old monster, holding back tears as he accepts the news that his parents have been murdered.

For his own good.

My heart suddenly aches for the child he once was. How can I begin to understand this man?

Oblivious to my thoughts, Synomea continues to open each container, naming the magic the contents perform. There are eight in all. He makes me repeat all he has said, and when I stumble over the names or magics each powder performs, he forces me to start over once again.

It seems like hours have passed before he's satisfied I've completely learned the powders and their magic.

"With these magics and our combined sorcery, we shall have dominance over all of Zanea." A vein bulges in his neck. "But first, we must find the crescent crystal."

His hands tremble and his face turns the color of crushed mulberries. Despite the confidence from the Ta'sha, my knees weaken.

Synomea grunts and growls. The Zumar enter the room and take me away, much to my relief. The longer I'm around Synomea, the more alarmed I become. I don't even want to think about what might be going on in his mind.

I throw myself onto the four-poster bed and stare at the carved ceiling. Such a feeling of hopelessness and fear overwhelms me, as if this strange world is closing in, attempting to destroy me.

The magic of the Ta'sha is now a part of me, forever running through my veins. A voice within my soul, a power the egg released, tells me this is true. Drinking more of the Ta'sha fluid will enhance my sorcery, but the magic is eternal. It has always been there.

Or could the Ta'sha have been a hallucinogenic drug that's making me feel this way? I still have no proof I can perform any kind of sorcery.

Yet I perceive things around me in a way I never have before. As the warriors brought me to my room we walked past a pair of servants, and I sensed their thoughts as clear as if they were my own. It was brief, as I withdrew immediately, embarrassed at having intruded.

Before leaving Synomea, I felt like I had sensed his thoughts. If so, does that mean he can read mine?

I turn onto my side on the bed, my body and mind so weary I can barely move. As I drop off to sleep I remember the silver disc, but I'm too exhausted to make sure it's still under the bed.

I fall into a fitful sleep, and I dream.

*Creatures roam the wasteland—my dream beasts! Lion, Bear, Bull, Tiger, Serpent, and Scorpion.*

*I smile. At least some things remain familiar, even in this dreadful place . . . and yet . . . and yet the beasts seem almost . . . human.*

*The thought startles me. I reject it, but . . . Lion prowls the wasteland, tail twitching. He swings his golden head to search the night sky, the breeze ruffling his mane. So majestic. So proud. Like Erick.*

*Bear, loping at Lion's side, enormous and shaggy. Could it be Cole? Protective and vigilant, obviously loyal.*

*And Scorpion, always the monster, glitters golden red beneath the twin moons. I could almost believe it's Synomea, but not quite. The rhythm of its walk, up and back, up and back . . .*

*I blink. My eyelids feel heavy, like fingers press down upon them.*

*Lion passes Scorpion, unconcerned, because they're friends. They've always been friends. I'm so sleepy I barely notice Scorpion change direction. What—what is he doing? Tail raised, stinger pulsing—no! Lion! My mouth opens, but no words escape.*

*Scorpion drives his stinger deep into Lion's flank.*

*No!*

*Bastard! How could he?*

*I know I'm screaming, but I make only dry whispers. I'm like the air, like leaves in the wind, helpless as Lion roars in pain. The sound reverberates in eerie waves.*

*Bear whirls and, with one swipe of his tremendous paw, bats Scorpion across the wasteland.*

*Hooves thunder across the lava rock. Bull!*

*Lowering his massive head, Bull charges Scorpion, tries to smash it against ebony cliffs. My breath jerks in time with Bull's snorts. Yes. Get him. Get him!*

*Missed.*

*Lithe Scorpion dodges back and raises that awful stinger. Bull attacks again, slamming against the venomous beast. The two tumble as one, plunging down a sheer bluff to jagged rocks below.*

151

*Fingers drift before my eyes. My hand, outstretched, as if to catch Bull.*

*I want out of this dream, but relentless images pound at me like angry surf.*

*Serpent—and for the life of me, I can't find anyone like Serpent in my mind—shimmers. Its sleek skin ripples as it slithers close to injured Lion. Comforting. Soothing. It wraps its slender body around Lion's neck, and squeezes . . . stealing Lion's breath, his waning strength.*

*Tiger claws at Serpent's head, sinking sharp fangs into scaly flesh.*

*The creatures vanish, but still I am not free.*

*I look to the sky and see Sickle moon. Strength, power that can be mine!*

*Incredible evil emanates from Sickle, evil that threatens to overcome me.*

*Screams rise in my throat as Sickle comes closer and closer yet.*

*Surrounding and imprisoning me.*

*Never to let go.*

## October 26

*Erick*

We are in yet another cave after another long night of walking across this hellish place.

As soon as it is dark again, we leave the safety of the cave to start another night's trek. Using the spiritual powers that have been cultivated since we were born, Van summons the Old Magic to search for a water source on our way. It is past midnight when we find a small spring. The water is bitter, but our magic tells us it is safe to drink. We refill our flasks and continue our journey.

I attempt to contact Taryn with the l'apitak as I walk, but she never responds. Does she still have it? What have the beasts done with her?

Hours pass with only the sound of our footsteps for companionship. My head and arms ache from my fall our first night here, but the pain has lessened. Van remains silent. I believe she is thinking about that vision she had yesterday.

If it truly was a vision, what could it mean? Blood on the sword Navran? She believes Navran symbolizes me; the sickle moon, Synomea. And the crescent moon—did the wizards not say to seek the Crescent? Who or what could it be?

Visions. If such things truly exist.

But even as I tell myself so, I remember the dream where I could never reach Taryn. At the end of the dream I saw the Zumar. Could it have been a vision, warning me of her capture by the warriors?

Odd sounds meet my ears, interrupting my thoughts. Clicks and chirrups, and a sound like countless insects scuttling over rocks. As I strain my eyes, a prickling sensation erupts at the base of my spine. Van halts at my side.

"There." I point to the moonlit path before us. "Movement over that rise!"

Rats? No. Spiders. A swarm of enormous spiders, glowing a wicked red in the dusky night.

"Erick! Beware the spiders' sting!" Van rips her sword from its sheath.

Navran throws sparks as I wield the blade. Van and I stand back to back.

The clatter of the monstrous spiders grows. Hundreds—no, thousands of the beasts, so loud I can hardly hear my own thoughts. Precious moments and then the creatures, some as big as Trendorian rats, draw around us. They glow from tendril to shell, like the lights of hell itself.

Van slices into the first beast, the crunch of sword through carcass churning my gut. The trenchant odor of skunk assaults my nostrils and my eyes burn and water.

In the motion I have practiced since my childhood, I swing my own sword. Navran gleams and the runes blaze. A rush of incredible power surges through me.

A green glow bursts from the crystal in the lion's mouth on my weapon. Lightning flashes from the blade.

The power flows along my arms and Navran's fire sears every beast in an arc of emerald flame. The boom of thunder echoes across the lava fields.

Then silence.

Smoking carcasses surround us. The malodor of charred flesh hangs in the air. I hear nothing but blood roaring in my veins. My arms vibrate. I wield the blade like a mammoth, a giant! With one stroke, I might slay Synomea's entire fortress!

*Damn!* Already the sword chills in my hands, the symbols quiet and dark.

Van's pale face fills my gaze. "It is true," she whispers. "You are Erickson's heir, just as our father thought. The wizards said the magic was Lion's to wield, and they meant you."

"Gods!" I shove Navran into its sheath. "I am no lion, and I have no use for ancient prophecies and feeble incantations."

Sweat on her face glistens in the moonlight as she leans against a rocky wall. "You have trained for this since birth."

I shake my head and sigh. "Aye, I have trained many long days, many long hours, as all my ancestors have. But I have never felt the power as strong as this moment. I cannot command it. It commanded me."

"Even so, we may yet have a chance against Synomea." With the back of her hand, Van wipes sweat from her forehead and looks at the carcasses around us. "These spiders are a danger I did not expect. I knew them to dwell only in Trendoria."

I blink the burning ache from my eyes. "How do you know of these creatures?"

"They are beasts of Sorcerer Kyriz in Trendoria, and are quite poisonous and deadly. I learned of the spiders from Quenn, who encountered them on a foray to Kyriz's realm. We are fortunate we received no bites." Using the tip of her sword, Van flips a spider husk. "These pinchers, long and needle-sharp. They are hollow, to inject poison into their victim. They cannot penetrate leather, but bare skin, aye."

155

Hair at my nape crawls and I long to breathe air free of the beasts' stench. "Come. Let us leave this place."

## *Taryn*

The clomping sound of boots jolts me from my thoughts as I tie the sash of my robe. I hear the scrape of the bolt and then the door opens. I try not to flinch at the hideous face of the Zumarian as it enters the room and tosses sandals at my feet.

Why did it bring these? With one eye on the warrior, I slip the sandals on, then follow it out the door. The sandals slap against the stone floor as the Zumarian escorts me to Synomea. Fortunately he's on my good side, so I can hear him.

The sorcerer is waiting outside the green room's massive doors, and he smiles like he's genuinely glad to see me. "Come, Ta'reen. I have much to show you of our realm."

He folds my arm tight within his and pulls me close to his side. Inwardly I cringe from his touch, and I want to crawl out of my skin to get away from him. But this is my *father*, my heart echoes. There must be *some* good in him.

One darkened hallway looms after another as we walk through the building, an occasional torch allowing enough light to see by. The fortress keep is not nearly as large as I imagined, with only two stories. The green room and mine, along with several other drafty bedrooms, encompass the top level.

"Where does that lead?" I indicate a wooden door to the left of the green room and an enormous window. Torches are mounted on the wall between the door and the window.

Synomea's gaze flicks to the door and back to me. "Of no interest to you, my dear. It is but a long-forgotten part of the keep that remains unused."

He's lying. I know it. Why doesn't he want me near the door?

We head down a set of abrupt steps to the lower level. The great hall serves as nothing more than another shadowed room with dingy tapestries shrouding the walls, unlike the vivid décor of the green room. Eerie silence drapes the hall and it's obvious my father isn't into entertaining.

Servants scurry around attending to their duties as we enter the kitchen, bowing their heads and avoiding our eyes. Dried meats, plants, and burlap bags dangle from the rafters. In one corner huddles a crate brimming with Ta'sha rock-eggs, next to a door that I think leads into the same turret I noticed upstairs.

Mmmm, delicious smells fill the kitchen. The odors are different from what I'm used to, yet familiar—like roast beef, mashed potatoes and gravy, and biscuits. My stomach rumbles and my mouth waters. A wave of homesickness washes over me and I sigh.

It's probably just poodle rat stew and dry bread.

Synomea guides me out of the keep, into an enormous courtyard he refers to as the inner ward. Even the sun barely shines here. Volcanic ash smudges the sky and a sickly green light filters through. Smells of sulfur irritate my nose and I sneeze.

The sorcerer and I drift into the courtyard, where he points out stables, slaves' barracks, and servants' quarters. It's absolutely appalling and my heart sinks. Every board on the buildings is weatherworn and every building is dilapidated. If it ever storms in this place, people could drown in those houses or wash away like twigs in a torrent. How could he force anyone to live this way?

Two Zumarians oversee slaves cleaning the grounds and feeding livestock. The slaves are dirty and worn, dressed in ragged brown and gray robes, with no emotion and no feeling on their faces. I wonder about that until I remember Synomea's mind-control powder. The sorcerer must be using the powder to make the slaves do what he wants them to. I flinch as one warrior snaps a whip, the sound cracking in the air like a gunshot.

We near a set of holding pens, and I hear the sounds of snuffles and grunts. Snouts poke through holes in the fence, dripping with snot. The beasts look like a cross between a javelina and a porcupine, and reek of manure and filth. A sick feeling grips my belly. The animals are in the same boat as the slaves.

Synomea draws my attention to the surrounding curtain wall. "It is twenty-five feet tall and fifteen feet in width."

My gaze travels its expanse, noting an occasional unmanned watchtower. Not even a warrior lookout is on the walks below the parapet. I gesture to the wall. "Are you concerned about attacks?"

The sorcerer sneers and laughs. "None would dare. I could crush them with a single thought! My powers are far too strong for challenge. I remain aware enough, daughter. Never fear. I will keep you safe until you are well able to defend yourself."

Once more, a strange shadow passes across his face. For a moment, he looks old, bent, and incredibly tired. His eyes are suddenly the eyes of that little boy orphaned by his grandfather's brutality. I feel a twinge of pity for him—and a trickle of truth seeps into me, as if draining into my mind from a brief connection with my father's essence.

He is still strong, yes. A powerful sorcerer. But he's not as strong as he once was.

Perhaps at one time he could crush with a thought, but his powers are weakening. Day by day, he's losing much of the magic he once had.

But can I possibly know that? Am I starting to imagine things?

Is he aging, sliding downhill like Gran did in the last year? Maybe that's why he's so cruel to these people.

He caresses my arm as we walk. "I also have released beasts to roam the lava fields that will kill any interlopers before they reach my fortress."

Beasts? What if Erick comes across any of these creatures?

Synomea halts and searches my face. "I was surprised to see Lord Erick attempt your rescue. No one has been foolish enough to try such an act for decades. Of course, he paid for it with his life, did he not?"

Did he read my thoughts? That I was thinking about Erick? I raise my chin and attempt to play along. "Yes. I saw you knock him from the cliff."

The sorcerer narrows his eyes. "You must prove your loyalty is now to me."

I swallow and try to think of something that will gain his trust. "You are such a powerful sorcerer and you are my father. How could I not admire you?" I hope I'm not overdoing it, but thank goodness he just grins and ushers me on.

We continue walking until we're near the gatehouse at the front of the fortress, Synomea naming the various things I'm unfamiliar with. A portcullis bars access to the fortress, but rust covers the metal and the wood is splintered. It doesn't look like it's been used for years.

"How are you so certain this place would be safe if an army or something attacked?" I ask.

"The dull-witted people of Newold and its sister villages are nothing to be concerned with." He laughs, a sound like the yelping of coyotes. "They are content and lazy, and ready for their slaughter."

I feel sick in my heart and soul at his words. *Slaughter.* Perhaps nothing about this man is good after all.

"And do you not remember mind-flight?" he continues. "On occasion I visit the wastelands to ensure no creature approaches, be it man or beast. 'Twould take days to reach the fortress once a being enters the lava fields. An army would need at least a week. Should any endeavor to attack, I have many ways to be rid of them."

Synomea points to the rear of the compound. "Ah, there is much of interest this way."

He pilots me through a postern, a door in the curtain wall behind the keep, and then we are outside the fortress. To our left, a bizarre garden flourishes. Row upon row of strange vegetables suffuse the field, including the queer mushrooms we ate during that first meal I had with my father. Plants of purple, orange, and red thrive in the dark soil, which surprises me. How could anything survive in this hateful place? Slaves hoe the rows and irrigate by carrying water in wooden buckets.

To our right a path leads to the pit mine, and in the background the distant volcano spits ash into the sky. The sulfuric smell nearly chokes me.

A water tower that rises beside the mine is enormous. Zumarian warriors stand guard over slaves who bear huge baskets on their shoulders. The slaves plod up the steps and disappear through the postern door into the fortress. More captives return from the wide doorway, baskets empty, heading back into the mine.

No sunshine, no laughter. Just gloom and despair.

My soul sinks as teens trudge by with enormous loads. Their clothes are tattered, their bodies covered in filth.

Taking a deep breath, I try to calm down and choke back my anger. "These people you abduct from Earth—Oldworld—why do you take them so young?"

He smiles and settles his arm around my shoulders. "When I first created the portal and began bringing Oldworlders to work in my mines, I discovered only the young can adapt to Zumaria's climate."

I want to yank myself away from him and run as fast as I can. Instead, I remain as still as possible and watch the workers lug the baskets. "What happens when they become adults?"

"After several years, the mind-control powder erases all thought and will, and the rigors of this world transform the larger, hardier humans into Zumarians. The rest die."

My face goes numb as I turn back to Synomea. "You mean the warrior beasts were once . . . human?"

He shrugs as he watches the workers trudging from the mine. "'Twas an unexpected benefit. The powder does not have the same effect on those I have taken from Newold. Thus, I decided to take only Oldworlders from desert climates, as they best serve my purpose."

Synomea says everything like it's no big deal, as if he's talking about the weather or a football game. But he's talking about people, not weather and football. They're kids. Regular kids. Maybe even kids I went to high school with who mysteriously disappeared. They're probably here, nobody knowing their fate—nobody suspecting *my* father is responsible.

A hard lump forms in my throat and I try to swallow past it. "Can—can they ever be returned to their human form, once they become Zumarian warriors?"

"No." Synomea's arm feels like a lead weight around my shoulders. "Those that work in the mines could never be human again. They are nothing but burned-out husks after years in the rigor of this climate, combined with the powder." He raises an eyebrow. "Does this bother you, Ta'reen?"

My stomach roils and I think I'm going to be sick all over the sorcerer's robes. Those Zumarians . . . they were human. Erick and the other knights are killing *humans*. Warriors who were once teenagers, like me.

"Ta'reen?" His voice barely breaks into my thoughts, but I hear the note of warning in his tone. "Does it bother you?" he repeats.

I lower my lids as I push the rage deep within. *Yes!* I want to scream. But I can't let him know how upset I am. When I look at him again I say, "How long have you been doing this?"

"Twenty years ago, I visioned your birth and your rise to power at my side. Shortly after your birth I began abducting Oldworlders. I had taken only a few humans at a time from Oldworld to escape notice." His grip tightens around me. "During the past two moon cycles, I have increased the number of Oldworlders I have taken by threefold."

That lump in my throat is growing bigger. "Why did you start taking so many more?"

He smiles down at me like I'm a prized possession. "'Twas time to put your destiny into motion. With our combined sorcery, the powders, and the crescent crystal, all of Zanea will be ours."

"I see." It's my fault—all of this is because of me. Because Synomea visioned I would serve as a sorceress by his side.

*Powerful, so powerful.*

Disgust at myself nearly tears me apart.

The sorcerer visioned my powers as his grandfather had seen Synomea's greatness. *"I have visioned your future . . . You will be a powerful sorcerer, revered by your followers and your many children, feared by all others."*

My voice is flat as I speak. "These slaves, what do they excavate?"

Synomea gestures to the workers. "The slaves mine rock that contains raw power. Once the rock is mined, I use my sorcery to create the powders I have been teaching you to use. Once we have the crescent crystal, 'twill be all we need to rule Zanea."

---

It's early evening and I'm in the green room, waiting for Synomea. I press my forehead against the cool glass and run my fingertips over its surface as I stare outside.

The darkening gray sky heightens my loneliness. I stare at the bleak landscape, an endless ocean of black rock, yet it can be no bleaker than my heart.

I miss Tucson, my home, my classes, and Jen, but most of all I miss my grandmother. I wish I could hug her again, kiss her papery-soft cheek and tell her how much I love her. How different things were a little over a month ago, and I wish I could go back to the way things were.

But then I would never have met Erick. Why can't I have it all—my life back the way it was and Erick, too? Except I would want to remember Erick every waking moment, and be with him every chance I could.

Did I really get a glimpse of Synomea's dark thoughts yesterday? Is that something I can do with practice? Yet today it seems more like a dream. Like this is all a dream—a nightmare—and soon I'll wake up.

A voice on my right side startles me, sending shockwaves throughout my body. I whirl to see Synomea standing behind me, a smirk on his face.

"What did you say?" I ask, trembling. I hate when people sneak up on me, especially when it's on my right side, where I can't hear very well.

He studies me for a long moment and frowns. "You have little or no hearing in this one ear."

I raise my chin and glare at him. "What difference does it make?"

The sorcerer's frown turns into a scowl. "I had no idea you were defective in any way. Obviously your mother's inferior human genes are to blame. It is most unfortunate, but there is nothing that can be done for it."

A hot flush spreads over me as I glare at him and clench my fists.

"Is there anything else imperfect about you?" he asks, his eyes narrowed.

"Nothing's wrong with me."

My father can go straight to hell before I tell him about the Ménière's and the vertigo.

He raises an eyebrow, then snatches an ebony box from the table of powders. "The time has come to show you a vision of the past . . . so you might better understand your purpose." He slides off the lid to reveal malachite dust, places the box on the table, then takes my arm and drags me toward him.

Synomea dips his fingers into the green stuff, swipes it across my forehead, then grabs my head between his hands.

My skin is on fire. Melting.

*Everything around me wavers, then becomes clearer. I realize I'm in a house. A man and a woman face each other.*

*"You're not Roland, are you?" The woman clutches her abdomen as if she's been punched.*

*The man stays in shadow, but I can see his sneer. "No. And it is too late for you, milady. For now you are my bride, and my child grows within your belly."*

*The woman crumples to the floor and buries her face in her hands. After a moment, she looks up and I see her tear-streaked face.*

*Mother? It's my mother, Stacie. I recognize her from Gran's pictures.*

*"Who are you? What have you done with Roland?"*

*The man steps into the light. At first he appears as someone I don't know, yet is almost familiar to me. Then his features alter as I watch.*

*It's my father, Synomea.*

*He kneels and grabs Stacie's shoulders. "Roland is dead. It is sufficient for you to know me as Ian Simons."*

*My mother sobs, tears pouring down her face. "Oh, God, no. No! You killed him, didn't you? Why? Why did you kill Roland?"*

*"Enough!" Synomea slaps her so hard her head snaps back. "You are nothing more than a means to carry my child. Ta'reen will one day serve by my side, as sorceress of Zanea. This I have seen."*

*My mother doesn't move, an expression of complete shock on her face. "How—how do you know this baby isn't Roland's?"*

*"Your mind is too easy for me to read, my lovely. I know you never consummated your relationship with Roland before I took his place."*

*"No," she whispers. "I will not carry this child for you to destroy."*

*My father smirks. "You have no choice." He pulls a jade vessel from a pocket and sets it on the floor. He knocks the lid off and I see the pink mind-control powder.*

*Synomea grabs Stacie by her hair and drags her close to him. She tries to fight him as he spreads the dust over her face with his free hand. The powder vanishes, blending in with the color of her complexion.*

*"You are my loving bride. You shall do as I bid and bring into the world this child. Our child."*

*Her face goes slack, then she smiles. "Yes, Ian. I am yours." Adoration. Total adoration as she gazes up at him, like in the photograph on my bureau.*

*Like a wax portrait held to flame, everything melts again, colors mixing and swirling . . .*

When I open my eyes, I'm shaking so hard my knees threaten to buckle. Synomea pushes me into a chair and I want to vomit. The look on my face could only be one of revulsion.

"You are surprised, my Ta'reen." He strides to the table and closes the ebony box.

Surprised? I'm terrified. I want to scream and rage at him.

No, not a word—or I'll never escape. Sweat trickles down my neck as I realize he could be reading my thoughts.

He smiles. "You do know I could use the mind-control substance on you, if you refuse to cooperate. Do you not?"

Even while I fear he can read my mind, I feel like I'm sensing his thoughts again. A flash of something comes to my mind—that this powder wouldn't work on me, because I am a sorceress. But am I really?

I nod, as if I believe him, hoping he doesn't know what I've been thinking.

"You now have knowledge of the reason for your existence. I created you to rule at my side. The woman Stacie served merely as a vessel in which to carry you."

*Created.* Like a piece of equipment. I nod again, my head moving up and down in a stiff motion, trying to keep my own mind as blank as a piece of paper.

"Upon the woman's . . . death, 'twas necessary to leave you to be fostered by your Earth grandmother until the age of metamorphosis. I had no desire to raise a child, and you were of no use until this time. 'Twas the only reason I allowed your grandmother to live."

*Allowed.* Did he cause her death after I turned seventeen? Please, *no.*

He strokes my hair. "So you see, my dear, you are mine."

My body goes rigid and my head buzzes.

"You have much to learn." Synomea grasps my hand and pulls me to my feet. "Now I shall teach you the spell to throw an invisible barrier between you and what you may need to hide or protect yourself from."

He narrows his eyes. "Of course, this could never be used against me. Do you understand?"

167

"Yes," I croak, my mind still reeling from all he's been telling me. But is he lying about the shield spell? If only I can learn this spell and hide from *him*.

Synomea moves his hand and then I don't see him. I gasp and step back. All I see is a slight shimmer in the air where he had been standing—and everything else as it was, as if he simply disappeared.

A flicker, and then he's right in front of my eyes again.

My father smiles at the shocked look on my face. "A shield spell solidifies the air wherever you choose, making an effective barrier and camouflage."

He presses his cold fingertips on my eyelids. "Close your eyes. As I explained yesterday, 'tis but a simple matter of concentration and will, and mastering the elements. Imagine you have erected a barrier between us. Feel the solidness of it. Know that it hides you from your enemies."

Part of me still doesn't believe I am a sorceress and can perform any magic. Yet another part, the part released by the Ta'sha, does believe.

"I said concentrate!"

I focus, my eyes shut, drawing on my years of meditation, and imagine for that moment I can perform magic. Something kindles deep within me, but it's faint and I can barely feel it.

Hair along my arms stirs and I know the sorcerer has come closer yet. "Imagine the barrier. Picture the elements answering your command."

Over and over he makes me practice the exercise, and he gets more furious by the moment at my failure to master the spell.

"Enough!" Synomea finally shouts, and my eyes pop open. "Sleep now. The morrow brings even greater lessons."

## October 27

### Erick

*I walk into a green velvet room. A woman stands at the other side of the chamber, her back to me. She is dressed in crimson robes, her red-gold hair swept atop her head. I notice the delicate curve of her ear, the soft line of her neck. Skin as smooth and pale as fine porcelain.*

*Familiar . . . yet not familiar.*

*A priestess?*

*No. This woman must be a mighty sorceress.*

*In heady ripples, I feel her power. It swells over me in waves, one crashing after the other.*

*Seducing me.*

*Imprisoning me with her sorcery.*

*Deceiving me.*

*Her robe slips to reveal one white shoulder . . . and the mark of the crescent moon on her upper arm.*

*I cannot stop myself—a force draws me. I walk toward the sorceress, but my steps bring me no closer. The velvet room grows, lengthening. Furlong after furlong I travel. She has knowledge I must possess—I must reach her!*

*My breath comes in gasps. My limbs ache. But the sorceress is farther away than before.*

*Then she stops before a pair of velvet drapes. Before I can reach out to her, she pulls the drapes aside to reveal a doorway, and vanishes.*

*I hurry after her into another chamber, but she is gone.*

*And at the center of the room is my sword, Navran.*

I wake, expecting to see the ceiling of my bedroom, but then memories return. Van and I are in another of the wasteland's thousand caves, at least three days from Zumaria. By the strength of light outside, I know it is late afternoon. I hear my sister's soft breathing nearby.

The strange dream haunts me as I gaze toward the mouth of the cave. A green velvet room and a sorceress. What was the meaning, if dreams indeed have meaning beyond their strange imagery? So odd, that crescent mark on the sorceress's arm.

The call of the sorceress was strong, beguiling. But, deep in my soul, I know I would never go to anyone but Taryn.

My heart belongs to Taryn alone; I shall never stop until I rescue her from Synomea. Then I shall seek vengeance for all he may have done to her. And for the murder of my father.

I never could see the sorceress's face, yet I almost thought it was Taryn. But why would I dream of her as a sorceress? Why would I feel she is deceiving me? And why would she show me my own sword in a strange room?

*Erick! Where are you?*

*Taryn!* I sense she summons me and shove my hand in my pocket to retrieve the l'apitak. But the moment my fingers reach the disc, Taryn is gone. I continue to call to her with my thoughts, but she does not respond.

*Damn!* I grit my teeth and curse to the gods. This contact was more brief than the last. What has happened? Why can she not respond?

## Taryn

After my morning bath, and Maria and Meg have left, I'm alone once again. I go to the window of my bedchamber and stare at the glowing cone of Mount Zumar . . . my new home, if Synomea has his way. Somewhere deep inside me I feel the surge of lava in the volcano's womb, the push and pull of forces beyond my grasp.

Never in a million years would I have imagined the things that have occurred over the last couple of weeks—especially the past few days. Knights, beasts, slaves, a father who happens to be a sorcerer . . . it's all hard to digest. But here I am, without the slightest idea of what I'm going to do to get out of here.

Or of who I really am.

*A sorceress?*

Ta'reen, daughter to a cruel sorcerer? Am I a freak, like the man who fathered me? I feel dirty and contaminated after seeing some of what he has done, knowing I'm of his blood.

If I am a sorceress, as Synomea insists, does that mean I'm evil, too? Is that why I've been having these cravings for power? Am I beyond salvation? Tears prickle at the corner of my eyes and pressure fills my head. No! I refuse to feel sorry for myself.

What happened to plain old Taryn, straight-A student who was too shy to speak to cute guys? The girl missing her grandmother, her only family, and struggling to take one day at a time? The girl with no social life to speak of, just a best friend named Jen, who's probably worried sick right now, not to mention her foster parents.

And Erick. What I would give to be back on that porch swing, cuddled next to him and feeling his hand stroke my hair. How stupid I was to ignore him, to refuse his explanation the last time I saw him. What an idiot I was to let him go without saying goodbye.

I close my eyes, take a deep breath, and begin to meditate. When my mind clears and I'm relaxed, I start to work through my situation. I need to think of something I can do to get out of this mess. But I'm so afraid.

What if the sorcerer is speaking the truth, and I am a sorceress? I've denied it, but I've also felt that intense glimmer of power within my soul, especially since I ate the Ta'sha egg.

Maybe I should try the spell he forced me to practice last night—I remember the feeling deep inside me as I attempted the spell. What if I can learn how to do it on my own?

And don't let on I know how . . .

My lips curve in a half-hearted smile. Yes. I'll try.

I remember what Synomea told me: *"It is but a simple matter of concentration and will, and mastering the elements. Imagine you have erected a barrier . . ."*

With more enthusiasm and energy than I gave my effort before, I attempt the spell. Even after several tries, nothing happens, and I work even harder at it. I remember what he said about solidifying the very air around me, imagining it answering my commands. A tingling sensation radiates throughout my body. My excitement grows as I feel the barrier in front of me. I open my eyes and see a slight shimmer—and then nothing.

I frown in frustration, but then it occurs to me that I saw the shimmer and felt the barrier, even if it held for only a few seconds. That means I *can* do it! I just need to practice.

It takes a few more tries and then I feel the barrier with my senses. My eyes are still closed, but I can feel the solidity of it, the strength of it. I open my eyes and can see nothing around me except for the glimmering barrier. I'm alone in a kind of sparkling tube. With one finger I reach out to touch it, and my finger sinks into the wall. It feels strange, reminding me of when I was a little girl and would stick my finger into the gelatin mold Gran made for dessert.

I'm so caught up in my excitement that the sound of the bar scraping across the door barely registers in my good ear. I freeze and catch my breath. What if it's the sorcerer?

The door creaks and closes. "Milady?" Maria calls. "Meg, check under the bed."

I heave a sigh of relief and the next thing I know, the barrier vanishes. Maria has her back to me and Meg is peering under my bed.

"I'm right here."

Maria yelps and whirls around, and Meg bangs her head on the bedframe.

"Where were you?" Maria asks, her hand at her mouth and her eyes wide.

"Ah . . ." I gesture toward the window. "Behind the curtain. I was looking outside."

Maria's face goes slack with relief. "I—I thought . . . never mind. We came to see if there's anything you need before we start our daily cleaning duties."

"No, thank you." I shake my head. "I'm fine, really."

Meg stands, rubbing the top of her head. They each make a small bow and leave the room. How it breaks my heart to see them acting that way. Scared of me. Scared of everything. They don't deserve to live like this.

No one does.

After they've gone, I turn my thoughts to Erick. I've been afraid to use the disc to contact him. What if Synomea can hear me and learns Erick is still alive, like my heart believes? Yet I get the feeling that somehow the sorcerer can't read my thoughts, and it frustrates him.

This once I'll try the disc and make sure Erick is okay. I hurry toward the bed, almost tripping over my robe in my haste. I'm relieved to find my clothes are still under the bed where I stashed them. I grab my jacket and thrust my hand into the pocket. My fingers feel the coolness of the l'apitak and I draw it out.

*L'apitak?* Where did that come from? Such a strange word, but it seems right.

The now-familiar warmth creeps up my arm to my chest, only it's intensified, mingling with my own growing powers. *Erick! Where are you?* I call as I start to close my eyes.

At that instant, an overwhelming sensation of evil passes over me.

Synomea! I know it's him, and more than that—I know he's coming to me!

I drop the l'apitak into my jacket pocket and thrust everything back under the bed. Even though I'm not touching the disc, I'm close enough that I hear Erick calling me, and it tears me apart not to respond. He *is* alive!

As I tighten the belt of my robe, I force all thought from my mind. If I can glimpse what runs through the sorcerer's head, I'm sure it's possible he can see what's in mine.

Or perhaps not. Maybe it's a strength I possess that he doesn't. Could it be? I wonder if there's a way to test it, to find out. Without getting myself killed, that is.

I dodge to a chair and watch the door. In a few moments the metal bar scrapes across the door and the hinges creak as the door opens.

"My beautiful Ta'reen." Synomea walks in through the door. He leers and expands his arms, as if to encompass everything around us. "Does this room suit your tastes?"

What, this velvet prison?

"Yes." While I lie, I brush away a strand of loose hair and strive to maintain eye contact. "It's very nice."

To survive, I have to let him think I've given in to him completely and he can trust me. He's watching, taking in everything I say and do. The Ta'sha has given me confidence, but not enough to banish this growing fear of the sorcerer.

Synomea comes closer to me and I struggle to look calm. "We have much to do today, Ta'reen," he murmurs loud enough for my good ear to hear when he reaches me. "Much to do."

We go to his chambers, where the sorcerer insists I eat more Ta'sha eggs for breakfast, and I don't argue. I feel their power the moment the first drop touches my lips. The high of the release is intense. It makes me feel like I'm filled with magic. Like I can do anything. It's beyond the power I felt when wearing my crescent necklace. This is so real.

When we have finished our breakfast, Synomea picks up a butter knife and takes it to the table of magical powders. He motions to me and I follow him across the room to where a fire crackles in the hearth.

"We will start with an exercise in levitation." Synomea sets the knife on the table. "And then move back to working on the shield spell."

There's no way I'm going to let him know I've started learning how to throw up a barrier—that's a secret I plan to keep.

"It is a simple matter to perform levitation," he continues, never taking his eyes from my face. "As with the shield spell, you must master the elements and use them to do your bidding. With both spells, you are commanding the very air around you. You can lift objects with the air or even conjure up a wind storm."

Synomea gestures to the knife, and with a flick of his finger, it rises off the tabletop. Another slight movement and it settles back to the table. "This is but a small measure of what you can do with levitation."

He motions for me to come to the table. "Do not focus on the knife. Focus on the air around it. Command the air to lift the knife."

The Ta'sha still fills me with that wonderful vibrating sensation, and I feel I can do it. I stare at the knife, willing it to move, but it does nothing. I concentrate on the air around it, trying to push it, lift it, *anything.*

Synomea seems to be in a more tolerant mood today and isn't getting mad at my failure. I even get the feeling that in his own twisted way he feels we're family, and he actually cares about me.

The sorcerer forces me to repeat the levitating exercise until I want to scream with my own frustration. My head aches and my back hurts.

Finally his patience wanes and he clenches his jaw. "Perhaps I should have raised you here, rather than waiting until you reached the age of metamorphosis. Living on Earth for these many years of your life seems to have caused more of a problem than I expected."

"Maybe I have no magic," I say, hoping it will make him want to send me back to my home.

He narrows his eyes. "Then you would be as good to me dead."

I feel blood draining from my face as I stare at him. If he doesn't see me perform magic, will he kill me? Is that really all I am to him?

"However," he continues, his green eyes glittering, "the powders would not have worked on you if you had no magic. They have worked for you and thus you are indeed a sorceress. If you are not truly flawed by your mother's blood, then it is simply a matter of training and time."

*Flawed.* My throat works, but I hold back the words I want to scream at him.

Synomea grunts to the Zumarian warriors at the door and they come to escort me to my room. "Rest, Ta'reen. We will continue your lessons later."

---

After dinner, the sorcerer takes me to the fireplace. "Before you retire for the evening, another past vision I will share with you." He draws me forward so I am standing inches apart from him.

The smell of burnt sugar surrounds me. Every fiber of my being cries out with revulsion at his nearness, at the touch of his hands on my shoulders. If only I could throw that shield spell between us now and make my escape! If only I knew some other spell that would strip him of his powers.

I force myself to remain as still as possible and not betray the revulsion I feel at his touch as he wipes the emerald powder across my forehead. But I gasp when he grips my head with his hands to force another vision of the past into my mind.

Warmth creeps over my body, then everything around me melts and swirls . . .

*An explosion! Flames soar, the intense heat searing my arms. Sweat soaks my temples, my nostrils filling with smoke.*

*"Ian! Help me, please!"*

*I whirl. Behind me . . . it's my mother! Trapped in the blaze.*

*"Please don't leave me, Ian!" A wall of flames hedges her in. She can't get through! She collapses to the floor, choking, gasping for breath.*

*I reach out to her, as if I can pull her from the fire, but I have no substance. My hand melts through the air.*

*A presence at my side—Synomea.*

*"Help her!" I scream.*

*The sorcerer laughs and walks away.*

The blaze fades from angry red to orange to yellow, the colors swirling like melted crayons.

And then I see only emerald velvet and that I've returned to the green room. The caustic smell of burning hair and flesh clings to my robes.

I stumble to a chair and collapse. Repeatedly in the crackling flames of the fireplace, I see my mother's face . . . and hear her screams. I feel ill, my stomach clenching in angry bursts.

Now I know there can't be good in this man who fathered me. How could anyone be so ruthless, so vicious? Synomea murdered my mother. He killed the man she loved, and I'm sure many others. No doubt he'll kill me if I give him a reason.

Do I even care if I die? What is life, if I'm sentenced to spend it with the devil himself? What if he forces me to repeat his cruel acts and to rule as he does?

And I know he will. That's his plan.

My next thought sickens me further. What if I like it?

Cold hands grab my face and force me to look up.

"Tell me your thoughts, Ta'reen." Synomea's eyes narrow.

Do I sense his exertion, trying to read my mind? It's as if I feel his frustration and his anger—that he's trying, but he can't do it.

He can't read my thoughts.

Silence shrouds the room as I battle my emotions, fight what I want to scream out loud, but don't. What am I thinking? I want you to pay for all you've done, for every cruel act ever committed. I want you to die a thousand deaths, in every way you've murdered others.

Yes, I want you to die a slow, fiery death. I want you to burn alive and feel the flesh singed from your bones while your black heart still beats and you smell the stench of your own demise.

There. Can you hear me, you bastard? Can you hear me?

"What are you thinking?" he says, his voice a growl and a threat.

My bottom lip trembles in my fight to remain silent. I can't avenge these lives if I'm dead, if he kills me for wanting to see him obliterated. For that is my mission.

Revenge.

Perhaps my own soul is lost, and maybe I've lost forever the one I love with all my heart. Somehow, I'll make the sorcerer pay.

I bury the rage, storing it deep, to use when I take him out—or die trying.

My thoughts startle me. My own father. Could I kill my own father, even if he is the most evil being in this universe? Could I actually kill anyone?

And would that make me as evil as he is?

The reality of my situation sinks in and my body turns to jelly. What am I going to do?

"Answer!" His cruel mouth twisting, Synomea grabs my shoulders and digs his fingers into my flesh. "Tell me your thoughts, or I will force them from your mind."

"I understand everything now." I hold his gaze, daring him to try and search my true feelings. "As you said, pain is necessary to prepare me for what lies ahead. I realize my pain must be turned into power."

For a moment he stills, and then his lip curls and he laughs. "A sensible wench you are." He releases me and moves to the table of powders.

"It is true irony you consorted with Lord Erick." Synomea grins, the cruelty in his smile sending chills down my spine. "For his father was Roland—the man I disposed of, the man who was once your mother's love. Had I not killed him, Roland could have been your father, and Lord Erick your brother."

My head swims and I grip the chair's arms to steady myself. Nothing prepared me for this, on top of all the horrible things Synomea has told me and all I've seen. *He murdered Erick's father.* But if he hadn't, Erick could have been my brother.

For a second a sickening thought slips through me. What if Synomea is lying? What if Roland really fathered Erick *and* me? I push the thought from my mind. No. I know I am of the sorcerer's vile blood. I have the birthmark that proves it. And my eyes are the same green flecked with gold as Synomea's. No. Erick isn't my brother.

The vision flashes in my mind of Synomea admitting to my mother he wasn't Roland. Before my father transformed to his own form, the face he had worn was familiar to me—because he had looked almost like Erick.

And, yes, how truly ironic I've fallen hopelessly in love with Erick. It's so hopeless that now I'm certain we'll never be together. How could he love the daughter of the man who murdered his father? The daughter of one of the most despicable creatures ever to live? And when Erick learns of his father's love for my mother, it will certainly seal the casket on our relationship.

My eyes ache, but I refuse to cry. When I'm alone in my room, I can release my true feelings. Right now, everything depends on living a lie.

"Ta'reen?" Synomea says after the long silence.

My knuckles grow white against the dark wood of the chair I'm sitting in. Behind the sorcerer, the ebony box levitates a fraction above the table, then settles and rocks in place. My eyes widen and blood rushes to my head. Did I make it rise?

I look back at the sorcerer. "Erick—he's nothing to me . . . now," I manage to say just as buzzing starts in my ear.

Synomea stares into my eyes, as if daring me to say more.

But in the next moment, pain slams my head and everything starts to spin as the vertigo assaults me. Cramps seize my stomach as I slide onto the floor and vomit. I can hear nothing but the buzzing, which is shriller than the screaming of a police car's sirens. Vaguely I feel fingers digging into my shoulder before everything goes black.

## October 28

*Erick*

At best it is only two hours until dawn. All I see is endless black stone, and Mount Zumar seems little closer than it did before. Gods, but will we ever reach Synomea's fortress?

To our right, the rock wall glitters in the moonlight. A strange sparkle, like a thousand pieces of crushed black glass.

A stench like rotting flesh fills the air and I grimace. What could that smell be?

And there . . . do I see two rubies in the wall?

The rubies blink.

My gut clenches and I rip my sword from its sheath.

Before I can warn Van, its tail swings from the wall to strike my twin across her legs. She screams as she is flung against a cone of rock. Her breeches are shredded and blood spills from her thigh.

"Van!" I shout, my heart thundering.

A force slams into my arm, ripping Navran from my hand, and a leather-like wing scrapes my face. Rows of spikes fly toward my head.

"Watch out for the tail!" Van yells.

I drop and flatten myself to the ground, and lava rock bites into my palms. Air rushes above my head as the tail sweeps by. I roll toward where Navran glints in the moon-light, trying to get to it before the beast can attack again.

Roaring, the creature bounds from the wall. The light from the twin moons reveals the triangular head of the Tren-dorian dragon—a beast ten times the size of a horse, and the deadliest dragon on all of Zanea.

A beast that shouldn't be here.

The dragon lumbers between my sword and me, keeping me from my weapon. Again, the creature bellows as it comes closer, and its teeth gleam in the moonlight. Its foul breath is hot on my face and reeks of putrid meat.

Van drags herself toward Navran, her face twisting with agony. It is as though she can barely find the strength to move.

Blood rushes in my ears as I crouch and withdraw the dag-ger from inside my boot. The dragon swings its tail and I try to leap from its path. Pain sears me like hot iron through my flesh as a tail spike gouges the wound on my biceps. The dag-ger flies from my hand.

I try to stand and see Van is behind the dragon, on her knees, holding her sword in one hand and mine in her other. She tosses Navran to me and it rattles across the rock.

The dragon's tail slices the air above me, and I flatten my-self to the ground. I roll toward Navran, stone grinding into the wound in my arm. A wave of dizziness from the pain nearly overwhelms me.

My sister stumbles to her feet and raises her sword. As I reach for Navran, Van hobbles closer to the beast. The dragon watches me and does not see Van.

"No, Van! Get back!" My hand closes around Navran's grip. Before I can wield my sword, Van lunges forward and runs her blade through the dragon's eye.

183

The creature shrieks and whips Van with his wing, slinging her against the wall. My twin crumples to the ground, motionless.

Rage engulfs me. My vision narrows and I raise my weapon. I no longer feel pain—no longer feel anything but fury.

My arms burn with power flowing from my sword throughout my body. The crystal on Navran flashes green and the runes blaze, and I wield the weapon as I have been trained my entire life. Lightning bursts from the blade and thunder rumbles across the wasteland.

An emerald glow captures the dragon. A giant bubble.

The beast screams. The sound is muffled, as if coming from underwater. Fighting to break free of the light, the dragon thrashes and topples onto its side. The beast screeches again, then collapses into a pile of charred bones.

Green light vanishes and the fire in my body goes cold. The odor of burned flesh fills the air. From the dragon's smoking skull, my sister's sword rises like a grave marker.

"Van!" I run to my twin. Fear squirms like a snake in my belly. When I pull her to me, her eyes are closed. Blood coats her face like a black mask.

"Wake, Van. Please wake." I hold her quiet body in my arms. For the first time since I was a boy, tears course my cheek. "Gods, help me!"

With a shudder, Van opens her eyes, and my heart cries with relief. As I stroke loose hair from her face, blood wets my fingers. A gash crosses her temple and it bleeds freely, but does not look deep.

"The beast?" she murmurs. "Is—is it dead?"

"Thanks only to you." Exercising great care, I ease her head to my lap. "Lie still. It is my turn to take care of your wounds."

"We—we must seek safety. Where there is one Tren—Trendorian dragon, there is—is always its mate." She gasps as if it causes her pain to speak.

"First, I must see that you have no other injuries, and I must stop the bleeding from your thigh." I feel along her ribs and back. "Does that cause you great pain? Have you shattered any bones?"

Van groans. "No. Only bruises and the breath knocked from my lungs. But I believe nothing is broken."

I put my pack behind Van's head and ease her so that she lies down. Her features are drawn, but her eyes are clear. I locate my dagger, then use it to cut lengths of cloth I find in her haversack.

"Hold this to your temple," I tell her as I place one strip along the cut on her head.

She presses the cloth to the wound, then winces and bites her lip when I pour strong medicine on her thigh. The tea tree scent is pungent, and for a moment I can no longer smell the rotten stench of the dragon. Van's leather breeches are torn and the wound is deep, but clean.

Once I finish tying the bandage around her leg, I tend the injury at her brow. Thank the gods, the blood is clotting and the bleeding has slowed, but it may leave a scar. I wipe blood from her face as gently as I can with another cloth.

After I finish, Van sits up, bracing her back against the rock wall. "Your arm. Let me help you." She reaches for the tea tree oil, then applies it to the gash on my biceps. It burns, but it cannot be as bad as my sister's leg.

When we are done, Van limps to the dragon and I follow her. "Navran did this?" she asks as she withdraws her sword from the smoldering carcass.

I nod and put my arm around her shoulders. "But only because you returned the sword to my hand and because you stabbed the beast in its eye. If not for you, we would both be dead."

She shakes her head. "I never saw the dragon. I should have suspected it when I caught the odor of rotting flesh. But my thoughts were elsewhere and I was careless."

"Let us debate this later. We must seek shelter and leave the carcass before the dragon's mate returns."

A haunting bellow echoes across the wasteland, and Van does not argue.

My sister refuses to allow me to carry her as we start toward Mount Zumar. I insist on helping her walk, and support her from one side. We make fair progress together, even with her limping. I am wary, but see no sign of another dragon.

The air is thick with ash and sulfur, and I long for a fresh breeze off the Vandre Peaks—for forests thick with game, rolling meadows, and Vandre Lake's crystal blue depths.

When we return, what will wait for us? Will we be banished from the land we love? Newold, our home.

If we return. If we do not perish here in this cursed wasteland. I pray the wizards guided me true and that we do not face a hopeless battle. I have no fear for myself, but for my sister and for my friends.

And for Taryn. Ah, for one kiss. To hold her in my arms again. Is there hope for us?

## Taryn

A niggling in my brain stirs me from my dreams. I'm so sleepy, so tired. It's a hazy, drugged feeling. Vaguely I remember having an episode of Ménière's. My throat is still raw from throwing up and my head aches, but at least the vertigo is gone.

Wait. There's a presence in the room, like someone is nearby. But my eyes feel too heavy to open and my limbs too weak to move.

A hand on my shoulder. "Wake," a deep voice says near my good ear.

I strain to lift my lids, but weights drag them down.

"Mmmm," I murmur.

"My love, wake," a voice says close to my good ear.

*My love?*

I manage to open my eyes. Moonlight from the twin moons streams through the parted curtains. Someone stands above me. Someone familiar, yet . . .

*No. It can't be.*

"Erick?" I whisper.

He takes my hands and pulls me up in bed. I slide my legs over the side and stand, and he draws me close. A sickly sweet smell swirls around him.

My limbs quiver, but with all my strength, I press my palms against his chest and push. "No. No!" I twist out of his arms and back toward the window, putting space between us. "You—you must go. *Now.*"

At first he appears angry, then confused. He strides toward me. "I am here to save you. We must leave this place."

*Don't touch me.* I keep backing away and attempt to keep the waver from my voice as I reply, "I—I can't be with you anymore, Erick."

"But—"

"Leave or—or I'll tell Synomea you're here!" I search for something to tell him that will make Synomea believe he has my loyalty, that I no longer care for Erick. "My life—my life is the sorcerer's now."

I tremble as I wait for his reaction. I can't read his expression and I can't sense his thoughts. Is it anger I see on his face? A sneer?

"Then I shall never seek you again." He turns on his heel and walks through the bedroom door. He closes it behind him, and then I hear the scrape of the bar as he locks the door.

Every part of my body shakes, dry heaves racking my chest. I race for the bath, stumbling over the divan in the semi-darkness. I make it just in time to vomit into the depths of the tub.

How dare he? Did he think I wouldn't know? Does the bastard think me a complete and total idiot? Synomea—as if he could impersonate Erick, transformation powder or not!

How can I share that monster's genes, his blood? How can I stop someone with that much power?

The real Erick will never want to touch me once he learns Synomea is my father. I'm sure he'll be repulsed and sickened that I'm the sorcerer's daughter.

I'm probably cursed to spend the rest of my life with this hideous creature, and doomed to serve at his side.

Is there nothing I can do? His foul blood sears my veins—will I become as evil as he?

*No!* I won't give in and I won't give up.

I've seen glimmers of the magic Synomea says I have. Surely I can learn to use it against him, to trick him as he has tried to trick me. The sorcerer is so confident, so full of himself. Perhaps I can use that against him. Yes. I'll do everything I can to learn from him until my powers are greater than his, and I will destroy him.

I curl up in a ball on the stone floor, the cold seeping into my bones.

---

"Milady. Milady Ta'reen." I barely hear the words as gentle hands rock my shoulder.

I awake with a start, icy terror shooting through me.

"Oh, Maria," I say in relief. "Thank God, it's you." I push myself up and hold my head in my hands. My head pounds, the morning light hurts my eyes, and my body aches from sleeping on the stone floor.

"Are you okay, milady?" Maria strokes my arm, her touch comforting me.

I nod. "I'll be all right. Please call me Taryn."

"Well . . . only when his lordship is absent." She takes my hands and pulls me to my feet.

A million needles prick at my right foot. "Ow. Please help me to the bed, Maria. My foot's asleep."

With her assistance, I hobble to the four-poster. I collapse on it and close my eyes.

"You were ill last night, mila—Taryn. I'll get a wet cloth for your head."

"Don't have to," I mumble, but I hear her robes swish upon the floor, then the sound of water being poured from the pitcher on the table.

When Maria returns, she places the moist rag against my forehead. It's cool and eases the pain in my temples. "Thanks," I say with a small sigh.

"How about a bath? I cleaned the tub and drew warm water while you were sleeping on the floor."

I peek out from under the cloth and see her chestnut eyes watching me. "I'm so sorry you had to clean that up. I intended to do it this morning."

"No problem. Remember, here I live to serve."

How does she manage to keep a sense of humor?

"Don't say that," I reply gently.

Maria goes to the tub and sprinkles crystals into the water. "Come, take a bath and you'll feel better. It'll be easier to face his lordship."

Maria leaves while I take my bath, giving me a chance to dwell amongst my own dark thoughts. I lather the raspberry-scented soap on a cloth and scrub my body. When I'm finished and have cleaned my hair with shampoo, I try to work out what I need to do next.

Meditation. That should help. I close my eyes, take a deep breath, then exhale. Again, fill my lungs with air, and release. I melt into myself, searching, reaching for the place Synomea said is within me. The place that holds the magic he says is mine.

But is such power within my grasp? And if it is mine, is it black sorcery? I fear that if I learn how to perform the magic he wants me to, I will become the same as Synomea—evil. Or can I control it and use it for good, to defeat the vile sorcerer?

Surely I will remain true to myself. I am Taryn, not Ta'reen. I've lived a good life, raised by a special woman.

Without thinking, I reach for the comfort of my pendant, but of course it's not there and my heart sinks further into despair. Where could it be?

*Gran.* I miss my grandmother so much. Did she know about Synomea? I close my eyes and remember the words she said on my birthday. *I wish I could better prepare you for what lies ahead . . . your future.*

And Synomea—did he cause her death? What was it he said? *Your grandmother served her purpose.* My stomach clenches as if a Zumarian squeezes it within its claws.

*Gran, if somehow you can hear my thoughts, I want you to know how much I love you and how much I miss you. Now I understand why you didn't tell me you were dying, because you knew how afraid I would be. How alone I would feel without you.*

*I pray I can find some way to defeat this monster . . . and salvage what's left of my soul.*

---

After I finish my bath and I'm dressed, I practice the shield spell. This time I take care to listen in case anyone comes to the door. Once I get the hang of it, the spell becomes easier and easier to perform.

When I feel I've mastered putting shields around myself, I practice throwing them around different objects in my room. First a chair, then a table, then the bed. It becomes a kind of game, like the way I've often considered my schoolwork. I've always enjoyed working to master some of my favorite school subjects, and I find I feel the same way about learning this spell. Next, I'll try levitation.

I realize I'm actually looking forward to learning more magic, that I crave this power even more, and that scares me. Does it mean I'm starting to become like my father?

Just as I throw one last shield spell around the bed, I hear the bar scrape against the door. Synomea! Again, somehow I know it's him. I drop the shield encircling the bed and hurry to stand by the window and look out, as if that's all I've been doing.

"Ta'reen."

I turn to face the sorcerer at the sound of his voice.

"Come, daughter, and we shall dine." He holds out his hand and I force myself to walk across the room to him.

Synomea takes my arm and guides me down the drab hall from my chamber to the green room once again. Intermittent torches sputter and hiss in the breeze we cause as we pass.

When we walk into the green room, I glance at the drapes across the room and I wonder what's behind them.

We sit at the dining table, and thank goodness servants appear with food so I don't have to talk for a while. Tonight the main course is a creature that looks like a crab-sized tarantula. A servant sets down a plate containing the entire beast, complete with multiple eyes.

Synomea eats his as you would crab or lobster, so I imitate him. I drink the bitter wine and my fears settle as I concentrate on eating and swallowing each bite without gagging. Oddly enough, the spider crab smells of brine, but tastes like refried beans. Maybe I'm just homesick for Mexican food.

"Yesterday you became ill after your last lesson," Synomea says when we've finished eating.

My face burns as I look up from my plate and meet his eyes, but I say nothing.

His gaze narrows. "It has something to do with your defective ear, does it not?"

"Maybe it was something I ate." I try to keep my tone even.

Synomea slaps the table with his palm, rattling the silverware and causing wine from his glass to splash onto the tablecloth. My eyes are drawn to the spill as it seeps into the cloth like black blood.

"Look at me!" he shouts.

When my eyes meet his, I see the fury on his face and I know that now is not the time to hedge or lie.

"I have a condition known as Ménière's disease." I clench my fists in my lap. "It has taken most of the hearing in my right ear. Sometimes I get severe episodes of vertigo—where everything whirls and I get so dizzy I can't stand. I get confused, disoriented. It makes it impossible to function and causes me to throw up, like I did last night. It might happen once a year, or every day. It can last for minutes or days, I never know."

"There is no cure?" His tone has a lethal edge to it, and I wonder why he's so furious.

"No." I shake my head. "Only medication that can help fend off the vertigo."

"And do you have this medication with you?"

My mind flashes to the tablet box in my jacket pocket and I realize with some relief I do have a small supply of my meds in one of the compartments.

But I say, "No. I didn't know I would be going anywhere."

Synomea studies me with his chilling gaze, and I strain to keep from squirming in my chair. "This is most unsatisfactory news. I did not realize you would be . . . damaged. Is this something that can be passed on to your heirs?"

*Heirs?* Heat flushes my face and a buzzing starts in my mind that has nothing to do with the Ménière's. "Possibly," I whisper. "It is hereditary. My mother didn't have it, but my grandmother did."

Synomea glares and throws his napkin onto the table. "Nothing can be done for this now. It is too late." He stands and motions for me to follow. "Come. You have much yet to learn."

With a lump in my throat, I follow him to the fireplace where he opens the cloisonné box. "We shall search for Lord Erick and determine if he lives," he growls. "And learn if other Haro knights are in Zanea."

A knot of anxiety grows in my abdomen as Synomea paints my palm, forehead, and nose with the blue powder, as he did the first time we did mind-flight together. If the sorcerer finds Erick and any knights, I'm sure he'll kill them.

I remember his words from the first time he showed me this power. *"Pay close attention and you will be able to lead the next mind-flight."*

Can I reach them first and put up a shield to protect Erick? And if I do, will Synomea be able to tell what I've done?

My fear for Erick propels my mind-spirit from the room so fast that somehow I know I've left the sorcerer behind. The excitement that fills me is beyond belief. I can't believe I actually have the power to separate from him!

I fly over the black rock . . . searching . . . searching . . . I find him! Erick's in a cave, with a woman. They are both injured, but alive. I throw a shield around Erick and the woman, just like I practiced in my room those dozens of times. I leave to explore the lava fields for more of the Haro. Synomea gains on me, and I can almost feel his spirit-breath on my neck.

On and on I search, looking for any sign of other Haro knights, but I see no one else.

Wait—there. Erick's friend Cole, and a woman. I fling another wall of protection around them. On my way back to the fortress, I stumble across two more men and block them from Synomea, too.

I flee, racing over the wastelands, until I find my way back to the green room.

Synomea's lids are still closed when I lift mine. A few moments more and his eyes pop open. Sweat crawls down my back and blood throbs in my ears as I struggle to look calm and keep my mind blank. For endless seconds he stares at me, and I'm terrified he knows.

"It was all I could do to keep up with you." He takes my chin in his hand, his eyes boring into mine. "You command more power than I would have thought possible."

His grip tightens, his thumb pressing into the healing wound on my chin, sending waves of pain through my jaw. "Did you see . . . anything?"

"No." I try to shake my head, but his grip is too tight.

He releases me and I stumble back, almost hitting the table of magical powders.

"Clumsy wench!" Synomea lifts his hand and I flinch, sure he's going to strike me. Instead, he shoves me away from the table. I trip on the hem of my robe and land on my bruised tailbone.

My eyes water as pain shoots along my backside. I stare up at him, afraid of what he might do next.

"Have you any concept of the disaster," he shouts, "should the slightest amount of these powders mix?" His face is livid again, but I can tell he's fighting to gain self-control.

A sensation overwhelms me—that it's not anger he feels, but fear. Fear of what would happen if the powders mixed. Why would that be so bad? Would they blow up or something?

But for the life of me, I'm too terrified to think of a word to say. All I want to do is get away from him.

"Get up!" He picks up a silver box from the table. "Next I shall teach you future vision." He opens it to expose crystalline powder. "Come, Ta'reen. *Now.*"

I struggle to make my limbs cooperate and push myself up from the floor. Each step feels like my arms and legs are weighted with iron shackles. When I make it to his side, he takes my forefinger and dips it in the substance, which smells of soot.

"Touch each eyelid with this," he commands.

As I dab my lids, my hand trembles. The magic grabs hold of me at once, ripping me from my physical body. I'm trapped within shimmering light, then whirling iridescent colors, and transported to the lava fields.

*It's like being inside a crystal ball. Everything's skewed, out of focus.*

*Lion—my Lion is at my side. I turn my face to the heavens, to the twin moons.*

*Sickle moon, blood red, dominates the black sky, choking the night with ominous power and evil. Crescent moon, once petite and far away, sails closer, growing larger and larger, until it reaches Sickle's side.*

*A wind storm. Glittering colors, like Synomea's magic powders, swirl around the moons. Faster and faster.*

*Crescent waxes full, glowing a brilliant white, blotting out the horrid red of Sickle.*

*Sickle withers with age, fading until it vanishes.*

*Winds die and I see only Lion, crying. Tears roll down his magnificent face, trickling into his mane.*

*Crescent's light wanes—and then all goes dark.*

Release. Like being dropped from a tower into the coldest water imaginable. I gasp. Open my eyes.

Synomea stares at me, like he's struggling to penetrate my thoughts and attempting to rip the vision from my mind. I sense his rage and the fear within me grows. He's so close I'm overwhelmed by the odor of evil.

"Tell me, what did you see?" His words are bitter-edged.

If he wants to know so much, why doesn't he use the powder and look for himself?

The answer hits me like an anvil. He can't do it. Synomea has lost the ability to vision the future. For this, he now needs me.

Synomea . . . needs . . . what I can do. He needs what I have seen. I can't let him know what I saw, even if I don't have any idea what the vision means.

"I—I didn't understand it." I search for something to tell him, anything but what I saw. If Synomea is Sickle, and Erick is Lion, then I must be Crescent . . .

"Your comprehension does not matter. Tell me what you visioned." His face turns livid, veins bulging at his neck.

I swallow hard. "A—a red sickle moon, a white crescent, and a lion."

He grabs my upper arms and squeezes so hard he bruises my flesh. "And?"

My mind races to find something that will please Synomea. I take a deep breath and say, "The sickle destroyed the lion, while the crescent remained at the sickle's side. Then the sickle grew to encapsulate this entire planet." My knees tremble and a rivulet of sweat runs down my back. "W-what does it mean?"

Synomea grins and releases my arms. "It means, my dear, that all proceeds as planned."

## October 29

*Erick*

Green dawn creases the sky by the time we find a cave, and Van is exhausted from the skirmish with the dragon and the long trek afterward.

The cave is clear of game or beasts, and fortune is with us—a pool of water is at the back of the cave, fed by a small spring. The water runs clean and pure, and we will have enough to flush our injuries without using any water from our flasks. After ministering our wounds, we eat a portion of the last of our rations: a couple strips of dried meat, a hard roll, and cheese.

We rest, but every hour or so I rouse myself and wake my twin to make sure her head injury is not too serious. Her eyes remain clear and her temper intact.

When I nudge her at midday, Van says, "Wake me again and I shall feed you to the next dragon myself." Her voice is thick with sleep, but her skin has regained its healthy hue and her thigh no longer bleeds through the binding.

I start to fall asleep, but cold spreads along my limbs. Taryn. I feel her. As if her soul is tortured. As if she cries out in anguish. I pull out the l'apitak and call to her, but she does not respond.

Gods! I must get to her this night. We are close now, and I dare not wait for the others. I must rescue her this eve, whatever the cost to myself.

I sleep, then wake again. Van breathes in soft sighs nearby. As I turn toward her, my head throbs and my hands and arms ache.

A dagger carves my heart at the sight of the blood-encrusted wound above Van's brow. Her shoulders rise and fall with each breath, her mahogany tresses loose around her pale face. With her features relaxed in sleep, she looks as though she should be my younger sister, fifteen at best, rather than eighteen and my twin. She resembles the portrait of our mother, a true beauty.

Van is my only family, save Rufus and Unay, who are not related to us. Should anything happen to my sister on this quest, I would never forgive myself. I could have lost her to the dragon and I could lose her still to Synomea's wicked sorcery. Why did I not force her to stay in Newold?

I know I could have done nothing to stop her.

I remember what the wizards said. *"Your love and your blood shall live to breathe beyond castle walls."* Surely their cryptic message meant Van is to complete this quest at my side.

Van opens her eyes as I watch, and she smiles. "What is it? Do you dare risk waking me and having me feed you to the next dragon?"

It is good to see my sister smile and to hear her attempt at humor.

"No," I reply. "But I am glad to see your eyes. The injury to your head was nothing more than a scrape."

She winces as she rolls toward the cave's mouth. "The sky darkens. I am afraid a storm will be upon us soon."

"Van."

She turns back to me. "What?"

"You must stay outside the fortress. I will go the route the wizards told me and bring Taryn to safety. Then we shall meet with our friends and revise our plans."

"No." Her lips are tight, her eyes hard. "We go together, or not at all."

I clench my fists and scowl. "For the love of Nar! Do you not understand how it would kill me should anything happen to you?"

Van frowns. "Do you not understand how much I care for you? I will not send you to the beast's lair alone. Together we shall rescue your love, and together we shall fight Synomea."

"Pah!" With another scowl, I roll onto my back and stare at the cave's black ceiling.

"You must sleep. It is at least four hours yet 'til sunset."

Van's voice has a soothing quality, but I resist. "I cannot."

Rustling sounds, then Van's face appears above mine. "Erick."

As I open my mouth to answer, she drops liquid to my tongue that tastes of dirt. I grimace. "What—?"

"I do this for your own good."

The cave seems to spin around me, then all goes black.

---

The rumble of thunder wakes me and I roll over to look out the opening of the cave. Outside it rains so hard it is like a curtain of water. A rock-fire Van has lit burns with the Old Magic. It gives off no smoke, but fills the cave with a green glow and gentle warmth.

201

My sister brushes her wet hair and grins. "Sleep well?" She looks refreshed and must have bathed. A scab forms on the wound at her temple and bruises cover her arms.

I grumble as I get to my feet, "It is good you yet have your sense of humor." Surely I have lost my own.

I go to the back of the cave and wash my face in the pool, the water cold and rousing. Ah, for a bath in our manor in Newold. I settle for cleansing my limbs with the lump of soap my sister left on a rock. The soap smells of pine and mountain breezes, reminding me of the forests of my home.

When I return to Van's side, her hair is braided, her wounds tended, and food is set out for our dinner. We sup on dried meat, the last of the cheese, and dry bread.

"I contacted Cole with the l'apitak," she says as we finish our meal. "He and Finella have met up with Basil and Gareth. Cole curses your impatience, but they will continue to the east of Mount Zumar, where they will be an hour's walk from the fortress. They should arrive late tonight. We can meet them there."

Van and I will dispatch to Cole's na'tan once we recover Taryn. We will be close enough to them for the dispatch. It is a difficult thing to do without the aid of Haro Command.

I want to beg my sister to change her mind, to stay outside the fortress as I had asked. But I know it is an argument I would lose. Again.

By the time we are ready to venture out, the rain has lessened. It stays slight until it nears the mid of night. Mount Zumar is closer yet, and it will not be long until we are inside Synomea's fortress.

As we walk, the twin moons peek through clouds, offering some light to travel by, and the glow of the volcano serves as a beacon. Dragons fear the rain, thus we have no concern for the mate of the slain beast this night.

Raindrops pelt us and wind picks up as we clamber down yet another hillside. I go first, with Van following behind me. We are almost to the fortress—I can see the curtain wall, blacker even than the dark sky.

*Erick!*

Taryn calls to me. Joy leaps within as I hear her voice in my thoughts.

*Erick . . . where are you?*

As I ease down the slope, I shove my hand in my pocket and withdraw my l'apitak. *Taryn! Thank the gods, you are safe. I shall be there soon. Tonight.*

The hillside gives way beneath my boots.

Van screams as my feet slide out from under me.

Landslide!

I claw at fleeing stone as I struggle to stop my descent. Silt fills my mouth and my eyes. Rocks tear my flesh. I hear nothing but a roar in my ears as the landslide sweeps me downward.

Faster, faster. Tumbling. Flying. Drowning.

At the bottom of the hill I slam into the ground, my face landing in muck. Something crashes into my shoulder and lands on my back. Pain rips my arm. Everything settles and is quiet.

A movement, and then I realize Van landed on my back. She rolls off and says, "Are you hurt?"

My body burns from new cuts. I spit pebbles and dirt, and wipe mud from my face with my sleeve. "I am fine. But quite tired of falling."

When I open my fist I discover the l'apitak is gone. "Damn!" I get to my knees and shake the filth from my face and hair. I know it is hopeless, but I glance to the ground to see if I might find the l'apitak, and of course see nothing but mud and rock.

Wind rages and a violent rain pours down. Lightning pierces the sky, the shout of thunder not far behind. It is so close, the air crackles with tension.

"We must seek shelter until this lightning ceases." Van stands and brushes mud from her face. "It is too close and dangerous."

The rain pounds so furiously it washes some of the muck from us. We run along the hillside until we find a group of boulders that serve as refuge. We crouch under the shelter to wait out the worst of the storm.

When lightning flashes again, my sister looks me over. "I am afraid we will scare the girl once she sees us."

I smile. Van can find humor in almost any situation.

"How shall we locate the girl once we're within the fortress?"

I shrug. "We will follow the wizards' instructions. We must search for a lion along this wall, and there shall find a passage. L'iwanda and L'onten claimed we would find Taryn in the dungeons. If she is not there—I will have to search for her, one room at a time."

While I look into the rain, lightning again lances the sky and I see the walls of Synomea's fortress.

And a pile of stones in the shape of a lion.

## Taryn

The pull of this magic is strong, seductive. It grows within my breast, threatening to take control of my being.

I wait in my room for his lordship to call on me again. I've paced it from one end to the other, stared out the window at endless black rock, meditated, and practiced the shield spell and have tried a little of the levitation spell.

The more I meditate, the stronger this feeling inside me becomes. A new voice in my head that is sensual and alluring is now telling me I can defeat Synomea. That I have the power to rule this world. Alone.

What is the wicked voice I hear inside of me? Is it some dark part of me that has been waiting for this time in my life? Waiting to become a powerful sorceress . . .

Like it's my destiny.

A knot of fear unravels in my belly. I'm so afraid I'm losing myself to this dark sorcery.

I hug myself, as if it might protect me against this evil stirring in my blood.

Heaven forbid, but I've noticed I'm even starting to sound different, like Synomea, in the way I speak, the way I think. It's been one week now that I've been here, yet I feel so much older. I don't know about wiser, but definitely older.

A plan has been stirring in my mind about how I'm going to get out of here. How I'm going to save Erick and his friends. And how I'm going to defeat the sorcerer.

Can I do it? I don't know if I can believe this voice inside of me, or if I can believe Synomea's assurances I am a powerful sorceress. But if I'm not, what is this burgeoning feeling growing within?

I've ignored the l'apitak, afraid to attempt contact with Erick because the sorcerer might somehow hear me.

But I'll have to try soon to warn him to stay away. I'm not sure how I will explain what is happening with me or what I should say. I wonder if he'll hate me when he finds out I am Synomea's daughter.

It doesn't matter any longer. I'll insist he must leave with his friends, while I try to stop Synomea. Yes, that's it. Tonight I'll tell Erick to stay away.

I love you, Erick. I don't know how I'll go on when this is all over.

With a sigh, I wander back to the window and stare out at the desolate landscape. How does one become a sorceress, fight evil, and then return to a normal life? Providing one annihilates evil and isn't destroyed in the process. Do I show up in my classes like nothing's happened, nothing's changed?

Or do I take up a new major when I enter college? Sorcery 101, Visions 105, Mind Control 150, and Defeating Sorcerers, Advanced, 200 level. Would that be in the College of Arts and Sciences?

I groan and go back to work on my plan, and try to learn if I can make something levitate. When I was upset with Synomea, the ebony powder box moved, and I'm sure I caused it.

And the vitamin holder! I must have made it rise above my countertop at home, even before the Ta'sha released my sorcery. A strange sense of relief pours through me, warm and inviting. I wasn't losing my mind when I saw it rise. And it reinforces the fact that the magic has been within me all along.

Can I do it again? I glance to the table with the pot of rosemary shampoo. I focus. Concentrate, Taryn.

Rise!

Nothing.

Again I try. The pot doesn't budge.

Deep breath. I close my eyes and meditate. I let the confidence the Ta'sha has released build up within me. I feel myself controlling the air around the pot, imagine the air cradling and lifting it into the air. Warmth spreads though my chest and limbs, my face flushes and my scalp tingles.

I raise my eyelids, and point my finger at the jar. A slight motion of my hand, as I saw Synomea do, and the pot levitates above the table. I curl my finger, beckoning. I draw it closer, and it floats straight to my waiting hands.

Triumph sweeps over me in a heady rush.

Again!

When I send the pot back, in my excitement I miss the table. The container crashes to the stone floor, pottery shattering and goo splattering.

Not that I care—I'm too caught up in the thrill, the power of making things move with my mind and my control over the element of air.

My plan grows as my gaze sweeps the room, looking for more objects to control. I start out small and elevate the hairbrush and a stack of towels. Next, I move to larger items and scoot the chair from one wall to another, then lift the divan.

Piece of cake. Now, I need something bigger.

The bed. I turn to it and dig deep into my sorcery. I'm a maestro, and the air around me is the orchestra. I hold my palms up, at my waist. Slowly, ever so slowly, building and building to a crescendo, I raise my hands. The bed wobbles. I feel its weight, so massive, so heavy. But I force it higher and higher, until it's at least four feet off the floor.

I grin and almost drop it. Again, a deep breath. I lower my arms fractions at a time, until the bed returns to its resting place.

A gasp behind me, just loud enough to hear with my good ear. Heart in my throat, I spin toward the door.

Maria. Her hand to her mouth, her face pale. "It's true," she whispers. "You're like . . . him."

"Shut the door!" I glance over Maria's shoulder to see if anyone else is behind her, but thank goodness, no one is.

"Yes, milady." A meek nod and she closes it.

I can't stop the anger boiling up inside me—fury like I've never felt before. "What do you mean I'm like him? *How . . . dare . . . you.*" I'm shaking, heat rushing to my face.

"I—I—"

"Don't you ever compare me to that bastard!" In my rage, a corner of my mind registers she's cowering on the floor, terror in her eyes.

An ice-cold wave crashes into me.

"Oh, my God. I *am* turning into him." I sink to my knees, completely numb. I can't see, can't feel, can't think. I sit there, staring at my hands.

Maria scrambles to her feet, and I hear her scuttling about the room. The jangle of pottery shards, the swish of cloth. For endless moments I stare at my hands but see nothing.

"Maria. Please come here," I say softly.

Immediately she's standing before me, and I see her brown robes scraping the top of her dirty, bare feet.

I look up and see her fear. "Please sit on the floor with me."

Maria settles on her haunches, her hands in her lap, her eyes downcast. As I reach toward her, she flinches.

I take both her hands in mine. "I'm sorry I yelled. Please forgive me, and please understand how frightened I am about what's happening to me and everyone else here. Yes, I'm his daughter by birth, and I can perform magic, but I'm truly not like him. I despise the beast, more than you'll ever know."

She nods, but still doesn't look at me.

"I could really use a friend right now." My voice trembles and I fight off tears.

Maria looks up with a glimmer of understanding. She takes me in her arms, and I cry so hard my body shakes. Tears wet the front of Maria's robe as well as my own.

Her gentle touch calms me as she strokes my hair. "I—I'm sorry, Taryn. I've known since the first day Meg and I met you that you're not like him."

I take a deep breath and catch her cinnamon and vanilla scent. "Thank you." I pull away and wipe my nose on the sleeve of my robe. "I hate him. You have no idea."

A wry smile. "I've been his slave for almost three years now. I have a pretty good idea."

Three years. Thank goodness the sorcerer doesn't use the mind-control powder on the servants in his castle as he does those who slave in his mine. Otherwise she would turn into a Zumarian. Not that goodness has anything to do with it. I think he enjoys seeing the fear in their eyes every time they're around him.

With the back of my hand, I swipe tears from my face. "What you've been through is horrible and completely unacceptable. I want to help everyone escape from Synomea. I have a plan, but I'll need your help to do it."

Her eyes cut to the door. "You must be careful what you say. He has ways of hearing things."

I follow Maria's gaze, then look back to her. "We do need to be careful. He doesn't seem to be able to read my thoughts, but he might be able to read yours, so the less you know, the better."

"Okay . . ."

The plan that has been forming in my mind has become much clearer. "I need a spoon, a napkin, and a tiny box with a lid or some other small container. Can you have these things here when I come back to get ready for dinner?"

Maria tilts her head, a confused look on her face. "I think so."

"Good." I attempt a smile. "You should probably go before Synomea gets here, so you don't have to run into the creep."

Maria looks hopeful. She gives me a hug and leaves.

While I wait for the sorcerer's summons, I work through my plan. I consider my options and discard those that probably won't work.

As I'm contemplating what I must do, I practice creating small windstorms in my room. It's a lot like lifting furniture and moving it through the air, because with that I must manipulate the air to move the object. Creating windstorms is actually easier, because I'm twisting the air itself.

At first I create little swirls of air that tease and tickle my hair, then larger whirls of wind that take my extra robes off a chair and whip them in the air like a mini tornado.

When I feel I've got it down, I go to the window to see if I can do the same thing at a distance and pray Synomea doesn't happen to look out his own window as I practice. I concentrate, and after a few attempts I find I can cause a cloud of black dust to swirl down below.

I locate bits of dead wood and rocks and practice moving those around, too. I find a couple of particularly good-sized logs and move them closer to where the green room is, so they're below the window of that room.

Can I move something I can't see, if I concentrate on it? Still looking out the window, I think about the chair behind me and imagine picking it up. I hear a sound, like the scrape of wood against stone. I imagine moving the chair beside the tub, and then setting it down. I hear a thump.

I turn around and see I've done it. I moved an object I couldn't see by picturing what it is and where I want it to go.

Finally, all the pieces fall into place.

All the clues are there . . . the cryptic vision of the future. Synomea's failure at reading my thoughts. The drain on his powers when he summoned me in my world. His need for the magical dusts to augment his sorcery.

His need for me.

*The powders. His fear* . . .

My spine turns to ice. Is there no other way?

From the snatches of thoughts and feelings I've had from the sorcerer, and from the future vision of the windstorm of powders, I'm pretty sure I know what will happen when those dusts mix.

My terror builds as I understand what I must do, no matter the consequences to myself. Unless I can think of something else, I believe it's the only way to stop him. I won't be able to live with myself if I allow him to continue murdering innocent people.

But do I have the guts to do it?

I sit at the dining table in the green room, eating dinner with Synomea. In my pocket, my hand trembles as my fingers caress the velvet bag Maria brought me when I returned to my room. She couldn't find a box, but the bag will work perfectly. Next to the bag the silver spoon and napkin weight my robe.

When he looks up at me, I fear Synomea will see straight to my soul.

Thankfully, his eyes seem distant and moody. Every now and then I feel snatches of his black thoughts, and I quaver.

Outside, a storm rages, rain pelting the windows. Flashes of lightning manage to pierce gaps in the drapes, and I jump at every crack of thunder. But the storm will be a perfect cover for what I'm going to do.

Is Erick out in this storm or taking shelter in a cave? How close is he? I must warn him to stay away!

The tasteless food sticks in my throat, but I eat like it's my last meal. It very well could be.

"What are you thinking, Ta'reen?"

His words startle me and I almost choke on a chunk of blue potato. While I flounder for something to say, I wipe my mouth with a napkin and struggle to meet his eyes.

"My next lesson." I glance at the table of magical powders. "There's so much to learn, isn't there?"

The sorcerer studies me like he's trying to read my mind. I get a strong sensation he resents not being able to know my thoughts.

His gaze narrows. "You are such a willing student. Why is this?"

Grabbing hold of what little confidence I have, I try to supply the answer that will satisfy him—one he will believe.

I force a smile and swallow. Hard. "You have shown me this is my destiny, and I have no other choice. I am a sorceress, and I might as well start learning to be a good one while I'm at it." I pause and brush a strand of hair behind my ear. "I've always been a top student and have a fondness for learning. I—I feel a thrill, and a sense of excitement from what you are teaching me.

"And power. I love the power." That part, I realize, is the truth.

He nods and smiles, his pleasure at my response obvious. "Of course. You are my daughter, and you carry the crescent. Certainly you would have succeeded in your education as a child."

Again, I get the feeling he cares for me in his own way. He is convinced it is my destiny to serve him, and that I will do so willingly once I understand my "place."

Synomea breaks a loaf of black bread and slathers a hunk with green paste that smells of garlic and dill. "I've been distracted with your education and have neglected my duties in finding the crescent crystal. On the morrow we will begin our search for the crystal, using mind-flight and future visions to aid in its recovery. Our time approaches and we must have it."

Trying not to squirm in my seat, I fidget with my napkin. "I don't understand how I came to have the crystal as a child."

A glitter comes to his eyes, and it's like I see a hunger there, a flame that consumes him. "It is a most powerful stone, once controlled by Lord Erick's ancestors. When I destroyed Lord Roland, I took the crystal from him and placed it with you for safekeeping until your metamorphosis."

My pendant actually belongs to Erick's family?

I want to look away from his gaze, but I force myself to maintain eye contact. "Why didn't you use the crystal when you had it?"

The sorcerer runs his tongue along his bottom lip, reminding me of a snake flicking out its tongue as it seeks its prey. "Both of our powers, yours and mine, are necessary to utilize the crystal's full potential. As I told you, I visioned you and our domination of Zanea. Seventeen years is but a blink of an eye in my lifetime. The years have been well spent in preparation for our rule."

Do I dare ask what I need to know about the crescent crystal? I reach my hand to my neck, as if I'll find the crystal there again. "How can this pendant be so important?"

For a long moment he studies me. My hands tremble as I wring the napkin in my lap, and heat rises within me. I hope my face isn't betraying how frightened I am he will see through me and learn what I plan to do.

Synomea sets his fork on his plate and steeples his hands on the table. "The crystal shall enhance our powers, Ta'reen. With it we can reach across the lands and Neguriän Sea to control the minds and souls of anyone not loyal to me and my sons."

I blink. *"Sons?"* Brothers? I have brothers?

He smiles, a cold smile that sends shivers down my spine. "You have many brothers, all by different mothers. Some of my sons are powerful sorcerers in their own right, scattered across this world. Most are nothing more than pawns with little magic. But all will serve me when my day comes."

My entire life I've been an only child, and he tells me I have a whole family out there.

I think about what he said. "What do you mean, pawns?"

"They do my bidding and serve as my spies."

"What about daughters?"

"You are the only daughter born of my blood, as I visioned," he says. "The one who will rule by my side. You will take a consort and bear heirs to our legacy."

I drop my gaze to my plate and pick up my fork. My stomach is roiling and I'm afraid I'm going to puke and ruin this chance to put my plan into motion. Even though I try to control my trembling, my food falls off my fork and I have to try again before I can get a bite into my mouth.

We eat in silence, and after a few minutes my nerves calm down. I take deep breaths and work through my plan until I'm ready to put it into motion.

While I pretend to focus on my dinner, I keep my face as blank as possible. I visualize the single window to the right of the doorway and one of the logs I moved this morning. Sweat breaks out on my forehead as I concentrate. I visualize picking up the log and then flinging it toward the window with my magic.

A muffled thump is all I hear. Fortunately, Synomea doesn't seem to notice.

As I spear another piece of blue potato, I picture the log. My head aches from concentrating so hard. I work through the motions, calling upon the elements, and hurl the log with the strength of a windstorm.

A crash shatters the quiet.

In pretend alarm, I look up at the sorcerer and widen my eyes. Synomea glances from me to the direction of the noise.

Without a word, he hurries into the hallway and closes the doors behind him.

I bolt from my seat to the table of powders, withdrawing the pouch and spoon from my pocket as I run.

Where is it? The crystal jar with purple dust.

There!

I glance at the doors. Still closed.

With shaking hands, I remove the lid and scoop a spoonful of powder into the pouch. After I cover the jar, I pull the bag's drawstring tight, then shove it and the spoon into my pocket.

The door slams and my heart stops. I whirl to see Synomea glaring at me.

"What are you doing?" He strides toward me, his face as menacing as the storm raging outside.

My throat is so dry my words come out in a rasp. "I—I'm making sure I have all the powders memorized."

I step back, but he grabs my shoulders, his fingers digging into my flesh.

"Is it truth you speak? Or lies?" His eyes burn as if willing me to ashes.

I blink and try to look as innocent and submissive as possible. "You're a great sorcerer. I—I'm sure you know my thoughts. You must realize I'm telling the truth, Father." I flinch as he drags me closer yet.

"Of course. But have you learned to mask—" He breaks off, and I sense his battle within. He'll kill me before admitting he can't read my mind, and he's afraid to say too much and give me any ideas.

"Never venture near this table without me at your side." Synomea releases me with such force I stumble and almost trip over a rug.

His gaze sweeps the table of magics. "A lesson you want. A lesson you shall have." A wicked snicker.

Oh, no.

"But none of these will we have need of this night." He moves to an open area before the hearth and motions to me.

The pouch and spoon slap my thigh as I join the sorcerer, and I'm afraid somehow he'll see through my robes into the pocket.

With one clap of his hands he extinguishes all light in the room, save the fireplace. He grips my shoulders and positions me so my back is to him and the flames, then releases me. The flames reflect in the mirrored wall across from where we stand, and I can see his face over my shoulder.

"Close your eyes, Ta'reen."

I comply, but prickles of fear creep along my spine at his nearness.

Synomea leans close to my good ear, his breath tickling me, his words soft and deliberate. "Deep within you is your pool of sorcery and your control of the elements. Draw from that well . . . build upon your power . . . nurture the magic . . . give it life."

He drones, low and hypnotic, and the allure of the sorcery swells. Heat spreads, expanding from the roots of my hair to my fingernails to every single toe. I hear only his voice; every other sound vanishes. My eyes still closed, I see nothing but silver ripples in my mind.

"Cup your palms before you . . . good. Picture a flame shimmering in your hand . . . desire its sensual warmth . . . feel the caress of its dance."

My palms tingle. I breathe in rhythm to the ballet skipping from finger to finger.

"Excellent. Open your eyes."

I gasp.

Purple fire. In my hands.

The amethyst glow suffuses the room as the delicate flame pirouettes and grows. Shadows leap and bound, joining in the fire dance. I visualize myself twirling with the light and dark figures.

Synomea's words draw me back. "Ah, I was sure you would prove to be an apt student, despite your failures at the spell shield and levitation. Those should come easily to you now."

He moves to my side and gestures around the room. "Focus on all torches and candles, seeking them out with your sorcery. Carry the flame with your magic and light them all."

I concentrate, imagining the fire lighting the torches and candles. The purple flame streaks across the room and the torches explode with life, sparks showering the furniture. It's like daylight until the flames settle to normal size. The candle at the dinner table didn't fare so well—it's nothing but a pool of melted wax.

"Hmmm. Next time, you must take more care," he murmurs, just loud enough that I can hear him in my good ear. "Not so hasty, little one."

My temper surges and I whirl around. "Don't you ever call me that again, you—you jerk!"

He raises an eyebrow. "Interesting how that name has such an effect on you. What meaning has it?"

I look away, trying to slow my breathing and soothe the rage within. "Nothing. It's just something I don't want to be called."

With cruel fingers, Synomea grabs my face, forcing me to look into his eyes. "Never forget who I am. You live and die by my word alone. Speak to me in that manner again, and you shall regret it."

My knees threaten to buckle as the sorcerer shoves me away from him and calls to a warrior. The Zumarian comes for me and then escorts me to my room.

After the warrior locks me in my bedchamber, I force myself to be patient—to wait until the keep is completely silent and hopefully the sorcerer has gone to sleep.

When I feel it's safe, I scramble for my clothes underneath the four-poster. I toss everything onto the bed, including the spoon, cloth, and bag of powder from my robe pocket.

I strip off the crimson gown, then dress in my own comfortable clothing. The texture of my jeans feels terrific, and my pink shirt is soft against my skin. It's wonderful to pull on my thick socks and tennies.

My pants hang, threatening to slide over my hips. Having giant insects and rats for dinner must be a fast way to drop a couple of pounds, or maybe magic is a good fat burner. I snatch the sash of my robe and thread it in the belt loops of my jeans.

Satisfied, I grab my jacket and search for the l'apitak. The instant I touch it, I feel Erick. How I wish I could escape with him.

No! I have a responsibility to Maria, Meg, and all the other people enslaved here. I'm the only one who can free them from the sorcerer.

At least I hope I'm right. And I pray I can do this.

I clench the disc in my fist. *Erick . . . where are you?*

Silence. Then that tingle travels from my palm to my chest.

*Taryn! Thank the gods, you are safe. I shall be there soon. This night.*

My heart leaps. No, not tonight!

*No, Erick, you can't come. It's too dangerous.*

No response.

*Erick!*

Nothing.

*Listen to me, Erick. You must stay away.*

He's gone and I feel a niggling of fear. Did something happen to Erick? Why doesn't he answer?

Well, that's great. I couldn't tell him to stay away, so now he'll walk straight into the beast's lair and it'll be my fault if anything happens to him.

I've got to get going. All I can do is complete the next step of my plan and urge Erick to leave when he gets here.

I must get to him before Synomea does.

After I slip my jacket on, I withdraw the vitamin box, take out the remainder of the meds for my Ménière's, and put them into one pocket of my jacket. I dump the vitamins onto the bed, then clean out each compartment with the cloth.

The vitamin smell brings back memories of home—Gran's kitchen, the flowery wallpaper, my favorite glass tumbler I used to fill with iced tea and lemonade. The simple, mundane chores of loading the dishwasher and taking out the garbage.

I wonder if I'll ever return to Tucson. My memories seem a lifetime ago, rather than days. I miss Jen horribly, and I even miss my foster parents.

With a sigh, I turn my thoughts back to Erick and accomplishing my mission as I shove the spoon and cloth into the other pocket.

Hoping the sleeping powder will work on the Zumar, I grab the drawstring pouch and hurry to the door. Since the warriors were once human, I think the powder will work. I kneel on the floor and peek through the crack under the door. Two sets of enormous boots, one to each side.

Here goes.

Taking care not to breathe it in, I sprinkle half the sleeping powder onto the floor. I blow on it, pushing it under the door and into the air with my sorcery. In my mind, I picture the purple dust swirling straight up to the faces of the warrior guards.

One thud.

Another.

Excellent! According to his lordship's lesson, the warriors should be out cold for a few hours. That's if it works on the Zumar the way it does on humans.

I concentrate on the bolt securing the door. As I pull it out with my magic, I hear the bar grate against the metal housing. I visualize the rod as it comes free, then lower it to the floor. A light clatter echoes in the hallway, and I catch my breath.

Everything is quiet, no one sounding an alarm.

When I push the door, it swings open and rams one of the warriors. The Zumar are so huge I have to stretch my legs to climb over them. My tennies make soft squeaks against the stone as I creep along the hall, praying the whole time the sorcerer is asleep.

Near the green room, a stray bit of broken glass crunches under my shoe. The sound is like chomping on a spoonful of cornflakes, and I hope it's not loud enough to draw attention. Thank goodness, most of the glass has been cleaned up, but a few shards glitter in the torchlight.

Eerie wails seep through cracks in the now boarded-up window, the storm still raging. Servants and slaves housed in the barracks must be drenched by now. I've got to do this right and help them all.

Hinges creak as I pull open the door to the green room, the creak so loud to my ears it might as well be over an amplifier. I'm afraid the sorcerer will catch me and then I'll never be able to carry out my plan.

It's dark in the green room. I'm thankful for the sorcerer's last lesson, and that for once I was able to get something right on the first try. In seconds a small flame dances in my palm, and with more care I send the fire to the hearth, igniting a small blaze. Even with Synomea absent, the heavy odor of burnt sugar permeates the place. I'm so sick of his smell— I'm sick of everything about him.

When I reach the table of magics, I pull out the vitamin box and cloth. After I take care to wipe remnants of sleeping powder from the spoon, I snap open the first cap of my vitamin box.

*S* for Sunday. I find the cloisonné box, take a spoonful of indigo dust, and in goes mind-flight. The plastic container is clear, so I'm able to see which powder I put in each compartment. I'm thankful for the hours of lessons I've had with the sorcerer and the knowledge I have of all these powders.

With a corner of the cloth, I wipe away the blue dust, and I'm careful never to use the same part of the cloth to wipe the spoon. Next is *M* for Monday, and mind control, the rose pink powder.

I continue adding magics to the box until each day of the week is full. The very last I'm hesitant to touch. *S* is for Saturday . . . and scarlet, the death powder. Do I really need this?

Yes. Without it . . . this may not work.

Each cap securely in place, I return the vitamin box to my pocket. I withdraw the bag of sleeping powder, the eighth dust, and spoon a little more in it for good measure. I slip the pouch back into my jacket pocket and clean the spoon.

The cloth is useless with all the magical dusts on it—I don't dare throw it in the fireplace because I don't know how the powders will react to fire. I search for a place to hide it, and finally tuck it into the fabric of a chair. I grab a clean napkin from the dining table and slip it into my jacket pocket.

A blast of cold air slams into my body—a sensation Synomea has awakened. The green drapes to my right . . . I've wondered what's behind them. I think that's where Synomea's bedroom is, and he probably senses something's amiss. I've got to get out of here.

I hurry into the hall. Before I shut the door, I remember to extinguish the fire in the hearth, smothering it with my sorcery.

Panic freezes my blood. I'm not ready to take him on just yet.

Where can I hide? I feel his presence, like he's coming closer. I spot the door to the turret across from the green room's doors and run for it.

It's locked!

What can I do? Concentrate, Taryn, don't panic. Can I manipulate the air to open the lock in the same way I moved the lever out of the door?

I take a deep breath and imagine going inside the keyhole and pulling the mechanism to unlock it. It takes a few seconds, and then I hear a click. The door opens when I grab the handle and then I dodge into total darkness.

After quietly closing the door behind me, I hold out my palm and within seconds it sports a tiny flame. A wave of dizziness sweeps over me. I'm standing at the edge of stairs so steep I can't see where they lead. Wood creaks with each step

I take down the stairs, and I hope it's not loud enough for anyone to hear. I pray Synomea hasn't discovered the warriors asleep at my door and that I'm gone from my room.

The spiral stairs seem endless. I pass one door I think leads to the kitchen, then finally reach a stone foyer. Another set of stairs leads down to my right, and a lighted room to my left. A hum and whirring noise come from the doorway, then the sound of rushing water.

Just as I'm about to peek into the room, I hear a Zumarian's growl. I extinguish the flame in my palm and press into the shadows. The stone is cold through my shirt and jacket, and dust tickles my nose. I wipe an enormous cobweb from my face and hope there's no giant spider over my head.

I lean toward the light, to see what's there. The room is familiar, like I've been there before. Occupying the center is a black platform, a cage to the side of it, and a Zumarian stands before something that looks like a set of controls. The air shimmers, and a black void appears above the platform.

The Zumar portal!

A warrior appears, gripping a girl, about my age, by both arms. She's slumped over, not even moving. Rows of gold bracelets slide down her dark arm, jangling like wind chimes. From behind she looks familiar.

It can't be . . .

The Zumarian throws her over his shoulder, and I catch a glimpse of her face.

*Jen!*

I gasp.

A hand clamps over my mouth.

# PART THREE

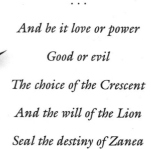

. . .

*And be it love or power*

*Good or evil*

*The choice of the Crescent*

*And the will of the Lion*

*Seal the destiny of Zanea*

. . .

## October 30, midnight

*Taryn*

Fear slices me as a muscular arm grabs my waist and pulls me deeper into the shadows, the hand still over my mouth. It happens so fast I don't have time to think, and I don't dare struggle or make a sound with the warriors so close.

My heart pounds as the Zumarian stomps from the room and through the doorway, walking inches away from where I'm held captive. As he goes by I catch the scent of Jen's baby powder perfume mingling with the beast's malodor. They disappear into the darkness, the sound of the Zumarian's steps farther away.

"Do not make a sound, Taryn," the husky voice says in my good ear, and his hands release me.

"Erick!" Relief flushes me in warm waves, and I can barely keep to a whisper. I whirl and wrap my arms around him, and he squeezes me tight. He's soaking wet and muddy, but it's wonderful to hug him again and to have him holding me. Absolutely no doubt is in my mind that this is my Erick and not another attempt by Synomea to trick me.

Erick seems as reluctant as I am to part. As soon as we pull away, I notice the bleeding cuts, the scabs on his arms, and the bandage.

"You're hurt, Erick."

"I am fine."

He leans down and kisses me. His face is cold from the rain, but his lips are warm, and heat radiates throughout my body.

Erick pulls away and says, "We must hurry."

My head feels light and a little dizzy from his kiss. I can't think of a word to say as he takes my wrist and straps something to it. My lips still tingling, I reach up and trace the scar along his cheekbone with my finger, imprinting his handsome face in my memory. This may be the last time I ever touch him.

I finally find my voice. "No. Even though I want to, I can't go with you. I don't have time to explain, but I must stay and destroy Synomea myself. You've got to leave before he finds you."

Erick flings his wet head back and searches me from head to toe with his silver eyes. With a gentle hand, he captures my chin. "You are injured, little one. I will throttle Synomea for harming you."

"It's a long story." I put my hand over his, where he's touching my face. "Please believe me, you must get out and leave me."

"No." Erick's eyes flash and he takes my hand.

I don't want to ask, but I must. "Erick—did you take—do you have my crystal pendant?"

"What?" He looks confused. "You no longer have the crystal?"

I shake my head. "It disappeared the night you came to tell me goodbye."

A flash of anger crosses his face. "You think I stole from you?" He rakes his hand through his hair and I can tell he's furious. "I would never!"

My face burns when I see how badly I've insulted him. "In my heart I knew it wasn't you. But it vanished, and I had to ask if you might have an idea who could've taken it."

He takes a deep breath, like he's trying to cool his anger, and then gives me his crooked smile. "We will find your keepsake."

A woman, almost as tall as Erick and just as soaked and muddy, appears from the darkness. Her eyes are the same silver gray as Erick's; she has a thick wound above one eye, and as many cuts and scrapes as he does.

"Hurry and bring the girl," the woman says. "We have no time for this." She grabs my arm and drags me toward the dungeon stairs, limping as she goes. "Come."

I try to fight her, but I might as well be struggling against an ox. "But—"

Erick gives me a gentle shove. "Follow my sister. Van will lead us out."

While I stumble after his sister Van, Erick tailgates me. I have to make him understand I must stay and help Jen and everyone else imprisoned by the sorcerer. We reach the bottom of the turret steps. A closed wooden door is to the left, a passage on the right.

I try to halt, pulling back on Van's grip as hard as I can. "I can't go with you. You've got to get away before the sorcerer discovers you."

Erick pushes me through the passage entrance. "I will not leave you."

It's hard to talk as I'm being dragged down the tunnel. "He'll never let me go. He'll kill all of your friends, everyone, to get me back."

"Are you so important?" Van asks. At last, she stops.

Erick nearly tramples me.

"Yes. I mean, no. Synomea is an evil monster, and I'll do whatever I can to defeat him, but there's something you should know." It takes everything I have to get the words through my lips. "I'm his daughter."

The silence following my words crushes down, and the look on Erick's face almost destroys me.

Shock. Revulsion.

I force myself to push aside my jacket and the neck of my shirt and show them the crescent birthmark on my upper arm. "See? I carry the sorcerer's sign."

"Come." Van grabs my arm again, as if she hasn't heard and hasn't seen, tearing me away from Erick. "We must reach the outside." Torches light the passageway so we are able to see.

Erick says nothing, but I feel him staring at my back as we run.

My eyes ache with unshed tears, but I shove them away. I knew this would happen all along. How stupid of me to hold even a glimmer of hope Erick would still care.

I draw on my inner strength to do what I need to do. After I see Erick and Van safely outside, I'll return and deal with Synomea.

Even limping, Van sets a pace that's hard to match. It seems like we run forever, along a narrow passageway, down steps, around a corner, on and on. My lungs burn and my mouth fills with the coppery taste of blood.

"The doorway lies ahead," Van urges. "We are almost to it."

When I open my mouth to speak, I choke on thick dust and cough. My eyes water, but I manage to clear my throat. "Where are you taking me?"

The woman glances back. "This passage goes outside the curtain wall. We shall be safe once we reach the outside, where we can dispatch."

I stumble over a giant root and almost fall, but Erick catches my arm. For a fraction of a second my eyes meet his. His expression is unreadable.

Van reaches the door and tugs on it. "It is locked. This cannot be. The Old Magic will not work!"

"Let me." I push her out of the way and grab the handle.

This time it's easier to dive into the keyhole with my sorcery. The lock clicks and I yank the door open and dash into the blinding storm. Rain pelts my skin, wind tears at my hair.

A flash of lightning illuminates the sky, and it takes me a moment to make out the shadows. Then it becomes clear. We're surrounded by Zumar.

Warriors grab Erick, pinning his arms to his sides. He kicks one warrior down, but another replaces him.

My stomach falls to my toes. Dread suffocates me. "Erick!"

At the same time, Van grabs my arm and taps the band Erick strapped to my wrist.

Just as Zumarian claws reach for me, everything vanishes.

It's like being on the octopus ride at the carnival—spinning round and round. I'm still screaming when we stop. I'm dizzy and afraid it's going to bring on an episode of vertigo.

The sensations stop and I fall back, once again landing on my bottom—only this time on sharp rock. Pain spikes me, but I force myself to ignore it. Even though it's raining, the air is so thick with sulfur I can hardly breathe.

"Erick! Where's Erick? We have to help him!" I barely hear my own voice above the screaming winds and downpour.

231

"Thank the gods, this dispatch went right." Van limps to me, grabs my hand, and pulls me to my feet. "Calm yourself, Taryn. We are no longer in the sorcerer's fortress. And my brother . . ."

She sighs. "Erick can handle himself. He must handle himself. Into the cave, quickly now, before the sorcerer locates us." She drags me toward looming shadows, and I wonder how she even knows where we are. Just before we enter the cave, she stops.

"Tell no one you are the sorcerer's daughter and show no one the sign. Is this understood?"

I nod. No problem—I'm not real anxious to advertise I'm the daughter of a monster like Synomea.

Even as my limbs still tremble, Van pulls me into the cave. Three men and one woman are gathered around a green fire made entirely of rocks. Swords flash as two men stand, but both relax when they recognize Van.

I blink away the light while I try to make out their faces.

"Where's Erick?" growls a big guy who I recognize from the night I met Erick. It's Cole, Erick's friend. He glances from me to Van.

"It is good to see you as well," Van says in a wry tone as she squeezes rain from her braid. "Erick was taken by the Zumar."

"Damn!" Cole shouts. "You were not to go in without us."

Van's lips tighten in a grim line. "We stumbled upon the signs the wizards prophesied and Erick would not wait."

Another guy, this one brown and shaggy like a dog, stomps his boots. "Lost, over an Oldworlder."

"I warned him of this," drawls a redheaded guy, who's leaning against the cave wall.

A gorgeous woman, lean and supple, stands and approaches me. She's as tall as Van, and I have to look up at her, as well as everyone else in the cave. I'm in the land of the giants. No wonder Erick calls me "little one."

The woman sweeps her slanted sapphire gaze from my head to my toes, then tosses her blue-black hair over her shoulder, and I notice her ear has a slight point to it.

She smirks. "He risked everything for her? This fat girl?"

My face burns, a hot flush spreading through my body. I'm painfully aware of all eyes on me, my drenched and grubby clothes, the bruises on my face, my disheveled French braid.

And I'm furious.

A boulder levitates behind the group as I clench my fists. It's a struggle to force it back down before anyone notices.

"Finella!" Van steps between the witch and me. "The girl's name is Taryn, and you will show respect for the one Erick has feelings for."

Make that the one Erick *had* feelings for. He's probably regretting that right about now.

But we don't have time for this.

"Listen." I raise my chin and glare at the bunch of them. "Whatever you may think of me, Synomea has Erick. We need to save him. Now!"

They look stunned that I actually have a voice.

The redheaded guy starts pacing back and forth.

"Come, Taryn." Van takes my arm and pulls me closer to the fire. "We can do nothing now. It will not be long until daylight, and we cannot risk detection."

"We can't leave him there." I shake off her hold. "The sorcerer might kill Erick. I need to get to him tonight."

With a heavy sigh, Van runs her hand over her hair, a gesture that reminds me of Erick. "We will be safe in the cave.

We are no good to Erick if Synomea kills us all. Tomorrow night we will carry out our plans."

Her silvery gray eyes, so like Erick's, meet mine. "I have reason to believe the sorcerer will ransom my blood brother before he kills him."

Oh. I get it. He'll ransom Erick because of me. I'm the bait.

Well, I'm a lot more than that, sister.

The redhead scoops up a rock and tosses it as he paces. "Why do you think this is so?"

This guy makes me uneasy—something about him gives me the creeps.

"Basil, it is enough I tell you that and no more." Van pulls me down with her to sit by the fire. "Even with Erick gone, it is still my command. Cole will serve as my second. You will continue to follow my instruction, and you will treat Taryn as one of us."

She nods to the shaggy guy as he crouches next to her. "What do you say, Gareth?"

"Aye," he grunts.

"Finella?"

The witch shrugs a slim shoulder. "Of course." A cat. The woman reminds me of a cat—with the personality of a serpent.

Van looks to the redhead. "Basil?"

He grins, still tossing that stupid rock. "Van, you know I live to serve you."

"Cole?"

His black eyes study me. He nods.

Last, she turns to me. "Taryn?"

I sigh. "Yes."

# October 30, morning

## *Erick*

When we rush out of the tunnel and into the blinding rain, two Zumarian beasts lunge at me from either side of the doorway. The beasts clamp their metal claws around my arms before I can reach my sword.

I struggle to free myself, lashing out with my boot and knocking one warrior down. I fight to grab on to Van's hand to transport with them, but the Zumarians hold me back.

Warriors leap at Van and Taryn as they shimmer and fade.

"Erick!" Taryn screams before she vanishes.

Rain hammers down, hard and fast, as I wrestle with the warriors who land blow after blow to my chest and head. A third Zumarian slams a fist into my belly, knocking breath from me.

Another warrior grabs me from behind, and pain rips me as he wrenches my head back. Surely he will snap my neck like a twig.

Thank the gods Van has escaped with Taryn.

The warriors hold me so tightly I cannot move. They growl, but we remain where we stand in the blinding storm. Waiting, but for what? The beasts reek, a foul odor like a dragon's lair.

Lightning flashes as Synomea sweeps through the tunnel door, his robes billowing in the storm like green flame. It can be no other but the evil monster himself. The wind whips his hair so that it looks as if he sprouts horns.

"Where is she?" A purple fire appears in his hand, illuminating the night. His face is wet from the merciless rain, and he is so close I could spit in his face.

And his eyes . . . they are the same green as Taryn's. Otherworldly.

*Her father.*

I glare at the bastard, but say nothing.

"Tell me where Ta'reen is!" The sorcerer raises his fist as if to strike me. Two warriors jerk my limbs, as though they will tear me apart. The other Zumarian's arm tightens around my throat and I struggle for breath, but I refuse to speak.

Synomea's face turns the color of Mount Zumar's endless volcano. He shakes so violently I wonder if he will erupt and spew lava before my eyes. He nods to the Zumarians.

The warriors strip me of my haversack and Navran, and even take the dagger from my boot. "To the dungeon," Synomea growls. "I will deal with you later. After I reclaim what is mine." He closes his fist around the flame, extinguishing its light, then whirls through the doorway and disappears into the darkness.

When the warriors shove me into the tunnel, I stumble and fall. They grab my arms and drag me until we pass the turret where I found Taryn. I would struggle, but the beating I received at their hands has left me with little strength. My body scrubs stone as they drag me down steps, through another wooden door. Hinges creak, and the warriors throw me into a dungeon.

When my skull strikes the stone floor, pain explodes in my head and white sparks float behind my eyes. I groan and roll onto my back, but the Zumar clamp manacles to my wrists and ankles, and I can no longer move.

The rusted click of metal and the dry rattle of chains echo in my head. Grunts and growls come from the beasts, then the thump of boots against stone. Hinges creak, and I hear the scrape of metal as the door is barred.

My head spins and my ears ring as I stare at the dark ceiling. My nose itches, but I don't have strength enough to scratch it, nor the means. The chains reach the wall and I am unable to move. A muddy haze swirls in my mind and I can hardly form a single thought for a while.

When my mind clears, I allow myself to feel some relief Van is safe . . . and Taryn.

Ice slices my veins as I remember the words Taryn spoke. *I'm his daughter.* Disgust rips at my soul at the thought of her being the flesh and blood of Synomea—the beast who has destroyed countless lives and slayed my father.

Just as fast follows shame at my feelings of disgust. It is not her fault she is the daughter of the sorcerer.

How could Taryn, the one I believe to be my heart's mate, be the spawn of that demon? But those eyes—hers are the same as Synomea's. If I had not seen him for myself, I would not have believed it to be true.

My dream of the sorceress had flashed in my mind when Taryn told us she was the sorcerer's daughter and showed us the mark. I was too stunned to speak, repelled by her words and remembering the feeling of deception I had felt in the dream.

Did Taryn know the Zumar were waiting for us? Could she have led us to a trap? Perhaps she expected us all to be captured, and was unaware I had strapped my na'tan to her wrist.

Still, I do not understand how any of this can be. I do not understand why she lived in Oldworld and yet is the sorcerer's daughter.

Like sunlight breaking free of clouds, I suddenly understand the strange things that have occurred with Taryn since I met her. She escaped the Zumar grasp and had flashes of memory of our times together when she should have remembered nothing.

Taryn is not of Oldworld. She belongs to Zanea.

But if she had been aware of this, if she had knowledge of her own heritage, Taryn would have realized it the moment the Zumar first touched her. When I visited her I would have seen this knowledge in her eyes, and I would have sensed it with the Old Magic. She must have been raised ignorant of her heritage.

Taryn claims the crescent crystal has been stolen from her. Who could have taken it? Or could it have been a lie so we would not know the sorcerer has the crystal?

My thoughts turn back to our flight into the storm. Gods—if only it was possible to dispatch from the confines of the fortress. One second more and I could have touched my sister and fled with Van and Taryn.

Is Taryn under the sorcerer's control? Will she lead Synomea to my friends? I can't believe it, but I know I must escape and go to them!

Every inch of me burns and aches. My body would not be so weak if not for the fall from the cliff, the fight with the dragon, and the landslide. I need to recover my strength. If the sorcerer does not kill me, somehow I *will* escape. And I will avenge my father's death.

I close my eyes. The pounding in my head is like the steady beat of drums at the feast of Nar. The dungeon smells of urine and filth. Insects scuttle around me, crawling over my arms and up the side of my face. I can only hope they are not the poisonous spiders known to frequent such places.

Welcome blackness envelops me like a lover's arms. I swirl into a dream world where I see Zumarian warriors with Taryn's face.

---

A heavy boot slams into my side and wakes me. I groan as pain shoots through my body. Warriors remove manacles from my wrists and force me to stand.

Once they have taken the shackles from my ankles, the beasts shove me out the door. I stumble and sprawl onto the floor. Anger burns in my gut, but I barely have the opportunity to get to my knees when two warriors take me by my arms and drag me through the doorway.

They haul me down the long passageway, up steps, and then to the turret where I found Taryn. I try to get to my feet before they start up the winding staircase, but they yank me forward, their claws digging into my flesh. From my chest to my ankles, the wooden stairs scrape and pummel my body.

The beasts wrench me through a door at the top of the turret, then lug me across a hallway.

And into the green velvet room of my dream.

But this time it is not the sorceress I see.

Synomea stands alone in the room, his hands behind his back and a furious scowl upon his face. The Zumarians fling me to the sorcerer's feet, then pull me to a stand. Their claws clamp so tightly on my arms they sink into my flesh.

Curse my weak body!

The sorcerer stands beside a table of containers, and while he stares at me he taps a wooden box with his finger. At his side is a chair with Navran lying upon the cushion, taunting me. The crystal in the hilt glitters in the light. Synomea glances from my sword to me and sneers.

"Lord Erick," Synomea says as he walks forward. I do not show my surprise that he knows my name.

When he stands a few feet away, his gaze rakes me from head to foot as though he might be determining the worth of a bull at market. He narrows his eyes. "Why would Ta'reen have interest in you?"

Does he mean Taryn? I grit my teeth, holding back words of disgust I wish to shout at him.

His eye twitches. "Tell me where she is."

"I do not know anyone named Ta'reen."

"She calls herself Taryn."

"I do not know where Taryn is, and if I did, I would never tell you." It is the truth. I do not know where my friends wait and I would not lead him to them if I did.

Synomea's face darkens. "You will tell me where my daughter is, or you shall die. The wench is mine to do with as I please. My blood fills her veins and her destiny is with me! Now tell me where she is."

*His daughter. To do with as he pleases.* If the Zumar did not hold my arms so tight, I would smash my fist into Synomea's pale face.

I struggle to control my voice. I cannot let him know of my feelings for Taryn. "Your daughter means nothing to me."

He grunts to the Zumarian beasts. A third warrior hooks his arm around my neck from behind. Synomea lunges and grabs my head between his palms. I feel his filthy presence in my mind, and my innards churn. The Old Magic tells me he seeks answers—but cannot find them.

The sorcerer pushes me away in disgust, and I realize it maddens him that he is unable to read my thoughts.

With every breath, his chest rises and falls. I smell his odor, heavy and sickly sweet. He appears to attempt to rein in his temper. "I will make you suffer, Lord Erick. If you do not tell me where my daughter is, I will make you plead for relief and then you will die as your father did."

Gods! Burning rage fills me. How I want to kill the bastard where he stands! But the warriors never loosen their grip on my limbs or my neck, and I can do nothing but stand here and listen to his foul words.

Synomea smirks. "Your father died a slow and painful death while he watched me take his form and snare the woman he loved as my bride—the woman who became the vessel in which to carry my child."

My thoughts cannot wholly grasp what he is saying. My father . . . the woman he loved. The Oldworlder woman my father was banished for? Synomea's bride . . . Taryn's mother?

He nods. "You understand."

A fierce ache spreads from my stomach to my bowels. Could Taryn be my sister?

No! It cannot be!

"I required the Oldworlder woman to produce my heir, and I visioned she was the one to produce a true sorceress to serve at my side. Your father was a means to my end. I waited as Lord Roland romanced the woman, so that I might take his place. I disposed of your father when he no longer had value, as I disposed of the Oldworlder once she bore my child."

Synomea's heir. His child. His eyes.

Even as anger grows in my breast, emotions battle within. I feel hatred toward this beast for what he has done to my father and countless others, yet relief that Taryn cannot be of my blood because she is the sorcerer's daughter.

"So you see," Synomea chuckles. "Your father died so Ta'reen could live."

Rage blinds me. If these warriors did not restrain me, I would rip him to shreds with my bare hands. Give me one moment with my fingers around his neck!

The sorcerer's smile grows impossibly crueler. My attempts to reach him are futile, as the filth who hold me give no ground.

"And to think, Lord Erick," Synomea says. "You have been killing those you try so dearly to save."

I grind my teeth as the Zumarians maintain their grips on me, and glare at the bastard. He grows addled, to be sure.

He nods to the beasts that have their claws clamped firmly onto my arms. "Those who have you in their grasp now were once the young of Oldworld. After many years on this planet they gradually become the Zumar." Synomea leans closer. "And you murder them."

My skin grows cold. Lies. Aye, he speaks naught but lies.

Yet even as my mind rejects his words, I realize them to be true. My gut sickens. Every time I have killed a Zumarian, I have murdered one who was once of Oldworld. And even now—if I survive—to save my kin and other Oldworlders, I may be forced to kill more of these pitiful creatures. Perhaps they are better off dead than to live such a life. But how can I make such a choice?

The sorcerer laughs as he surely sees the anger flash across my face. Then his features grow stone cold. "Tell me where my daughter is," he says, "and where you have hidden the crescent crystal."

He truly does not have it? "I do not know where it is." Could one of my friends have betrayed me and taken the pendant from Taryn?

Synomea scowls. "I demand you tell me where the crystal and my daughter are, or I will torment you until you scream for mercy."

I stare at him, refusing to answer.

Synomea's face turns the dark shade of his wrath, and one eye spasms. "Tell me!"

The warriors' claws clench my arms harder, until I no longer have feeling in them. "I do not know where Taryn or the crystal are. You may torture me until I die, but you will never have your answer. I would not tell you if I did know."

Synomea shakes, his body trembling like leaves in a storm. He grunts to the warriors and they drag me to him as he turns to the table of containers. The Zumarian's grip on my neck tightens and I can hardly breathe, so secure is the arm against my throat.

The sorcerer takes a puzzle box from the table and withdraws a peg. He pushes aside the lid and reveals a scarlet powder within. "This will bring a slow, painful death, as it did to your father."

At his words, sweat breaks out on my body, but I work to keep my expression impassive.

He slips the peg into the box and sets it on the table. "One touch of it to your forehead and you die, for there is no cure."

Synomea picks up an ivory bowl and removes the cover. A reddish brown dust lies inside. "When I spread this across your forehead, you will feel the most excruciating pain you have ever felt in your miserable, insignificant life. The agony will continue and continue, and it will feel as though it shall never end."

Even if I could tell the beast the answers he seeks, I wouldn't. But the look in his eyes curdles my blood.

I do not speak.

"So be it," he says.

Synomea dips his forefinger in the powder and advances. I refuse to close my eyes or flinch. I refuse to let him know the fear twisting inside.

The moment he touches my forehead, flame engulfs me. My head burns, my body is on fire. Pain sears every fiber of my being. A thousand knives stab me and flay my flesh from my bones.

I jerk, thrashing against the grip of the Zumarians. Cries spill from my throat. A screech fills my ears.

Blood oozes from my nose. From my mouth. From my ears. My heart slams against my rib cage.

*Gods! Help me!*

---

*Taryn*

How do these people sleep on stone? Granted, I did spend one night on a dungeon floor, but I was unconscious. I turn to lie on my back, the small blanket Cole gave me tucked under my head. He's at the mouth of the cave on watch, then it'll be Van's turn. Of course, no one would let me do it—so much for treating me as one of them.

Snores from the knights fill the cave. It sounds like a monster truck rally and smells like a boys' locker room. I'll never get to sleep, not that I could anyway.

All I can think about is Erick. No matter how I try, I can't reach him—the l'apitak is useless. I don't even feel his presence when I touch it. No tingle, no warmth.

And what about my pendant? I never did believe Erick could've taken it, but then who? It must be someone connected to everything that's happened. Could it be one of these knights?

Whatever happens next, I'll stop at nothing to free Erick, and then deal with Synomea. And after that, nothing will matter, anyway, because it's likely I won't survive.

I no longer am afraid of what I must do.

The realization surprises me. For so long I've lived in fear —fear of losing my hearing, of not fitting in, of being alone. And fear from all that has happened to me since that first night the Zumarian tried to take me.

Fear that has made me doubt myself and my abilities.

None of that matters anymore. There's only me now. Me and the right thing to do, fear be damned.

I wish I could see what's going on with Synomea and Erick. Wait—mind-flight! I have the dust and I can try to use it on my own. But what if someone wakes and sees me? I roll over toward Van, who's facing me, her chest rising and falling as she sleeps. She has such an incredible inner strength that's obvious by the way she carries herself. She's so pretty, her eyes the same silvery gray as Erick's. She has some of the same mannerisms, but those are the only resemblances I've noticed.

If Van hates me for being the daughter of her father's killer, she hides it well. She's been so nice, sticking up for me when everyone else would just as soon tie me up and leave me to rot in this cave. If Van would wake, maybe she could help me.

She opens her eyes and looks straight into mine—a coincidence? No. It's like we're linked and she knows what I'm thinking. Van scoots up and motions for me to follow to where Cole is keeping watch. We're at the edge of the sleepers, so we don't have to step over anyone to get to the entrance, which is far enough we should be able to talk without being overheard.

Cole raises his brows, but gets up and heads into the cave. A man of few words, I've gathered. As he passes me, I feel a strange sensation, almost a magnetic pull. I shake off the feeling and crouch down at the cave's entrance. I almost wish I could hear his thoughts, but somehow I can't get a read on anyone in this group.

The storm has ended, and all around us rain-washed lava rock gleams in the dull sunlight. I rest with my back against the cave wall and study the strange device on my wrist that Erick called a na'tan. Pale green symbols crowd the na'tan's surface, but I don't know what any of them mean.

When I glance up at Van, I see her wince as she sinks down, favoring her injured leg. The soft light raises chestnut highlights in her hair. "What are you thinking, sister?" she asks.

Her use of the familiar term floors me, and I can tell she means it as a form of acceptance. She's loving, like Erick, but so different. She has a calm, soothing personality, yet there's a spark in her eyes that shows she's definitely not someone to mess with.

"I'm sorry Synomea killed your father." It isn't what I meant to say, but there it is.

*My father killed your father.*

Resting one hand on her knee, Van relaxes against the cave wall. Her black leather pants are ripped at her thigh, and a bloody bandage is tied around the wound. I catch the sinus-clearing smell of tea tree oil.

"Taryn, do not let that trouble you. It was a long time ago, when Erick and I were babes. His death was no fault of yours."

Outside, the sun forces its way through clouds of volcanic ash, and I feel its warmth. "You know I love Erick, don't you? I'd do anything to save him."

"Aye. He feels the same for you."

A long shuddering sigh, and I realize how tired I am. "After what I told him, I doubt he cares for me now."

Van leans forward and takes one of my hands. Hers are cal-loused, her fingers long and tapered. "Erick is passionate and headstrong and, more often than not, reckless. But he is a good man. Even if he is confused by your admission, he does love you."

I nod, but can't help thinking he's finished with me. That's if we make it through this alive. Once again, I reach for the comfort of my missing pendant, then drop my hand to my lap. "Why are you being so nice to me, especially after finding out who my father is?"

"I love my brother with all my heart." She squeezes my fingers. "Because you are important to him, you are also im-portant to me. You had no choice in who fathered you, and you were not raised by him." With a smile, she continues, "I sense you do love my brother and will do whatever you can to save him."

"Thank you for your trust." I return her smile, trying not to fall apart at the thought of Erick now in the sorcerer's hands. "I need to confide in you, so you'll understand what I must do."

Van releases my hand and settles back against the cave wall. I launch into a terse explanation of what happened over the past week, since the night when the Zumar captured me. I'm blunt, not glossing anything over, even the truth about her father and my mother, and Synomea's deceit, because it's important she knows. I push up my sleeve to show her the birthmark again, and she flinches.

"I believe all you say, even without the sign. I thank you for your trust." Van glances into the cave like she's making sure no one listens. "I, too, have something to share with you."

She tells me about a couple of wizards named L'iwanda and L'onten and a prophecy of the Crescent and the Lion, and the Crescent's choice.

*"By the fire of Navran and the power of the crystals,"* she recites, *"on Allhallows Eve, under the light of the moons, loyalties will be tested and blood shall spill. And be it love or power, good or evil, the choice of the Crescent and the will of the Lion seal the destiny of Zanea."*

When she's finished, I study her gray eyes. "You believe I'm the Crescent of the prophecy."

"Aye."

"And midnight tonight is Allhallows Eve."

She nods.

I take a deep breath. She's laid a lot on me to think about.

"What is it you need to do now, Taryn?"

"Mind-flight." I pull out the vitamin box. The rainbow of powders looks benign and almost beautiful through the plas-

248

tic. I pop open the tab for Sunday. "I need to see what Synomea's up to, and if I can find Erick. Just keep an eye out so no one comes near while I do this."

I dab one finger in the powder and snap the lid of the box shut with my free hand, and stuff the holder into my jacket pocket.

She watches as I spread the indigo powder from my wrist to the pad of my middle finger, then down my forehead to the tip of my nose.

Warmth spreads throughout me, and then I'm flying across the wastelands. In a matter of moments I'm in the fortress, heading straight for the green room. In through the doors . . .

*NO! Erick!*

When I realize I'm back from the mind-flight, I'm in Van's arms, sobbing uncontrollably. She strokes my hair, whispering soothing words I don't understand and rocking me the way Gran used to when I was little.

"It's all my f-fault. All my fault! I—I should have made you both leave, at once!"

"Shhh, Taryn. No blame lies on you. Erick never would have left you." She hesitates. "Tell me, does he live?"

I nod and sob, and she exhales her relief. Indigo tears spill onto my shirt, and I've smudged the powder all over Van's arm. Strangely, I have the presence of mind to pull the napkin out of my pocket, and as I wipe the watery dust from Van and myself, I tell her everything I saw. Her mouth grows tight and she stiffens with anger.

"That monster! That bastard!" Van clenches her fists and her eyes flash fury.

She takes a deep breath, leans back, and lowers her eyelids. For a long moment she doesn't speak. Finally she says, "We can do nothing now. We must sleep." She opens her eyes and checks the sun's position. "Half a day yet remains."

I tuck the tear-soaked napkin into my pocket. "I can't sleep. Not after what I've seen."

Gracefully, Van gets to her feet and disappears into the cave, then returns with her knapsack. She digs in it, then pulls out a small vial. "If you cannot sleep, at least relax. A little on the tongue will calm your nerves."

It smells of California poppies and chamomile, but tastes like sour dirt. Even as I stand to go back in the cave, I know I've been had. My head spins, my feet feel like bricks, and Van supports me as my legs turn to spaghetti. As soon as she lays my head on the blanket, I'm out.

*Lion is missing. All my dream beasts prowl the lava fields except him.*

*Blackness shrouds the night, not even the light of the twin moons to see by.*

*Yet I visualize each beast so clearly. I walk beside them, an eerie green mist swirling at my bare feet, pointed rocks jabbing my soles.*

*They don't know the power I hold, don't know how dangerous I am.*

*Bear roars, a plaintive cry that echoes across the wasteland. Tiger limps beside Bear, turning her elegant head to see what lies behind. Yes, her. Tiger is Van.*

*Bull, Serpent, and Scorpion follow Bear and Tiger. Friends? They've always been friends. These beasts must be Cole, Finella, Basil and Gareth, but I can't quite make out whom each represents, except Tiger.*

*Who is Scorpion, the traitor? And Serpent, who wishes to own Lion, who wrapped its body around him in my past vision?*

*Something glitters in Bear's paw. Something familiar . . .*

## October 30, afternoon

*Erick*

Thunder fills my head. Drums of Nar pound, the beat strong and never-ending. Pounding. Pounding. Pounding. Louder and louder yet, until I fear my brain will ooze from my ears. My flesh burns; agony sears me. Surely my very soul is on fire.

Even the torchlight creeping through the window's bars is too bright for my eyes. I squeeze them shut, then try to open them. Again and again I lift my lids a slit, then close. Over and over I work to be able to keep my eyes open. I do not know how long it has been before my eyes no longer cringe from the light.

When I can keep my lids open, I look around the dungeon. The slightest movement sends fresh bouts of pain throughout my body, but I force myself.

One muscle, then another, screams agony. First, my head and my neck. The drums hammer louder, but I ignore them. I move my fingers, one at a time, down to my thumb, and each cries its pain as though Synomea smashed every bone.

Now my wrist. It is torture to move it, but a shred of hope takes hold as I realize the beasts did not manacle my arms. In his arrogance, the sorcerer surely thinks I will be too weak to escape his prison.

Time passes as I struggle to regain control of my body and to build the strength I shall need. To fuel my determination, I remember the sorcerer's leer and his wicked laugh as he tortured me. And with satisfaction I recall Synomea's fury when I still did not answer his questions even as I writhed in agony.

I do not know why he did not kill me with his scarlet death powder or why I still live—unless he intends to use me to draw my friends to him. It is likely they will attempt my rescue.

When I have moved every muscle in my body, I still cannot rise from the floor, my body feeling as if encased in lead armor. Sleep calls me, seducing me. I try to fend it off, but it drags me deeper and deeper, into the darkest pit.

---

A rattle wakens me, followed by the drums throbbing in my head. Keeping my eyes shut, I bite back a curse. The scrape of metal against stone rakes my mind like the clawed hands of the Zumar.

When it is silent again, I open my eyes, blinking away the light, and am pleased I am able to keep them open. Pain spears me as I turn my head to see a tray of food has been shoved under the door. My belly rumbles and cramps seize me. Even my innards torture me yet.

My muscles still ache, daggers twisting in every one. But I force them to move. Ever so slowly, I roll over. Even if I do not eat, I need to move, need to regain control over my body. I drag myself to the tray. If I take what is there, Synomea will know I can move. But if I do not eat, I may not have the strength to recover.

Shards of glass feel imbedded in my flesh, shifting and slicing with every movement I make. As I crawl, I notice dried blood on my hands. My face itches as my sweat mingles with the blood caked beneath my nose and on my lips.

By the time I reach the tray, my body sinks into exhaustion and I cannot lift my head. I rest my brow on my forearm and spiral into blackness.

---

Bristles poke my face and I open one eye to see an enormous rat. All the anger that has been building up within, all that I have been unable to vent, spills forth. I sweep my arm from under my head, and shove the rat away from me. It gives a loud screech, then scurries into a dark corner. I see its red eyes blink, then the creature disappears.

The moment of anger costs me. I grit my teeth at the pain that vibrates my arm and shoulder. Damn! Will this torment never end?

This time I will sit, no matter the consequence. Gods! Every fraction I move tortures me. My breath comes in heavy gasps. My body burns hot, a raging fire sweeping over me. Beads of sweat roll down my forehead to my eyes, causing them to sting and burn. I blink, but dare not rub them.

At last, I am up, my back to the wall beside the tray. Swords stab my lungs with every rise and fall of my chest, and an anvil lies on my breast. I close my eyes, fighting off the black sleep that wants to claim me again.

When my heart no longer threatens to burst my rib cage with its pounding, I force my eyes to study the tray. The rat beast must have enjoyed a good portion of the bread, but left the pottage alone. At least I think it is a vegetable stew, though the things inside it are of strange colors and textures.

My hand trembles and pain wrenches my body as my fingers close around the bread. I tear off the end untouched by the rat and bring it to my mouth.

Gods! Curse Synomea! Even my jaws and teeth ache as I chew. Slow bite after slow bite, I finish the strange-tasting bread.

I lean over the tray to eat the pottage. My hands do not have the strength yet to lift the bowl, so I raise the wooden spoon. The stew is cold and tastes odd, but it calms the rumbling in my belly and I feel more of my health return. The cup of water is almost too heavy to lift, and I spill some of the fluid onto the stone floor. It is bitter, but assuages my thirst.

With the movements of an aged man, I recline my head against the wall and notice the pain racking my body has lessened.

Now to find some way to get close enough to the sorcerer, find Navran, and run the blade through the bastard's gut.

When I am rested, I work to stand, bracing myself against the wall. My muscles refuse me. The feeling of glass ripping my flesh is my constant companion, but I cannot stop, cannot yield. My kneecaps feel crushed, beaten by a sledgehammer and ground to pulp, but I continue. Every small movement is a victory. Every fraction brings me closer to vengeance.

At last, I am on my feet. The wall still supports me, but I stand. Sweat soaks my body and it is difficult to breathe. I attempt to take a step, but my knees threaten to buckle.

I wait. Wait to reclaim my strength. Wait to master my body.

I take a deep breath and push away from the wall. My muscles tremble and crumple. My head strikes stone. Darkness descends.

## Taryn

When I wake, it's late afternoon. Green fire still brightens the room, but the knights are outside the cave entrance.

"Sleep well, Taryn?" Van's smile is warm when I come outside, but her eyes are shadowed.

"Yeah, thanks." I attempt a smile and jerk my thumb toward a group of boulders. "I need a moment's privacy behind a lava rock."

She nods and as I pass Cole, I feel that odd magnetic pull again. As I head past all the knights I can feel them watching me, the "Oldworlder" girl. I bet they're all wondering why Erick would fall for someone like me.

But I don't care anymore. I am who I am, and I no longer feel insecure about my appearance. What they think of me no longer matters. What anyone thinks of me, for that matter.

Except Erick. Inside, I know Erick cares about me. There's a connection between us, strong and vibrant.

Before I return to the cave entrance and have to face all of the knights, I lean back against a rock wall and close my eyes. I feel a need to postpone the moment I'll have to be around those men and women. I want a few moments alone with my own thoughts.

It's my fault Synomea tortured Erick. If only I had insisted they leave! If I had run back to the sorcerer, Erick could have gotten away. Then he wouldn't have gone through what he did at my father's hand.

In my dream last night, Bear had the crystal. What did it mean when Serpent wrapped its body around Lion in one of my previous dreams? Does Serpent wish to kill Erick or own him?

I open my eyes, intending to start back to the cave and return to the others, but Finella rounds the corner and blocks my path. "Erick has no real feelings for you," she says with a smirk. "He only desired the crystal."

By force of habit I reach for my pendant, then drop my hand. "That's not true."

"You are nothing to him." Finella's smile is cold. "Erick loves me."

My thoughts buzz and for a moment I feel lightheaded. I close my eyes. Did Finella steal my pendant to give to Erick, because she's in love with him? I take a deep breath and open my eyes. "Did you take my crystal?"

Shock crosses her face, and I can tell she's genuinely surprised by my question. "Watch your tongue, Oldworlder."

Who has my crystal?

I sigh and try to rein in my emotions. "What do you want, Finella?"

She tosses her head back. "I want you to leave and return to your own world."

"I am of both worlds. My mother was from Oldworld. My father is from Zanea."

"You lie!"

"Taryn speaks the truth."

Finella and I whirl to see Van standing behind us.

Her lips are tight, her gaze deadly, the wound on her temple an angry slash against her pale skin. "You will cease these attacks upon Taryn. She is one of us now."

For several seconds Finella stares at Van, her jaw set, her eyes defiant. Just when I think she's going to walk away, Finella says to Van, "Only for you." Her gaze flicks back to me. "Is it true? You do not have the crescent crystal?"

I nod. "I dreamed last night that one of you has it."

Finella's face flushes. "How dare you!"

"Do you know who?" Van asks, her tone low and controlled.

It clicks. The boot print like Erick's, only bigger. That he knows where I live and had plenty of opportunity to come to my home, probably right behind Erick. And the magnetic pull I felt when I passed him—my crystal calling to me.

"I think Cole has it," I say.

"You lying filth!" Finella shouts.

"No. Not Cole." Van's face pales and she shakes her head. "He would never steal from another—least of all Erick's love."

"Stop defending me, Van. I took the damnable thing." The deep male voice comes from behind us, and we all spin to see Cole.

"Cole?" Van whispers. "It is true? You stole the crystal from Taryn?"

The guy hangs his head. "I did it for you and Erick. You mean more to me than—" He drags his hand over his mouth and sighs. "I was wrong."

"How could you?" Van clenches her fists and walks up to Cole. "You as good as betrayed us!"

Finella looks from Cole to me. "He only did what each of us wanted to do, but dared not."

Van spins on Finella. "It was wrong!"

Cole's face crumples. He looks so sad, my heart goes out to him.

I reach out and touch his arm and feel the pull of my crystal, even stronger than before. "Cole, thank you for your honesty."

He looks at me, his black eyes meeting mine. "My apologies . . . Taryn."

With a smile, I say, "In all truth, if it wasn't for you, the sorcerer would now have the crescent—because he would have taken it after he captured me."

A flicker of relief passes over his face. He reaches into his pocket and pulls out a leather pouch, and I hold out my hand.

Like warm summer rain, relief pours through me. Everything and everyone around me ceases to exist as the crystal slips from the bag to my palm.

A charge like lightning rips through me the moment the pendant touches my hand. Intense energy. Wind picks up and swirls around us. Faster and faster. My sorcery is far more powerful than before. I close my eyes as magic flows within my veins.

Incredible, frightening thoughts swirl in my mind.

*I am powerful. I rule this world.*

When I lift my lids, I see Finella holding her fingers to her mouth, her eyes wide, her black hair floating in the wind. Cole steps back. Van stands straight and tall, her gaze never wavering from mine.

Finella drops her hand. "Her eyes. By the gods, they glow!"

"She is a sorceress," Cole murmurs.

258

Van nods. "Aye."

I barely hear them. Chittering insects, dirtying insignificant ground. What do they matter now? What did they ever matter?

*No!*

The sorcery rages within me, a tempest. A hurricane. Battering my soul, demanding entrance—

*No. No!*

*I am Taryn.*

*Daughter of Stacie.*

*Granddaughter of Laura.*

*I reject the wickedness of my father.*

*I reject his ways, his endless evil.*

*I am not the Sorceress Ta'reen.*

*I am Taryn.*

*Taryn!*

Van, Finella, and Cole come back into focus. Humans. Beautiful, breathing humans. The energy within me calms. Or, rather, I lock it away deep within and refuse its call. In my mind, I fasten a lid of immeasurable weight atop the storm and give it a latch only I can open. A bit at a time.

My hair settles about my shoulders.

The wind dies . . .

Finella sighs and her shoulders relax. "The glow is gone." She looks to Van. "Tell me what this means."

"Taryn is the Crescent the wizards spoke of. The one who will deliver us from Synomea."

"Or rule in his place." Finella scowls. "The prophecy speaks of the Crescent's choice."

"No." Van gazes at me, trust in her eyes. "Taryn will choose what is right."

Cole grunts, and I can't tell who he agrees with.

After I clasp the chain around my neck and the crystal lies at my throat, I ask Finella and Cole, "Do you stand with me, or not?"

Finella glances to Van, and then to me. "If Van stands with you, then I shall also."

Cole nods. "Aye. For Van and Erick."

"Do the others know?" Finella asks.

Van runs her hand over her braid. "No."

"And we can't tell them." I wrap my fingers around the crystal at my neck. "One of them is a traitor."

Finella's cheeks redden and her eyes flash. "Do not dare to accuse one of us!"

Cole furrows his brow, his gaze intent on me.

Van's eyes widen. "Who?"

Did I make a mistake in saying that? What if Finella or Cole is the traitor? But no—the traitor is Scorpion. Now I'm sure Cole is Bear, who had the crystal, and Finella is Serpent, who longs to have Lion for her own.

I shake my head. "I'm not sure."

"Lies!" Finella says.

Like enormous claws strangling my chest, my anger mounts. The lid on my sorcery rattles. No, I cannot afford trivial emotions now. Such little irritations will have to go.

"We don't have time for this," I say. "Are you with me, or not?"

"Aye," Van replies without hesitation.

Cole folds his arms and gives a single nod.

Finella stares at me for endless seconds. She shakes her head and sighs. "Only for Van and Erick. Aye."

## October 30, evening

*Erick*

> *By the fire of Navran . . . and the power of the crystals . . . on Allhallows Eve . . . under the light of the moons . . . loyalties will be tested . . . blood shall spill . . . and be it love or power . . . good or evil . . . the choice of the Crescent . . . and the will of the Lion . . . seal the destiny of Zanea.*

The scrape of the tray against stone wakes me once again. I remain still, the wizards' words echoing in my mind. I have no concept of the true passage of time, yet something tells me it will soon be Allhallows Eve.

The Crescent—Taryn must be the Crescent!

Is it her choice that will seal Zanca's destiny? Then we may well be doomed since she is Synomea's daughter.

Yet my heart cannot believe Taryn is evil—cannot believe she would betray me, would betray our love.

When it is quiet, I pull to a sitting position. My mind spins, but it soon passes. Drums no longer beat upon my skull, and I can bear the ache in my limbs. It seems the evil sorcery has worked its course and is leaving my body.

Sitting with my back against the wall, I eat from the tray. The fare is the same as before, except the pottage is lukewarm rather than cold. This time when I stand, my legs tremble but hold me. With care I stumble around my prison, testing my strength and stretching my limbs. I am not yet re-covered, but I am closer.

To get out of this dungeon and to retrieve my sword, I must form a plan. Synomea displayed my sword in his velvet room, as if to gloat over stealing it from me. In his arrogance, I am sure he would never believe I could recover it. I will do everything in my power to regain what belongs to me and to have my vengeance.

That vengeance burns heavy in my gut, outweighing the fire that still blisters my limbs.

I test the strength of the door and check the hinges. All appear solid, the fastenings made of iron. The cell is dark, and it is difficult to see. Slowly, I work my way around the room, searching for some way to escape.

The rat I saw earlier was as large as Xen when he was a pup. Where could such an enormous beast have come from? I continue working my way around the cell until I come to the darkest corner. A stench rises from the floor, but I see noth-ing in the darkness. I crouch and run my hand over the filth. Just as I am about to abandon my search, my hand brushes over a hole in the rock floor. It is perhaps the size of a small plate.

Cool air comes up through the hole, and the stink it car-ries is overpowering. I pull at the surrounding rock and find it crumbles a bit in my hand, a brittle material that was used to patch a larger hole.

Hope glimmers within me. The torchlight spilling through the door's bars is too weak to reach this corner, and it is too dark to see what lies below. But the smells of urine and waste tell me it must be the sewer.

Never before have I welcomed such. My body still com-plains as I work at enlarging the hole, but I ignore the pain.

Sweat pours down my face as I work. My hands bleed and my fingers cramp. I begin to wonder if it shall ever be large enough to make my escape.

Finally, the opening is as large around as my shoulders, but I will need light. I select one of the larger rocks I pried from the opening, then close my eyes and draw on the Old Magic. I set flame to the top of the stone; the warmth of the rock-fire nears my fingers, but does not burn me.

I hold it in the hole so I can see. Rock-fire is not true fire, and holds no peril near dangerous fumes. The flames reflect on a green surface several feet below, and a path wide enough for a Trendorian rat slopes into the darkness.

After I set the rock-fire beside the opening, I test the sides of the hole. The edges crumble, pieces falling into the sewage. I am not sure it will bear my weight. The Zumar have already brought my dinner, so I hope they will not return for some time, and will not discover my escape until it is too late.

While I ease my legs into the hole, I take a deep breath. I try to steady my boots on the rat path, but it crumbles. My muscles scream as I lower myself through the opening.

Rock disintegrates beneath my palms and I fall into the blackness below. I land on my feet, but my legs are still weak and I slip onto my backside in the muck. Sewage surrounds me, sloshing my face, seeping into my tunic and breeches. I struggle to get to my feet, slip and flail, but manage to brace myself against a wall.

For the love of Nar, the stench is overwhelming and I can hardly breathe. The rock-fire still burns above, close enough I am able to grab it from the edge of the opening. Thank the gods it did not fall, for I see no other stones in this place.

After I take the rock-fire from its purchase, I slog through muck in the direction I believe the turret lies. I must find my way into the keep and to the velvet room where Synomea holds Navran. As bad as I stink, I fear the sorcerer and the Zumar will smell me before I can recover what is mine.

With one palm along the wall, I tread carefully, my other hand holding the rock-fire. Its green glow exposes only more moldering stone around and above me. Several times my boots slip, and I struggle to avoid falling into the waste. My clothing is wet and heavy, my boots filled with sewage, and my many wounds burn. Even if I should live through my encounter with the sorcerer, I may die from infection.

I hear nothing but the sound of my own breathing, my boots sloshing, and a steady drip coming from ahead. It serves as a beacon, and I work toward it as I try to ignore the stench of my surroundings, my itching face and limbs, and the feel of sewage coating my body.

Ages pass as I travel through waste. At long last, I see light ahead and hear a steady whir and hum, then silence. When I reach the light source, I am below an iron grate, and water or sewage drips from the opening. Torches spit and hiss, and their glow flickers in a shadowed room above. No other sounds meet my ears. No movement above. I look for some place to set the rock-fire, but find none.

Using my free hand, I pull on the grate. It refuses to budge. My frustration mounts as I struggle with the grate. I try to use both hands, but the rock-fire slips from my grasp— it tumbles into the sewage and its fire extinguishes. With my hands around the bars of the iron grille, I drag downward with all my strength, but to no avail.

"Damn!" I curse before I can curb my tongue. I stop to listen for movement above, but silence meets my ears, thank the gods.

The darkness ahead taunts me. Without my rock-fire, I will be as blind as serpents in the Neguriän Sea. At least they have cunning and intelligence.

For the love of Nar. Cunning and intelligence, indeed! Surely the sorcerer's powder addled my brain and has made me daft.

This time when I grab the grille, I push up with all my strength. I hear a thick sound, like the suck of mud, then a rusted scrape.

For endless seconds I hold my breath, but nothing stirs. When I push the grate aside, the clatter of metal against stone follows. I wait again, but I hear only silence.

Water trickles on my face as I grip the edges of the opening and hoist myself upward. My muscles vibrate and complain while I work to raise my body through the opening. When I am finally sitting on a rock floor I rest, my limbs crying relief. After I roll away from the opening, I replace the grate. I glance up and see I am in the Zumarian portal room.

The chamber is bare, save for a platform, the command, and a cage. Water dribbles from the platform's base to the grate at my feet. It is apparent the Zumar use water to power their portals. Interesting they do not rely completely on magic to dispatch to Oldworld, like we of Newold do.

I hear a whir and hum. Boots pound stone, coming my way. I dive into darkness.

## Taryn

Sorcery burns in my breast, fueled by the crescent crystal. Wicked thoughts consume me—that if I were to develop my magic to its full extent, I could squash these pitiful knights with just a breath. A whisper. The depth of my sorcery would be unimaginable.

What am I becoming? Why can't I control these terrible feelings coursing within me?

I walk with Van, Finella, and Cole around the corner of rock toward the other knights who are still in front of the cave. Which one is the Scorpion, the traitor? I've narrowed it down to either Gareth or Basil. How can I learn who Scorpion is before it's too late?

"I have a plan," I say as the knights and I move inside the cave and gather around the rock-fire.

Basil twirls his sword point on the cave floor in a constant rhythmic motion. His pale green eyes focus on me.

"Why should we listen to you?" The shaggy guy, Gareth, says.

"Because I wish it." Van eyes Gareth with a look that would wither an oak. "It is my command. You will follow my instruction, or you will stay behind."

Cole raises his brows and grunts. I'm not sure what that means.

Finella says nothing.

I hold my head high and look into each person's eye, one after another. "This is what we'll do."

When I've outlined each person's part in the plan, the knights look from one to the other and shake their heads, but they don't argue or complain.

After we review the plan once again, it's time to set it in motion. It's still light enough to see as Finella, Van, and I head toward the mine. Basil, Gareth, and Cole remain behind and will handle their part later.

But who is the traitor?

And do I have what it takes to pull this off?

Yes, I can do this. I *must*.

---

It took us a good hour to reach the fortress.

Finella, Van, and I creep close to the mine and crouch behind lava rocks, watching slaves bring their loads from the depths. I take careful notice of how they look—tattered brown robes, unkempt hair, and worn sandals.

I see a familiar form and it's all I can do not to rush over to Jen. She struggles with a basket of rocks she carries out of the mine toward the fortress. She gazes straight ahead with no expression on her face. Pink mind-control powder shimmers on her forehead.

My hands tremble and my skin prickles with fury at what Synomea has done to my friend. With great difficulty, I force myself to control my raging emotions and turn back to my companions. I pull out my tablet box and flip open the lid that covers the white powder. "Now the way this works—I put a touch of it to your forehead, and you will look like the slave I imagine you to be."

"What?" Finella backs away.

"Look," I say with irritation in my voice, "I can't go in there with you two towering Amazons—we'd stick out. And someone might recognize me. You've got to trust me or this isn't going to work."

Van settles next to me. "I'm ready."

I dab the powder on Van's chin, each cheek and forehead, and then I back away as the air around her sparkles. The wound vanishes from her forehead and the scratches from her arms. Her face shifts from oval-shaped to round, her gray eyes to hazel, and her hair from long brunette to shoulder-length blonde. Worn brown robes cover her black leather clothing.

Finella gasps. "What kind of sorcery is this?"

"Sorcery that will get us into the fortress without Synomea knowing about it." I put my finger into the powder. "Are you ready?"

She hesitates, then nods. I apply the dust to her face and almost grin as I watch her turn from slender goddess into someone rather short, dumpy, and just a wee bit homely.

Van snickers.

Finella raises a bushy brow. "What?"

"Um—that worked great," I say, glancing away from the hair on Finella's chin. I repeat the transformation process on myself. I choose someone a little more comely to transform into, and brown robes cover my own clothing. I reach underneath and find the tablet box of powders in my pocket.

"Your weapons should still be underneath those robes." I turn and focus on one of the water towers, the one beside the pit. "Now I've got to cause a little disturbance . . ."

I concentrate my sorcery, let it swell up within. Warmth floods my limbs and the crystal burns at my throat, intense power soaring through my being. With my magic, I command the elements and pull on the leg of the tower.

The tower rocks back and forth. Like a maestro, as I did in the bedroom, I wave my hands—pulling, pushing, pulling, pushing. Back and forth. Then I yank with all my might. The tower leg snaps, the sound like a gunshot echoing across the wasteland.

A creak of metal and wood, then a roar as the tower collapses and smashes to the ground. Water rumbles and then a wave rushes into the mine. Workers dash out, their clothing soaked, and I hope all are uninjured.

Zumarians growl as they surround the slaves like cowboys rounding up cattle. The transformed Van, Finella, and I slip into the commotion, mixing with the slaves. Even though I can't see her wounds, Van still favors her injured leg. The transformation must be only cosmetic.

The three of us try to keep together as we're herded into the fortress. After we are forced to stand in the courtyard, we're taken to a soup line. It's like in a prison camp movie, where we're served a meager meal of stew and bread. The bread is dry and the stew tasteless, like the stuff I'd been given in the cell, but I eat it to keep up appearances and to renew my strength.

When all the slaves have finished eating, the Zumarians usher us into the barracks. Males are put into one dilapidated building and females into another. My companions and I crouch in one corner of our barracks as the doors are bolted.

"How will we get out of here?" Finella asks when everything has quieted down and we hear only the sounds of snoring around us.

I roll my shoulders, trying to ease some of the tension. "It'll be easier to get out of here than it was to knock down the water tower."

While we wait, I search for Jen. I step over sleeping slaves, one after another, but I can't find her. There are so many! Hundreds. What will happen to them all if we don't succeed?

"Taryn, we must go," Van says as she comes up from behind me, but her voice is faint because she's on the wrong side of me.

"In a moment. I'm looking for someone." Just as I'm about to give up, I see Jen. She's lying asleep on a pallet, her face streaked with dirt, her feet muddy, and her clothes tattered.

Tears prick at the back of my eyes and I want to drop to my knees and cry. My beautiful, generous, loving friend—here, forced to work in the sorcerer's mines.

Synomea will pay.

# October 30, late night

*Erick*

While I hear the footsteps coming closer, I dive behind the cage and flatten myself to the floor. With one cheek pressed to stone, I watch as a Zumarian enters the chamber and goes to the controls. Water rushes the grate and a familiar humming noise grows, and I realize a portal is opening.

A warrior steps through the black portal with an Oldworlder slung over each shoulder. He tosses the two girls into the cage next to another human male. They all remain motionless, as it will be some time before the Zumar grasp wears off.

I hold my breath, hoping the beast will not see me in the shadows. My hair must surely be as black as my clothing, a fine camouflage. But if the beasts have a sense of smell I will be discovered, as I stink badly from the sewer. I long for my dagger or, better yet, for Navran.

The Zumarian returns to the void and vanishes with the portal. My nose itches and I can barely control the urge to sneeze. The other warrior leaves his station, comes to the cage, grabs one of the Oldworlders, then slings her over his shoulder.

The beast pauses and looks around the room, sniffing the air. With a growl, it turns on its heel and leaves.

Air whooshes from my lungs and I sneeze. I hold my breath, but hear no sound save the rushing water. The Oldworlders in the cage lie as silent as the dead. It must be the mid of night, with the warriors pillaging Oldworld of their young.

My gut sickens again as I realize these burnt-out husks were once children of Oldworld—that my fellow knights and I have been killing night after night.

I creep from the room to the turret stairs, and how well I remember them. It was not long ago my face kissed the wood as I was dragged up the stairs. And before that, this is where I kissed Taryn.

I still cannot believe the one I love is Synomea's daughter.

Aye, I still love Taryn. But it tears at my gut that she is the offspring of the vile beast who killed my father.

With a grumble of frustration, I turn my thoughts away from Taryn to the task at hand. My sodden boots make squishing noises as I climb up the turret to that velvet room where I hope Navran waits for me. It is dark and I must make my way with care.

Step by step. Closer and closer to the wooden door. My limbs ache, yet I feel amazing energy, my body celebrating the release of the sorcery. When I open the door it creaks, the sound so loud it harries my ears, and I am afraid the noise will alert Synomea.

Torches burn in metal brackets on each side of the doors to the velvet room. Fury blazes in me at memories of the sorcerer's torture.

I reach the doors and pause. What if Synomea is in this room? Even if I had my dagger, it would be no match for his evil powers. Precious seconds pass as I lean close to the door, but no sounds meet my ear.

When I ease the door open, I see the room is empty. A dying fire burns in the hearth, giving me enough light to see by. My boots squish as I creep across the endless length of the floor. It seems as though the room grows, as in my dream. I reach the chair where Synomea had displayed my sword.

It is gone.

Frustration sweeps me in a frigid gust. "Gods damn," I mutter. What can I do now? If the prophecy is indeed true, I need Navran to defeat this sorcerer.

Drapes are pulled back from a single window and moonlight spills onto the floor. I steal across the room to see what lies below. The moons are full and Mount Zumar glows. Shadows flitter across the wasteland, playing tricks on my eyes. Can it be? Do I see the forms of men moving toward the fortress?

Aye. Three large men ease toward the wall and vanish into the gloom.

Can it be my friends? Where are the others?

I must find Navran! Perhaps Synomea left my sword elsewhere in this room.

My frustration mounts as I search and search and search, below every piece of furniture, upon every table, in every corner.

Navran is nowhere to be found.

A noise outside the doors captures my attention. I crouch behind a chair, not daring to breathe.

"You have his sword?"

*That voice . . . it is so familiar. No, it cannot . . .*

"Of course," Synomea replies. "Where is Ta'reen?"

The voice is muffled, and I strain to hear the words.

". . . had hidden herself amongst the slaves, then let us in. The others are with her now. I believe they intend to set Erick free before they attempt an attack on you."

*Taryn is here? Gods, no! She has led them into a trap!*

"Lord Erick lies in the dungeons, surely too weak to be of any use to them." Synomea chuckles. "And now that I know where Ta'reen is, I will dispose of Lord Erick and the other Haro knights."

"This Taryn wench. You are certain she is of our blood?"

*It cannot be. My trusted friend—he has betrayed us!*

"Yes, my son," Synomea replies. "But unlike you, she carries the sorcerer's mark. With her at my side, I will rule all."

*I shall kill the treacherous bastard with my bare hands!*

My vision turns to red and I grip the back of the chair as though my fingers were wrapped around the betrayer's neck.

Silence, then the traitor speaks. "And what of me?"

"We shall discuss this later. To the courtyard. I must retrieve my daughter."

Footsteps. Then quiet.

For precious seconds I cannot move. A battle rages within. Do I warn my friends now? Or do I seek Navran, then go after the sorcerer and the traitor?

My greatest weapons are surprise and my sword. I must make use of both.

I scurry to my feet and start to head toward the doors, then notice the drapes that hang along the far wall, as if to cover a window.

My dream of the sorceress! I saw this very room and those drapes.

I backtrack, and pull the velvet aside to reveal a door. The moment I open it, a sickly sweet smell overwhelms me—the sorcerer's malodor. Candles, books, and vessels clutter the chamber, a canopied bed at the room's center.

And there, as in my dream, is Navran.

I rush to it and pull it from the sheath.

L'iwanda's runes glitter along the blade. I feel L'onten's magic, stronger than before. It fills me, centering my being, clearing my mind, sharpening my thoughts, strengthening my body.

I fasten my scabbard at my hip, then grab my haversack and slip my dagger into my boot. I do not sheathe Navran— I grasp my sword that has become an extension of my arm.

I hurry from the room and start to pass the window. A sight gives me pause.

In the courtyard, the traitor stands at Synomea's side.

One of my friends lies motionless at the sorcerer's feet.

---

## Taryn

After I use my sorcery to unlock the slaves' quarters, Van, Finella, and I sneak through shadows along the curtain wall to the postern door, trying to stay out of the light of the twin moons. The slaves' barracks are close to the door that leads to the mines. In his overconfidence, apparently Synomea still does not keep guards on watch.

Before I open the postern door to let in the other knights, I concentrate on reversing the transformation spell on myself. It's a strange feeling, like my features turn to putty. I glance down see the brown robes have vanished and I'm back in my jeans.

The postern door is locked, so I delve into my sorcery and release the locking mechanism. The door creaks as I open it, so loud I'm afraid it's going to bring the Zumar running.

Cole, Basil, and Gareth slip in the door.

"The Old Magic would not work on this lock," Cole grumbles.

Then the three pause at the sight of Van and Finella.

"What?" Finella asks.

"Who are these girls?" Gareth demands.

"Oops. I forgot." I turn to Van and put my hands to her forehead. Warmth fills me as I concentrate on reversing the magic of the transformation powder. Sparkles snap around Van and she grows taller and returns to her normal appearance, down to the scab on her forehead.

Gareth backs up. "Sorcery! Wickedness!"

Basil stands still as stone, watching me.

Cole shakes his head and grunts.

"Silence," Van says. "We must hurry. We do not have time for questions."

"What about me?" Finella says.

I sigh. I rather like her as a frumpy, pudgy girl. But I place my hands to her forehead and work the magic. Again the black-haired, blue-eyed goddess towers over me, and I feel like I'm the homely girl she transformed from.

"Come on." I motion for everyone to follow. "Erick's probably in the dungeon. We need to sneak into the keep and go to the turret that leads to the cells."

We stay to the shadows and slip into the kitchen. I light a small fire in my palm and the purple glow gives us enough light to see by. I take them to the door that will take us into the kitchen, then to the turret. I'm amazed at how quiet these enormous men and Amazon women are as they follow me. All are silent, save for the gentle sound of breathing, the occasional brush of clothing, and the faint tap of boot against stone.

276

Apprehension creeps up the back of my neck, as if someone is sticking needles into it like a pincushion. Is it Synomea, searching for us? Does he know we're here? I've tried to keep a shield around us, but it's been hard to concentrate on it all the time.

When I open the turret door, it creaks and I catch my breath. "Only two of us should go to the dungeon. The rest stay here."

"I will free Erick," Cole says.

"No." Van shakes her head. "Taryn and I will fetch Erick. You remain with the rest."

A trickle of sweat rolls down the small of my back as I glance at the knights. "Where are Basil and Gareth?"

We look at each other and I sense the uncertainty flooding everyone in tidal waves.

"They were behind me," Finella says.

With a grim look, Van says, "Cole and Finella, watch your backs. I fear one of our friends may be a traitor, if not both of them."

Van and I slip through the turret door, the purple fire in my palm lighting the way. Since we're starting from the ground floor, the distance is half as long as it was from the green room.

When we reach the portal chamber, I hear a low whir and hum. I clench my fist and extinguish the fire in my hand, and hold my breath as we stay back in the shadows and wait. A minute later a Zumarian strides by, carrying an Oldworlder over his shoulder. He moves into the darkness toward the dungeon and disappears.

As Van begins to step forward, I grab her by her arm. "Wait. Give me a second."

I close my eyes and let myself try to feel Erick's presence. Somehow I know he's not in there, or he's—no. I won't even allow myself to think that way.

Where could he be? Did he escape? Surely Synomea didn't . . . no. Please, no.

"Erick's not in the dungeon," I say to Van. "I'm not sure where he is. We should go back to the others."

Van's lips tighten and she nods. She still limps, but she makes better time than I do. We hurry up the stairs, through the turret door and to the kitchen.

Cole and Finella are gone.

"By the gods!" Van mutters.

The door leading from the kitchen to the outside hangs open, moonlight pouring in. We pass the wooden crate of Ta'sha eggs. I stop to crack one open and quickly swallow the fluid while Van watches me with a frown. I slip another egg into my pocket.

Power . . . such power!

A man's strangled cry meets my ears. Van and I hurry to the door, and my heart beats faster.

Synomea stands in the courtyard, illuminated by the light of the twin moons.

Gareth is lying at his feet, completely still. Cole and Finella are on their knees before Synomea, stripped of their swords and na'tans.

Basil is standing at the sorcerer's side, his cruel grin a perfect match to Synomea's own snarling smile. Obviously Basil is the traitor, the Scorpion in my dreams.

At least a hundred Zumar warriors stand behind the sorcerer.

Van tenses at my side.

I expect to feel terror, but a strange calmness eases my mind. The power from the Ta'sha, the crescent crystal, and my burgeoning sorcery all combine to make me confident and feel so, so very powerful.

Now is the time I have been working toward. I will confront Synomea.

This must end now. Tonight, everything ends for the sorcerer . . . and for me.

Can I do it? What if I fail?

Or what if I succumb to the sorcery—let it rule me so I might be a powerful and terrible sorceress?

I take a deep breath. Synomea turns his head and looks straight at me.

"Ah, Ta'reen. Come out, my daughter. And bring the Haro wench with you."

Van puts her hand on my arm, as if to hold me back. I shrug her off and step forward. She follows me into the courtyard.

The crystal burns at my throat and I feel the wicked sorcery swirling within me, stronger and stronger. It's like I grow taller with every step. I grasp the crystal in one hand, my other hand deep in my pocket, wrapped around the tablet box of powders.

"So, you have brought me the crescent crystal and the Haro knights." Synomea grins and gestures to the moons with one hand. "They turn. Soon 'twill be as you prophesied, my lovely, and I will rule this world with you at my side."

"What?" Van gasps and she stares at me, her eyes wide with horror, obviously thinking I've betrayed her.

The moons draw my gaze, and they change as I watch. No longer full and bright, they metamorphose into crescents.

Like my dreams. Even after the smaller moon stops changing, the larger moon thins and shifts from white . . . to pale ruby . . . to blood red.

I close my eyes. It's time.

"Bring me the crystal, daughter." Synomea's voice rings across the courtyard.

I grip my pendant tighter and open my eyes. "No."

# October 31
## *Allhallows Eve*

*Erick*

Blood rushes my ears and my thoughts sharpen. Navran grows hot in my hand with magic as the runes shift and change, telling me to hurry, guiding me, instructing me. The time is *now!*

I bolt from the kitchen and out into the courtyard.

"Release them!" I shout.

Taryn and Van turn to me as one. "Erick!" they cry.

Synomea scowls and steps forward. "You shall perish here with the other knights."

"No. It is you who will die," I say.

The sorcerer laughs, a sound that grates my spine. "Do you not realize the full measure of my powers?"

Taryn raises her chin and glares at Synomea. "You have lost much of your powers, haven't you? That's why you need me."

One of the sorcerer's eyes twitches. "You had best watch your tongue, Ta'reen. Once we finish with these fools, you will be punished for your impudence!"

She shakes her head. "You have little power left. And it drains you to use it. You have only the magic powders to carry out your sorcery. Without those, you are nothing."

Synomea trembles, his face darkening.

Basil says, "Look how she taunts you. Only I have been faithful to you. You have no need for her."

Rage fills me. "Bloody traitor."

"Synomea is your *father?*" Taryn says in a harsh whisper. "You are my brother?"

Basil scowls at Taryn. "You are naught but worthless Old-world scum."

Synomea grunts and growls to the warriors. The Zumar close in and I see their sightless eyes, their hanging flesh. I must not think of them as the humans they once were. There is no hope for them. They are but the walking dead . . . and I have no choice but to save the living.

Brandishing my sword, I charge past Taryn and Van toward the sorcerer.

The warriors surround me.

Heat fills me as I wield my sword as I have been trained from birth. The wizards' magic flows through me, rushing my limbs. The runes blaze brighter than ever before—so bright I see nothing before me but Zumarian beasts.

I swing Navran at the first warrior. A crack of thunder rumbles in the courtyard. Green lightning explodes from my blade. The bolt sears the first Zumarian. Then another. And another. Until they all lie in piles of smoldering bones, and the stench of cooked flesh surrounds me.

"Erick!" Taryn cries. "Watch out behind you!"

When I turn, I see Basil, his blade slicing toward my head.

Even as I raise Navran to block his sword, Gareth rises from the ground and lunges at Basil. "Traitor!" Gareth roars as he grabs Basil's arm and knocks the sword from his hand.

Gareth and Basil tumble to the dirt and roll toward Cole. Before I can come to my friend's aid, I see the flash of a blade.

282

Then Gareth lies still, a slit in his neck, his blood spilling onto the flinty Zumarian ground and his eyes sightless.

Fury consumes me as I charge toward Basil, but Cole reaches him first. Basil's mouth drops open, his eyes wide, as Cole runs his dagger through the traitor's belly.

When I turn to deal with Synomea, I stop cold.

He has Van by the throat.

The box of scarlet death powder in his hand.

The powder he claimed to have used to kill my father.

---

## Taryn

"Wait!" I shout. "I'll come to you . . . *Father*. Just let her go."

To the left of me, Erick flinches—he looks suddenly helpless. He opens his mouth, but he doesn't seem to know what to do or what to say. He's torn with love for his sister.

And his love for me. I feel it, as strong and tangible as the moons above.

Erick's love gives me strength. Strength to do what I must to save him, to save the people of this world, and to save those taken from Earth.

"Before I come to you, *Father*," I say, "I need to know about Gran. You gave her a sickness, didn't you? A sickness that would kill her after I turned seventeen. She knew, didn't she?"

Synomea's wicked grin churns my stomach. "As I told you, I allowed your grandmother to live long enough to raise you to the age of metamorphosis. She served her purpose."

"I see." I walk toward Synomea, fury building inside me. My anger rises molten and hot, ready to spew from me like the lava pouring from the volcano's mouth. I remember the words his grandfather told him in my dream and realize my father did exactly the same thing to me.

I take step after step, closer to my fate. "I understand now. It was to make me strong. You wanted me strong to meet my destiny, to take this world as our own. Your wisdom. My power. We can rule forever."

He smiles, looking almost handsome again, and like he feels pride for me. A loving parent, as I always imagined my father would be.

When I'm feet away from him, I release my grip on the crystal and hold out my hand. "Let her go. I'll join you." My other palm still cradles the tablet box.

The sorcerer grins. Even with his Zumarian soldiers lying wasted around him and his own son dead at his feet, in his arrogance he never doubts I will join him. He believes this to be my destiny. His destiny. The future he had asked me to reveal.

Only I know the real future. If I can do this right.

In my pocket, I pop open the lid of every compartment on the tablet container.

I gaze at Van, willing her to see what I want her to do. She tightens her lips and her gray eyes flash.

While I stretch out my other arm toward Synomea, I beckon with one finger.

The box of death powder flies from his palm and into my hand.

Synomea gasps. In the sorcerer's moment of surprise, Van drops out of his grasp to the ground and rolls away from him.

The sorcerer's eye twitches and his face turns livid. He raises his fist, his eyes on Erick, and squeezes.

Hands at his neck, Erick falls to his knees. He gurgles and wheezes, his face turning purple. Synomea is choking him with his magic!

Blood pounds in my head and my heart rages as I draw from my well of sorcery. Even as I fear for Erick's life, I know what I must do.

*And I know the consequences.*

Combined with the power of the crescent crystal, the call of the sorcery is incredible, mind-boggling. This world could be mine. I alone could rule it. It's my choice!

*My choice.*

Strange voices chant in my head, speaking the same words Van told me earlier. *And be it love or power . . . good or evil . . . the choice of the Crescent . . . and the will of the Lion . . . seal the destiny of Zanea.*

The moons bleed above, bathing everything in a crimson glow. I pull the tablet box from my pocket and hold it in front of me.

"Everyone—get far, far away." My voice, resonant with my sorcery, booms through the courtyard.

"Do as Taryn says," Van yells and pulls at Finella.

"No!" Synomea cries as he sees the powders. He seems frozen, like he's afraid of what I might do with them if he moves.

Erick collapses as the sorcerer's attention turns to me and he releases his power on Erick's neck. Cole grabs Erick under his arms and drags him away.

With the power of the crescent crystal and my sorcery combined, I call to the elements as Synomea taught me and spin the air around the sorcerer and me. The wind twists and dances, causing Synomea's robes to billow and my hair to fly about my face.

"*No!*" Synomea cries. "Daughter, do not mix the dusts!"

With my magic breath, I blow the powders from the box into the wind. They swirl and glitter between Synomea and me. Sparks snap in the air, a jagged rainbow of electrical currents, spinning faster and faster until a cyclone of the dust whirls between us. I withdraw the bag of sleeping powder and shake out the contents, adding its magic to the storm.

Synomea seems immobilized, his mouth slack with fear. His sickly sweet malodor, that burnt sugar stench, is swept into the winds, fueling my determination, reminding me of every evil deed he has committed.

The box drops to my feet, empty. The bag slides from my fingers.

The sorcerer backs away. "No, Ta'reen. We are meant to rule together! Do you not know what will happen should these dusts touch our flesh? It will mean our deaths!"

"I know." My smile is sad and wistful for what might have been.

Can I do it? The end for Synomea . . . my father. The end for me. The end of all the evil deeds this sorcerer is responsible for, and all that could yet happen.

Black sorcery burns in my breast, telling me not to do this. Telling me I can be a powerful sorceress with all these people to serve me. *Me*.

But I fight its sensual pull. Reject it, force it away. I am not evil. I will die before becoming a monster like my father.

The sorcerer smiles at my hesitation. "Come, Ta'reen. Drop the powders to the dust between us, and we can begin our rule this day. See?" He gestures to the moons that bloody the sky. "Soon the moons will join as one, and so will you and I. What say you, daughter?"

My resolve strengthens. "I say easy come, easy go."

A horrid screeching noise fills my ears and panic squeezes my soul.

*No! Not now. Not the vertigo. I must complete this task!*

The world is spinning, turning, and I fight to keep my balance; fight to keep from collapsing to the ground.

With everything I have, I release the windstorm of powders, and it surrounds the sorcerer and me.

I barely see Synomea stagger and fall to his knees, his hands to his chest. The sorcerer withers before my eyes. His youthful skin wrinkles and shrivels around his skull. His green eyes cloud. His hands curl like ancient claws.

Pain wrenches my body. A million ice picks puncture my flesh. On fire—I'm on fire. The torment blinds me and I no longer see anything but lightning flashes in my mind.

In the distance, I hear myself scream. White-hot flames blaze every cell as I collapse and writhe in agony. My body jerks in spasmodic bursts.

The horrid screeching noise intensifies as my world spins. I vomit like the volcano spewing lava in the distance, no longer hearing anything but sirens in my head, seeing nothing but flashes behind my eyes.

The world darkens.

I welcome the shadows—welcome the darkness that closes in on me.

## Erick

"Taryn!" I try to wrench myself from my friends, but I cannot get free. Cole holds my arms, and Van and Finella grasp my legs.

"Release me!" I cry as I watch Taryn collapse to the ground. I fight my friends but they do not free me until the dusts have settled.

I stumble forward and run toward Taryn. She sprawls on her side, motionless, her face to the dirt.

The sorcerer moans. He is nothing more than an old man, ancient and feeble. His mouth slackens and his head rolls to the side, his eyes wide and sightless. He gives one last breath, the rattle of death, and he is no longer among the living.

Fear sears my being. Does Taryn live? Will she too have withered and died as the sorcerer did? Gods, *no!*

I kneel beside her and drop my sword to the ground. "Taryn," I whisper as I touch her shoulder. She does not move. My throat thickens with grief as I gather her in my arms and cradle her to me. Her face is pale yet beautiful, as always, but her body is lifeless. She does not breathe and her head hangs back, baring the crystal at her neck. Green fire glitters within its black depths.

Tears come hard and fast from my eyes, spilling onto my love. I wrap my hand around the crystal. "*No!* You cannot take her from me!"

The crystal heats my palm. Its energy swells within my body, churning in my soul. I pour all my love for Taryn into the crystal, as if its magic has the ability to bring her back to me.

Emerald flames spark at my knees. Navran! My sword's power surges into my body and to the crystal. Wind whirls around us. Wind that binds Taryn and me, binds our magic, makes us as one. The wind blows Taryn's red-gold hair into my face and tugs at my tunic. Faster it swirls, faster . . . and then gradually the wind dies.

Taryn gasps and arches her back. Her eyelids flutter. "Erick," she moans.

"Taryn!" I crush her to me. "Thank the gods!"

"W-what—" she says, so faint I can scarce hear her.

She opens her eyes. Her beautiful green eyes. I stroke hair from her face and brush away the moisture on her cheek.

"Can you ever forgive me?" I ask, careful to speak in her good ear.

"There's nothing to forgive," she whispers.

"I love you, Taryn."

She smiles and brings her hand to my face, tracing the scar along my cheekbone. Her eyes are bright with her own tears. "I love you, too."

I bury my face in her hair, breathing in her scent of raspberries and moonlight. "I do not care where we live, be it Newold or Oldworld. But I shall never again let you far from my sight."

Taryn caresses wetness from my cheek, tremors running through her hand. "You would do that for me?"

"Please say you will be with me always, little one." I pull back to look at my beloved. "Say you will handfast with me. Say you will be my mate."

"You mean marry you?" Taryn's eyes widen and her lips tremble. "I—I don't know. I—we're so young. We're from different worlds." She shakes her head and my heart aches. "Let me think about it, okay?"

I manage a smile for her. "I will wait."

She smiles, a hint of mischief in her tired eyes. "But you've got to take a bath. You smell like you've been in a sewer."

Laughter from behind, and I feel a hand on my shoulder. I glance up to see my sister, Cole and Finella at her side.

"The girl is right," Van says. "You smell worse than the sewer rats of Trendor."

"To be sure, I do." I smile at Taryn. "May I kiss you, my love?"

Taryn slips her hand into my tangled hair and pulls my head toward her. "You never have to ask me."

How soft and sweet her lips! I am reluctant to end the kiss or to let Taryn out of my arms. But when she is ready, I help her to her feet. She winces as she stands, then sways. I catch her to me and hold her.

After a few moments, she says, "I'm okay now." She releases me and sees the destruction around us. "Oh, my God," she whispers.

My spirit weighs heavy as I look at my slain friend. "Gareth gave his life for me."

"You would have done the same," Cole says. He pushes Basil's corpse over so the traitor's face is in the dirt.

I kneel beside Gareth and press his eyelids down. "Thank you, my friend."

"The Bull," Taryn says. I glance up at her, wondering what she means. "In my dreams, Gareth was the Bull that fought the Scorpion, Basil, to defend you."

I remember the wizards' warning of a Scorpion—it must have been Basil they meant.

Taryn turns and stares at the sorcerer's shriveled body. "I knew if I combined all the dusts at once we both would die. I never expected to live."

My blood chills. She sacrificed herself to rid our world of Synomea.

I stand and put my arm around her shoulder and draw her head against my chest.

Taryn holds her hand to the crescent crystal, and her voice catches. "He deserved to die after all he's done and all the people he's murdered. But I'm not sure I can handle having killed someone . . . my father . . . even as evil as Synomea was."

Van lays her hand on Taryn's arm. "The sorcerer was at least five hundred years old. His sorcery allowed him to live long past his time. It was how he retained his youth."

Taryn gasps. "Five hundred?"

"Aye." I squeeze her tighter to me. "He should have died long ago."

Taryn nods, but says nothing.

Van runs her hand over her hair. "And what of your own sorcery, Taryn?"

I look down to see that Taryn's smile is sad and perhaps a bit wistful. "Gone," she says.

Finella looks to the sky and points. "Look. The moons."

Even as we watch, the red of the moons fades until they wax full and bright.

The smaller moon brightest of all.

# November 1, dawn

*Taryn*

Intense joy floods me as the sun rises and breaks through the sulfur-laden sky. Yet at the same time my chest tightens at the choices I need to make.

Wanting a few moments to myself, I walk away from the others into a corner of the courtyard, where I'm alone. Already the air seems lighter, like the death of Synomea has rid this place of all the oppression and ugliness that shrouded it, probably for centuries.

During my fight with the sorcerer I lost what little hearing I had in my right ear. I'm half deaf now, though I've told no one of it. What if the Ménière's takes the hearing in my left ear, too? If I choose to stay with Erick, I could be completely deaf in a strange world.

Somehow that no longer frightens me.

The thought that Erick wants to marry—or handfast—me makes my heart pound with happiness. Yet why couldn't I say yes the moment he asked me?

Could Erick and I make our relationship work? Could we be happy, coming from such different worlds, such different lifestyles?

Even though he offered, I could never ask Erick to leave his world for mine. He belongs on Zanea, with his family and friends, and in his own home.

My hand moves to the pendant at my throat as I watch the odd sunrise. Instead of the oranges and pinks I'm used to, here the sunrise is green, yellow, and blue. Could I get used to sunsets in this strange world? Erick told me Newold is beautiful, with mountains and lakes and forests. I would truly love to see his home. But live there . . . forever?

I was raised on Earth with all the modern conveniences I doubt they have in Newold. What of my doctors, my medicine? If I live with Erick, would I be allowed to travel to Tucson for these things? Perhaps even to visit Jen? To let my foster parents know I'm all right?

Clenching my fist around the pendant, I let my gaze travel the horizon. Do I even belong here and would I be accepted by Erick's people? My birth father came from this world, so I am half Zanean. But my father was Synomea, the most hated and feared person on this planet.

On Earth I have no real ties other than Jen. Nothing that is more important to me than Erick. Yet I need to consider my dreams of being a journalist and making a difference in people's lives. Can I make a difference on this world?

I realize I just did make a difference in a whole lot of lives. I defeated a wicked being and helped two worlds at once.

At what cost? That being I defeated was my own father.

*My father.* And now he's dead, because of me. But if he hadn't died, what acts would he have forced upon me? How many more people would have died?

My thoughts churn as I walk back toward the courtyard, where the Haro knights work to release all the slaves. Perhaps there are other things I can do in Newold that will fulfill my dreams and desires—ways I can help Erick and his people. *My* people now.

I smile at the thought.

When I come out into the courtyard, I see Erick leading Oldworlders from the slave quarters toward the keep, and my heart beats faster. Erick is so beautiful, inside and out, and he loves me.

He loves *me*.

Being with Erick feels so right. He fills that empty well inside of me, and I know he feels I am a part of him. The thought of making a home with him fills me with odd tingles. Having him there every day to love and cherish. Perhaps it's our destiny to have children of our own.

My home is where my heart and soul are . . . and Erick owns both.

Maybe Erick's people will allow me to stay for a while before I make a decision. I should be scared, but somehow I'm not. Scared I won't be accepted by Erick's people. Scared I won't like living in Newold. Scared of becoming completely deaf and living in silence.

But all I feel is a quiet confidence inside. I smile.

The sky lightens. Oldworlders continue to stumble from slave quarters one by one, a confused murmur surrounding us. The slaves who worked in the mines had always been under Synomea's mind-control powder, and now that his magic is gone they have no memories of what happened to them.

Servants in the keep had been allowed by Synomea to keep their memories. Twisted as he was, the sorcerer had delighted in wielding his power over them, knowing how much they feared him.

"Maria! Meg!" I yell as I see them come out of the keep. "We did it. You can go home!"

They run to me. We laugh and hug and cry.

"Thank you, Taryn," Maria whispers. "You saved us."

"It wasn't just me." I gesture to my companions. "It was also the Haro knights. And you helped, you know."

"Taryn?" A voice from the crowd says. "Is that you, girl?"

"Jen!" I turn and fling my arms around my friend, and hold her tight.

---

It takes countless hours to send everyone to his or her home through the Zumar portal, but fortunately the Haro are able to take large groups at a time. The knights use the Old Magic to erase the slaves' memories back to the moment just before the Zumar captured them. Their loved ones on Earth are sure to wonder how these people suddenly appear back home with no memory of where they've been, but there's not much that can be done about it. Those who have been here for over three years, but are not yet as far gone as the Zumar, may never fully recover.

And the Zumar . . . those that remained were put out of their misery. I can't believe they were once teenagers, like me. It made me sick, and still does, but there was nothing that could be done to help them.

Jen is the last to go. She stands at my side as I help operate the portal controls. I've explained everything to her, and Van has agreed to let Jen retain her memories as long as she promises to keep everything a secret. If I decide to live with Erick, it's possible I'll be able to visit Jen, but that will depend on how things go once we're in Newold.

When Erick returns from his last trip, he wraps his arms around me and kisses me hard. Even covered in scratches, filthy, and smelling like a sewer, he's beautiful to me. Lost in his kisses, I forget everything around me until I hear Jen laugh.

"Are you going to introduce me to the big smelly guy?" she asks.

I turn toward her, and I know my smile must be a mile wide. "Erick, this is my best friend, Jen. Jen, this is my big smelly guy, Erick."

Erick gazes at me with such a proud look it makes my head spin. "I have asked Taryn to handfast with me, and I hope she will agree. Soon."

I smile.

Jen shakes her head and grins. "I think you owe me a new pair of sandals."

# November 1, evening

*Erick*

It is late evening when we finish destroying the sorcerer's portal machinery and burying the dead. We are ready to dispatch to Newold. We do not know what to expect, be it exile, imprisonment, or otherwise, but we hope for the best.

Cole goes first with the wooden box that holds Gareth's body. Finella and Van follow. When all my friends have departed, I take Taryn's hand and we leave together.

I catch Taryn to me as we arrive at Command, then help her stand. She trembles, weakened from the dispatch. It was not so bad for me as the journey to Zumar had been, but I can tell it was not easy for her.

"Lord Erick." A voice cuts through my concern.

Taryn stiffens.

I jerk my head up and see the chamber filled with Elders' Council members in their pristine white robes, and Council Guard in blood red. My sister and friends stand to one side, heads high, hands behind their backs, Gareth's casket beside them.

Albin and Quenn stand on either side of Council Voice Osred.

Voice Osred steps forward, his face stern. "Lord Erick, you are accused of numerous transgressions of Council laws and Haro doctrines. Chief amongst these, you are accused of consorting with an Oldworlder and violating Council decree by traveling to Zumaria. You face exile from Zanea or imprisonment. How plead you to these charges?"

When I glance at Taryn, I see her fear for me, her eyes wide and her lips trembling. I put my arm around her shoulders and smile, then turn back to Osred.

"Of these things I am indeed guilty."

A murmur passes through the crowd. Osred nods to the red-robed guard and two soldiers approach me.

I hold up my hand. "First, there is something I must say." The guards pause as I look from face to face in the crowd. "For too long we have allowed ourselves to become comfortable with our lives, ignoring the evil flourishing in Synomea's realm. It was only a matter of time before the sorcerer's wickedness would have spread to Newold. We must not allow ourselves to be complacent any longer and put all we hold dear at risk."

"Despite what opinions you may have, you have broken our laws and you will be tried," Osred replies, his face a mask of ice.

"All hail the Lion and the Crescent!" booms a voice from the doorway.

Relief floods me as the sea of white robes parts and L'iwanda and L'onten glide toward Taryn and me.

When they reach us, the wizards turn to face the crowd. Council members, guards, and Haro knights bow in reverence.

L'iwanda spreads her arms, her palms to the ceiling. "Behold the Lion."

L'onten raises his hands. "Behold the Crescent."

"Who delivered us from wickedness."

"Saviors of Zanea."

The wizards turn to face Taryn and me, and kneel.

I hear gasps of surprise, then everyone follows the wizards' lead.

All kneel.

Taryn looks to me. "What?"

I take her hand and squeeze it. "I believe it means we will not be banished."

L'iwanda rises and turns to the crowd. "A traitor stands among us."

L'onten joins her. "Reveal yourself, Synomea's spawn."

Shock blasts me in a frigid gust. Taryn's face goes deathly white. I draw her closer, my hand on Navran's hilt. But the wizards' attention is elsewhere.

They point to Albin. Quenn's jaw slackens and she steps back.

Her eyes wide, Van covers her mouth with her palm.

Gut burning, I clench my hands into fists.

Albin's face reddens and he whirls and tries to shove through the crowd. Guards lunge for Albin and grab his arms. They drag him before the wizards.

"Confess your crimes," L'iwanda demands.

"Sorcerer's son," L'onten adds, passing his hand over Albin's head, surely using the most powerful Old Magic to draw a confession from the traitor.

Albin glares at the wizards.

His lip curls into a snarl and he speaks. "Basil and I were brothers, but of different mothers. We conspired to assist our father in retrieving his Oldworld daughter." He glares at Taryn. "Should Synomea have been successful, we would have served him well. Power would have been ours and all here would have been turned to dust!"

He narrows his hateful gaze on Taryn. "But our sister betrayed us and killed our father."

At the mention of Taryn being his sister, the crowd murmurs and disgusted looks mar the faces of those around us. Even as they hear she has destroyed the sorcerer, they condemn her for her blood.

Van steps toward Albin, her hands clenched. "You son of a bitch."

He shrugs. "You were naught but a means to our ends."

I release Taryn and lunge for the bastard, as does Cole. Before we can reach Albin, Van slams her fist into his belly.

He shouts his pain as he doubles over, and Van drives her knee up and into his chin. His head snaps back and he drops to the cold stone floor, a cry tearing from his lips.

"Filth!" Van's eyes flash. With her head high, she turns on her heel. The crowd parts as she strides out of the building.

"Enough!" Voice Osred comes forward. "Take this traitor to the prisons. He shall be tried for his crimes by tribunal."

I put my arm around Taryn again. She sags against me as the guard marches Albin from Command.

"The dead moon leaves many stones," L'onten intones. And like a wisp of smoke on a breeze, he disappears.

"Until each has been exposed to the light of day, Zanea remains in peril." L'iwanda vanishes like doused flame.

## One Year Later

*Taryn*

  *Beneath the warm sun, I dance. Damp grass chills my bare feet as I move under the shadow of the snow-capped mountain. Scents of rich loam and leather fill my senses.*

  *Lion walks at my side—and becomes Erick. He takes my hand, pulling me close to him.*

  *My Lion. My Erick. My love.*

  *The smell of raspberries and rose petals sweeps over me, and my blue and gold gown rustles in the light wind. The world is green and alive under the gentle sun.*

  *Cole stands at Erick's side, his normal scowl softened.*

  *Van is beside me, tall and beautiful, the scar at her temple pale against her tanned face. She feels joy for Erick and me, yet I see the pain of many betrayals still reflected in her eyes.*

  *Erick and I each hold a hand up and press our palms together. My lips tremble as I look into his steady, calm, silvery gray eyes.*

  *The wizards wrap colorful satin ribbons around our hands, like a maypole. The ends of the ribbons stir in the breeze when the wizards finish.*

  *L'iwanda presses her fingertips to my forehead, then Erick's. "Forever and always," she says.*

*L'onten touches my shoulder, then Erick's, with Navran.*
*"Lord Erick and Lady Taryn, you are as one."*

*Erick smiles and his eyes drink me in. "I love you, Taryn."*

*I can't imagine ever being happier. "I love you, Erick."*

*A sudden gust of wind rips through the meadow, bringing a*
*frost that chills my heart, withers what was young, steals all that*
*I love and bares my soul.*

*"Ta'reen," the wind cries. "Ta'reen . . ."*

I wake from my dream, my heart thudding so hard it
might burst from my chest. Moonlight from the twin moons
spills through the window, and black shadows creep in the
room. As if sensing my distress, Erick snuggles closer, wrap-
ping his strong arm around my belly.

Even as my new husband holds me, the crescent crystal
tingles against my throat and the secret embers burn inside
my soul. The Ta'sha egg I took from my father's fortress and
hid amongst my belongings lies heavy on my mind.

It's there, always close, tucked in some pocket or purse.
Tonight, it rests in a silken bag, just beneath the bed, where
Erick can't see it. The Ta'sha stays within my reach.

All the power—that intoxicating, endless power.

Waiting.

## THE END

## To Write to the Author

If you wish to contact the author or would like more information about this book, please write to the author in care of Llewellyn Worldwide and we will forward your request. Both the author and publisher appreciate hearing from you and learning of your enjoyment of this book and how it has helped you. Llewellyn Worldwide cannot guarantee that every letter written to the author can be answered, but all will be forwarded. Please write to:

Debbie Federici
℅ Llewellyn Worldwide
2143 Wooddale Drive, Dept. 0-7387-0808-9
Woodbury, MN 55125-2989, U.S.A.

Please enclose a self-addressed stamped envelope for reply,
or $1.00 to cover costs. If outside U.S.A., enclose
international postal reply coupon.

Many of Llewellyn's authors have websites with additional information and resources. For more information, please visit our website at http://www.llewellyn.com.

## L.O.S.T.
Debbie Federici
and
Susan Vaught

Is Brenden the Shadowalker who could save the world? Seventeen-year-old Brenden is happily on his way to San Diego for a short summer vacation. Stopping to use the restroom in a small town changes his life forever when everything familiar disappears and he finds himself in L.O.S.T.— one of many witch villages from different times (ranging from medieval to modern) and magically disconnected from the rest of the world. The golden-eyed teenage girl responsible for taking Brenden to this land of witches, hags, and sirens is Jazz, Queen of the Witches. She recognizes an inner power in Brenden that could save her people. Throughout their adventures, Jazz and Brenden share an irresistible attraction, yet they must devote their strength to defeating Nire, an ancient evil threatening both of their worlds.

0-7387-0561-6
312 pp., 5³⁄₁₆ x 8                                    $9.95

To order, call 1-877-NEW-WRLD
Prices subject to change without notice

## ShadowQueen (The L.O.S.T. Series)
Debbie Federici
 and
Susan Vaught

The Shadowmaster has been defeated and the witch sanctuaries are safe for now. But the effort has cost Jazz her life. Trapped in Talamadden, the land of the dead, the former Queen of the Witches is lost in a dark limbo until a spirit guide revives her memories. Desperate to reunite with Bren, she wrestles menacing harpies and shadows to find a way back to the living.

Meanwhile, Bren has become King of the Witches and is now in charge of the witch villages. But he abandons them to search for Jazz, his true love, despite the fact that crossing over to Talamadden would surely kill him. Will Bren and Jazz join up once again to fight evil forces intent on destroying the witches? Or will Bren's impulsive departure leave the witch villages vulnerable to the shadows?

0-7387-0827-5
312 pp., 5³⁄₁₆ x 8                                    $8.95

## Stay on the Path!

Llewellyn would love to know what kinds of books you are looking for but just can't seem to find. Witchy, occult, paranormal, metaphysical, or just plain scary—what do you want to read? What types of books speak specifically to you? If you have ideas, suggestions, or comments, write Megan at:

megana@llewellyn.com

Llewellyn Publications
Attn: Megan, Acquisitions
2143 Wooddale Drive
Woodbury, MN 55125-2989 USA
1-800-THE MOON (1-800-843-6666)

And be sure to check out Llewellyn's website for updates on new books from your favorite authors:

www.llewellyn.com